Web of Lies

Books by Brandilyn Collins

Hidden Faces Series

1 | *Brink of Death*

2 | *Stain of Guilt*

3 | *Dead of Night*

4 | *Web of Lies*

Bradleyville Series

1 | *Cast a Road before Me*

2 | *Color the Sidewalk for Me*

3 | *Capture the Wind for Me*

Chelsea Adams Series

1 | *Eyes of Elisha*

2 | *Dread Champion*

HIDDEN FACES SERIES

BOOK FOUR

Web of Lies

BRANDILYN COLLINS

ZONDERVAN™

GRAND RAPIDS, MICHIGAN 49530 USA

ZONDERVAN.COM/
AUTHOR**TRACKER**↗

ZONDERVAN™

Web of Lies
Copyright © 2005 by Brandilyn Collins

Requests for information should be addressed to:
Zondervan, *Grand Rapids, Michigan 49530*

Library of Congress Cataloging-in-Publication Data

Collins, Brandilyn.
    Web of lies / Brandilyn Collins.
       p. cm.—(Hidden faces series ; bk. 4)
    ISBN-13: 978-0-310-25106-4
    ISBN-10: 0-310-25106-0
    1. Police artists—Fiction. 2. Women artists—Fiction. I. Title.
PS3553.O4747815W43 2006
813'.—dc22

                           2005021093

Interior design by Beth Shagene

Printed in the United States of America

---

06 07 08 09 10 11 • 17 16 15 14 13 12 11 10 9 8 7 6 5 4 3 2 1

For my pals
Deb Raney and Robin Lee Hatcher.
Heh-heh.
Now you have to read it.

The devil ... was a murderer from the beginning,
not holding to the truth, for there is no truth in him.
When he lies, he speaks his native language,
for he is a liar and the father of lies.

JOHN 8:44

Acknowledgments

My deep gratitude, as always, to members of the Zondervan fiction team, who make my books so much better. And to Niwana Briggs, who has critiqued just about all of my manuscripts.

Citizens of Redding, thanks again for letting me "borrow" your city for this series. As with the other Hidden Faces books, I have fictionalized much about your area, including Annie's neighborhood of Grove Landing, some roads, plus the buildings and certain procedures of the Redding Police and Shasta County Sheriff's Departments.

Karen T. Taylor, the nationally known forensic artist mentioned in this story, is a real person. You will see Annie employ Taylor's recognized method for two-dimensional facial reconstruction from the skull. This method, as well as the study of skeletal remains to determine gender, height, race, etc., requires precision and often long hours of work. While *Web of Lies* includes overviews of these tasks, I have had to sacrifice some details in order to keep my story moving. In the end, this is a work of fiction, not a textbook. For an excellent text detailing two-dimensional reconstruction, plus all facets of forensic art, please see Karen T. Taylor's book, *Forensic Art and Illustration*, or visit her website at www.karenttaylor.com.

A Note to My Readers

*W*hen are you going to write another Chelsea Adams book?" This is a question I have heard countless times.

My first two suspense novels, *Eyes of Elisha* and *Dread Champion*, featured Chelsea Adams, a Christian woman to whom God speaks through visions. In both of these stories, the visions God gives Chelsea about murder and malice send her on labyrinthine journeys that she would not have chosen, but that God wants her to make for the sake of justice.

Fans of this Hidden Faces series have often added the same question in their letters: "When will we see Chelsea Adams again?"

And so the idea for *Web of Lies* was born.

There were some challenging hurdles along the way, however. The two series were written in very different formats, not the least of which involved character perspective. Annie's stories in Hidden Faces have been in first person. Chelsea's stories were not. As a result, *Web of Lies* evolved as a blend of both the characters and the varying points of view from these two series.

By the way, a note for those who haven't read *Eyes of Elisha* and *Dread Champion*: you'll find no spoilers for those stories within this book.

And now—off we go on another roller coaster ride. As always, strap yourself in, hold tight, and

don't forget to *b r e a t h e* ...

Brandilyn Collins
Seatbelt Suspense

Prologue

She was washing dishes when her world began to blur.

Chelsea Adams hitched in a breath, her skin pebbling. She knew the dreaded sign all too well. God was pushing a vision into her consciousness.

Black dots crowded her sight. She dropped a plate, heard it crack against the porcelain sink. Her fingers fumbled for the faucet. The hiss of water ceased.

God, I don't want this. Please!

But this one was strong; no stopping it now. Chelsea's legs jellied. She stumbled across the kitchen and collapsed into a chair.

The room went black. Chelsea gripped the edge of her seat with palsied hands—and waited . . .

First, an overwhelming sense of evil. It rolled over her, terrifying, oppressive. Crushing her lungs as though she'd been shoved into a black, airless cave. She struggled to breathe.

Far away through the darkness, a vague image began to shimmer. The kitchen chair fell from beneath her. Chelsea tumbled into the vision.

She landed . . . somewhere, with a jarring thud.

Chelsea blinked. Found herself staring at a dirty oval window filtering dim light into a small room.

Where am I?

Awareness grew. She sensed herself in someone's body, seeing the room through that person's eyes. Someone imprisoned, shell-shocked, and trembling. She felt bare feet against cold concrete. The place smelled dusty, close. Claustrophobic. The walls closed in. Panic seized Chelsea.

I have to get out, I have to get—

Wait. What was that, on the floor?

A barely visible figure. Hunched, with head down.

A sudden noise on Chelsea's left. Her nerves flared. She heard a male voice, scratching out whispers. Vile explanations, deathly threats too horrible to imagine. She cringed at the words, heart flinging itself against her ribs. *Let me out, let me out, let me out . . .*

A click, and red light filtered into the grayness. Slowly Chelsea's eyes adjusted.

The terror of the room froze her blood.

Thursday, September 22

Chapter 1

Our nightmare started with a mundane errand.

I was driving my SUV away from the Redding Municipal Airport, my sister in the passenger seat. She aimed a heavy sigh out the window. "I miss my airplane already."

I shook my head. "Jenna, your precious airplane isn't parked that far away from the house. Small price to pay for a few weeks, wouldn't you say? Just think how much you'll like the longer runway at Grove Landing."

"We don't *need* a longer runway." She couldn't hide the pout in her voice. "It's our neighbors with their fancy twin engines who just had to have more space."

So that was it. I threw her a glance, a sage smile crooking my mouth.

"What?" Jenna's velvet brown eyes glowered at me.

I affected a shrug. "Nothing."

"Don't tell me *nothing*. I know that look on your face."

Wow, she was in a mood today. "You're just jealous of those neighbors. You want a bigger plane."

"I do not."

"Uh-huh." Private pilots are a strange breed, never satisfied. They always want the next electronics system, the latest turbocharged engine. Whatever's better and bigger. Especially bigger.

Jenna huffed and folded her arms. We drove in silence.

"What's with you anyway?" I turned north, headed for Foothill High School to pick up my daughter, Kelly, and her best friend, Erin. School would be letting out in about five minutes. "You've been out of sorts all morning."

Air seeped from Jenna's throat. "Yeah, well, I have a reason. I'm mad at Eric."

"Oh." Trouble in paradise. "What happened?"

"He was a jerk last night. When it comes right down to it, all men are jerks." She frowned and turned away.

At one time I would have agreed with her, but no more. Not since Dave and I had started dating—if you could call our painfully slow process that. At any rate, Dave Willit was not a jerk. My voice softened. "Tell me about it."

"We need milk."

"Huh?"

Jenna pointed at a 7-Eleven ahead on the right. "Stop there so we can buy some milk. We're out."

My sister is seven years younger than I but bosses me like a nagging mother. The trait only worsens when she's upset. I've learned to roll with it. "Okay."

I slowed the SUV and turned into the small 7-Eleven parking lot, pulling up next to the walkway leading into the store. Three other cars filled spaces around us, two on our left, on the other side of the entrance walk, and one immediately to our right. Switching off the engine, I turned to Jenna. Her beautiful, heart-shaped face looked pinched. "First tell me what happened."

She focused ahead at the store. "We sort of argued."

"I gathered that. And?"

She turned to me, words spilling. "He went out with someone else! Which I suppose is his right, because we're not dating exclusively. But he lied to me about it, told me he *wasn't* seeing anyone but me. When I caught him in his little fib, he tried to squirm out of it by telling a bigger lie ..."

My peripheral vision caught frantic movement in the rearview mirror. I blinked, focused on it.

"... and I am so *sick* of men who can't tell the truth. You'd think for once ..."

Someone sprinted across the street toward the store. A young man. Caucasian. Shoulder-length blond hair.

"... I'm just not going to put up with it ..."

Wait. Another young man behind him, chasing.

With a *gun.*

My mouth opened but no sound came. I threw out my right hand, gripped Jenna's arm.

She stopped midsentence. "What—"

I whipped my head around. The first young man hit the curb, flew over it into the 7-Eleven parking lot. He raced toward our car, the second man barreling behind him.

"Get *down*!" I grabbed behind Jenna's neck, pulled her low across the console, and pressed on top of her. My eyes squeezed shut. Footsteps pounded past my window—

Thud!

A body slammed into the door of the building. I raised my head a few inches, peeked through the windshield. The 7-Eleven door smacked open, the man streaking through it into the store. He veered left, aiming for the checkout counter. His pursuer thumped past us, hit the door as it was closing and flung it wide. The first man reached the counter and dove over it. The store clerk shouted, jumped out of the way. Somebody screamed. In seconds the pursuer rammed into the counter, flattened himself upon it. Up came the gun.

Bam. Bam, bam. Bam.

"What's *happening?*" Jenna squirmed under me. I held her down.

The shooter pushed off the counter, twisted toward the door. He'd have to run right by our car ... and this time he might notice us. I pressed my head back down, air pooling in my throat.

Jesus, protect us.

The door slammed open. My heart slammed with it.

God, please ...

Footsteps pounded toward our car ...

And past us.

A wail from inside the store rent the air.

I counted to ten.

Cautiously I raised my head, glanced through the rear window. The shooter was racing across the street toward an alley. Soon he would be out of sight.

The whole thing couldn't have taken more than sixty seconds.

Jenna heaved herself off the console, forcing me up. Strands of her thick auburn hair were stuck to her lips. "What happened? What happened? Where's my gun?"

My sister carries a two-inch barrel Chief Special in her purse, identical to the one in mine. But it was too late. Screams staccatoed from the store. A woman staggered outside, yelling, "Call the police!" Jenna and I shoved our doors open and jumped out. I reached the woman first, gripping both shoulders to steady her.

"Are you hurt?"

She shook her head, sobbing. "But a man in there, and a boy ..." She turned wide, shocked eyes toward the store.

Jenna ran back to the car, grabbed her purse and snatched out her cell phone. I eased the woman down on the curb, then rushed into the building.

A teenage girl stood near the checkout, knuckles pressed to her mouth. I hurried around the counter. A man knelt beside the young clerk, now sprawled upon the floor, his face white. Blood oozed from his right thigh. Beside him lay the crumpled body of the young man who'd been chased. That man's face was turned away from me, his hair matted red. The left side of his head had been blown away. *Oh, dear God.* Two bullets had plunged into his back. He wasn't moving.

The clerk moaned.

"Just stay still; we'll call for help." The kneeling customer reached into his pocket and withdrew a cell phone.

"My sister's already called." My words sounded hiccupped, ragged. I moved around the customer and clerk toward the still form. Bile rose in my throat. I leaned down to look at the face, trembling in fear of what I would see. *Please, Lord, please*—I sucked in a breath. Nearly gagged. One cheek and an eye were gone. Obliterated. I steadied myself, swallowed hard. Felt for a pulse in his neck. Nothing. Checked for breath. None.

Numbly I straightened.

"How are they?" Jenna's voice, firm, controlled, came from above me and across the counter. Both her handbag and mine hung over one arm, a cell phone at her ear. My fast-thinking sister. Even in the chaos, she'd thought about securing our purses—and the guns inside.

I shook my head. "This one's gone."

The teenage girl rattled out a wail. The woman who'd staggered outside appeared behind Jenna, face flushed. My sister spoke the news into her phone, then looked to the young clerk. "Second man down, white, maybe nineteen years old. He's been shot in the thigh. He's conscious." She paused. "Yeah, I'll stay on the line. How far away are they?" She looked to me. "Police car will be here in two minutes. Ambulance in five."

I nodded. "Did you tell them who we are?" Any dispatcher in Redding would know my name.

"Yes."

"Okay." I glanced at the young clerk's leg. "Jenna, can you find me something to place against that wound?" I moved over to kneel beside him, gently touching his shoulder. "Hey. What's your name?"

"T–Toby Brown." He groaned. "It *hurts*!"

His pain squeezed my throat. "I know. Help is going to be here real soon. You'll be okay."

"I'm Ken." The man on the other side of Toby patted his hand. "She's right, you'll be fine. And we'll get that guy who shot you, don't you worry."

"Did you get a look at him?" I asked.

Ken shook his head. "It happened so fast, and I was in the back of the store."

"Annie, here." Jenna held a roll of paper towels over the counter. "I don't see any kind of packaged cloths."

"These'll do." I took the roll, tore off a long strip, and folded the paper towels over on themselves. Carefully I pressed them against Toby's oozing wound. He winced and I bit my lip. "Sorry. Just don't want the bleeding to get too bad."

He managed a nod.

"Toby, did you see the man who shot you?"

"Y—yes."

One for our side. I hadn't seen the shooter at all. I'd been too busy focusing on the gun in his hand. How stupid. Of all people, I should have noticed his features.

Toby whimpered, started to shake.

"I think he's going into shock." I looked to Ken, who wore only a short-sleeved shirt. Then to the girl. Even in the hot weather, she had on a light jacket. "Can you give me your coat? We need to keep him warm."

Words and actions flowed in those suspended minutes while we waited for the police. I covered Toby with the jacket, Jenna reporting everything to the 911 dispatcher. The teenage girl told us her name was Christine, and the woman identified herself as Mary. Neither of them had seen the shooter's face either. We all avoided looking at the dead body mere feet away. In its silent stillness, it screamed at me. Somewhere out there a mother and father, brother, sister, friends, would soon mourn him. Who was he? Why had he been chased like that—in broad daylight—and killed? Anger at the senselessness of his death coagulated in my chest. The man who'd done this *would* be found. And I'd do everything I could to help.

Toby's face cinched with pain. Ken and I soothed him, my heart clutching. I tried to distract him, asking his age. "Eighteen," he managed, every breath careful, his chest shuddering. I pressed my eyes shut. My own son was seventeen.

"Are you in high school?" I rubbed his arm.

"Yeah." He shivered. "A senior at Central Valley High."

Oh, God, help him. Stephen's a senior too. What if this had happened to my son?

Ken surveyed me, a look of recognition smoothing his face. "Now I know who you are. Annie Kingston, right? The forensic artist."

I kept my focus on Toby, feeling the familiar self-consciousness. "Yeah, that's me."

Christine gasped. "Oh, wow. You're the one the Poison Killer—"

"Listen." I held up a hand, glad for a reason to cut her off. Sirens sounded in the distance.

Jenna trotted to the entrance. The sirens wailed louder, suddenly upon us. "They're here."

Police burst through the door, two paramedics not far behind. In moments the store turned into a scene of bustling uniforms, voices over radio, revolving red and blue lights. Jenna handed me my purse, and with the other witnesses we were herded out of the store. From the parking lot we all watched as officers strung up yellow crime-scene tape. Before long the paramedics emerged from the store with Toby on a stretcher, loaded him into their vehicle, and bore him to the hospital. The man who'd been pursued by the shooter was pronounced dead.

Dead.

Even though I'd known, the official word pierced me. I grieved for the man and his family. And for the entire town. Only three months had passed since the Poison Killer was caught. Three months of calm in Redding, of newness in my own life. I was not ready to have that peace disturbed, and neither was our town. We had barely enjoyed enough time to heal from the evil of a serial murderer and all the national media that descended upon us when that case finally broke.

God, once again the people in Redding are going to need You.

My cell phone rang. I pulled it from my purse and saw Kelly's number displayed on the ID. *Oh great.* She and Erin would be wondering where we were. I didn't relish telling them what happened. The girls and Stephen were protective enough of me, after all I'd been through. With a meaningful glance at Jenna, I flipped open the phone.

"Mom, where *are* you?" my daughter demanded.

"Oh, we'll be there soon." Lightness forced itself into my tone. "I was just picking up Jenna after she flew the plane over to the Redding airport. Remember, she has to keep it there while they lengthen the runway at home?"

A sigh. "Okay, but will you hurry? Erin and I have lots of homework and we need to get started on it."

"Be there as soon as we can. Has Stephen already left for work?"

"Yeah. He had to be at the video store fifteen minutes after school let out."

Should I call and tell him what happened? I didn't want the news to filter to him from someone else.

"All right, Kelly. Just hang around with your friends, and we'll be there as soon as we can."

I hung up and slid the phone back into my purse. Jenna gave me an empathetic look. "You're going to have to tell them, you know."

I shook my head at the thought. *Here we go again. More disaster.* "Yeah. I think I'd better call Stephen at work while we're on the way to pick up the girls."

With the ambulance gone, officers Fred Sparks and Raymond Bradet, joined by homicide detective Tim Blanche, began questioning the witnesses. On the sidewalk behind us, a curious crowd had begun to swarm like stirred-up bees. Someone said my name, and it buzzed from one mouth to another.

"That's Annie Kingston."

"You know who *she* is."

Even though the town hailed me a hero, the whispers stung. My mere presence spelled extra sensationalism. I couldn't blame them; history was on their side. But I hated it.

My eyes grazed the crowd—and landed on Adam Bendershil, reporter from the *Record Searchlight*. He darted among people, jotting in his notepad. At that moment he looked up, and our eyes met. I turned my back on him.

Detective Blanche beckoned me and Jenna into the taped-off area, his face stern. "You see the guy, Annie?" His penetrating blue eyes bore into me. I suppressed a wince. Blanche was not one of my favorites at the Redding Police Department, to say the least. He was far too arrogant, with those raised eyebrows and a frequent curl to one side of his mouth. I didn't think he cared for me, either. I'd heard rumors of his cynical remarks about my belief in prayer and in God. Blanche was in his midforties, with three kids, the oldest of which had recently graduated from Foothill High. He had thick salt-and-pepper hair and a large mole on his left cheek.

I felt slack-limbed, shaky. "Afraid not. Everything happened way too fast."

He narrowed his eyes, almost in accusation, then glanced toward the store. "Well, let's hope the security cameras did *their* job. Should have caught it, as long as the tape's in good condition."

"I hope so."

Jenna mumbled agreement. The press of her lips bespoke her righteous anger over the entire affair. No doubt she was ruing her own failure to grab her gun and go after the killer. If I hadn't been on top of her, that's exactly what she would have done. Might have gotten herself killed too.

My sister and I gave our statements. It seemed to take forever. By the time we finished, I could barely breathe. Anxiety snapped at me like some salivating beast. *Get a grip, Annie; think of the poor victim. At least you and Jenna are alive.* But I had a bad feeling this wouldn't be the end of it. One man was already dead, another wounded. And we were witnesses.

We climbed into the SUV to head for Foothill High School, my heart skidding. Jenna insisted on driving. As we rolled through the parking lot, a television news van showed up at the curb. A man spilled out and raised his camera, the red light on. I ducked. Our car jostled as we entered the street. I could hear Adam Bendershil calling through my closed window. "Ms. Kingston, can you tell us what happened?"

After a few turns, Jenna touched my arm. "Okay, you can come up now."

I uncurled my spine and leaned back against the head-rest, wishing I could feel as strong as my sister. *God, I'm the Christian here. Help me rest in Your power.*

The scenes started rolling then. They always do.

In my head resides something akin to a film projector. During times of stress it tends to spit vivid images onto my brain's movie screen. Now it spewed sequences of

the shooter running straight toward our car, gun jerking up and down in his hand ...

Toby's pinched white face. "It hurts!" ...

A bloodied, shattered head. A cheek and eye—blown away ...

I squeezed my eyes shut. Forced the memories away.

From my purse, my cell phone sounded. I withdrew it to see Kelly's number. Pulling in a breath, I answered the call.

"Mom!" My daughter poured the impatience of a beleaguered fifteen-year-old into her voice. "What's *taking* you so long?"

Chapter 2

On our way to the high school, I called Stephen and told him what happened. I tried to keep my tone factual, but my son knew me too well.

"Mom, that's *awful*. Are you sure you're okay?"

Not really. "Yes. A little shaken by the whole thing, but fine."

"That guy with the gun—did he see you?"

"No. We were ducked down—"

"But still, it'll be on the news. They'll say you were there." His voice edged. "Now you're personally involved again. In another murder case."

I wanted to tell him to stop, that his fears were too close to my own. Instead I floundered for some soothing response that would calm neither of us. "Jenna and I gave statements, and when the guy's brought to trial, we'll probably have to testify. But that's all. It's not like last time."

Last time—when a serial murderer played chess with me, nearly killed me . . .

"Right." Stephen made a cynical sound in his throat. "Should I come home from work?"

Home? "No, of course not. There's no reason for you—"

"'Cause now I'm all worried. You sound upset, and I don't want you there by yourself."

Good grief, do I sound that bad? "I'm not by myself; Jenna's with me."

"Mom, I don't *like* this." He breathed frustration and angst into the phone. I could practically see his knit eyebrows, the set jaw. "Look, at least this time you can rely on me. Nothing better happen to you. I swear I'll kill *anybody* who —"

"Stephen, whoa! Nobody's going to do anything to me. This is *not* like the other times. Just please, calm down."

"Yeah, yeah, I'm calm." The words dropped like pebbles on cement. "I'm just telling you the way it is."

I hung up the phone and gave Jenna a nonplussed look. She raised her eyebrows. "I heard him. Feeling rather protective, isn't he?"

"No kidding." I crossed my arms. "Kid's scaring me."

"I think it's healthy. I mean, really, Annie, look at all the grief he's caused you. Thank heaven he's been scared straight for the last three months. I think it's only right that he'd turn some of his vehemence on anybody who'd try to hurt you. It's part self-defense and part ... I don't know. Atonement."

Interesting choice of word, coming from Jenna. But Stephen's real atonement would come when he stopped staying no to God. So far he'd managed to keep away from his old friends and drugs, and he'd gotten a good start on his grades this school year. But he needed God's help to stay straight.

We reached the high school, Stephen's diatribe still ringing in my ears. I dreaded telling the girls why we were late. Kelly was sensitive and more easily frightened than her brother. For the first month after the serial killer was caught, she was plagued by nightmares about what happened to me. And Erin witnessed her own mother's murder in their home a little over two years ago. These poor girls had been through enough.

My heart panged as I watched them cross the parking lot, chattering as usual—no doubt about important teenage social issues. The sight of them together always made me smile. They're both strikingly pretty—in very different ways. Kelly stands a little taller than Erin, but they're equally slim. Erin's white-blonde hair and fair complexion make her appear all the more ethereal next to my daughter's tanned skin and long brown hair.

The girls threw their backpacks in the SUV and slid into the rear seat. I turned around to say hello. Kelly took one look at my face and stilled. "What's wrong?"

How did my family do that?

God, here goes. Please help them be calm.

With a deep breath, I told them everything. Kelly listened, lips parted, brown eyes never leaving my face. Erin leaned forward, blue eyes round, a strand of bang caught on her lashes.

"That's *terrible*," Kelly breathed. "Those poor people who were shot." She shook her head. "Just think, Mom. If it had been a minute later, you or Aunt Jenna could have been in that store."

"Yeah." Erin's words swelled with awe. "God protected you."

My throat tightened. How quickly their faith rose to the surface. Both of them put me to shame. "Yes, He did."

Jenna stopped at a red light. I turned forward in my seat, thanking God they were taking it so well.

"Does Dad know?" Erin asked.

Dave. I hadn't even thought about telling him. Oh boy. Talk about someone who'd worry. "Not yet."

"Well, you better talk to him as soon as we get home. *I'm* sure not going to be the one to tell him."

Jenna tossed me an amused smile.

After we pulled into the garage, I headed across the street with Erin.

"Dad!" she yelled as she slammed her front door behind us. "Annie needs to talk to you!"

We passed the kitchen, walked down the hall toward his office. I stepped through his door as he came around his desk to meet me. I took in his square jaw, the green eyes and blond hair, and my heart performed its little Dave dance. "Hi, Annie." His face creased into a smile.

The air between us fibrillated. I felt the ancient quiver of high school years, when I was Erin's age and endured my first crush.

I halted a few feet away from him, sensing Erin behind me. Dave and I hadn't displayed much affection in front of our children. Although the girls wouldn't have minded. In fact, if they had their way, we'd be walking down the aisle tomorrow. Dave waited, gazing at me with an adoration he didn't even try to hide. Then he looked over my shoulder toward his daughter. I turned to see Erin standing in the threshold.

"I'll leave you two alone." She raised her eyebrows at her father with the wisdom of fifteen years. "Now listen. Annie needs to tell you something. But everything's okay, so don't freak out."

She pulled away and disappeared. I heard the rustle of her clothes, her cushioned footsteps as she headed toward her bedroom.

Surprised once more at this child's fortitude, I turned back to Dave. He gave me a questioning look, then held out his arms. I stepped into his embrace and hung there, just *feeling* the strength of him. Wishing I could float in this soothing sea without the detritus of my past. Music kicked on in Erin's bedroom, filtering through the wall. I pulled back, looked into Dave's face, seeing the concern in his eyes.

He ran a knuckle down my cheek. "What happened?"

His question dredged up the old insecurities. I shrugged out of his embrace. Why was I always the first one to do that?

"It's nothing bad for me, really. I mean, *I'm* okay. But Jenna and I witnessed a shooting. Some poor young man is dead; we don't know who he is yet. And a clerk at the 7-Eleven was shot. He's only eighteen."

Dave sucked in a breath. The *oh-no-not-again* worry crimped his face. He led me to his large leather armchair and eased me down. Sitting on the matching ottoman, he faced me. "Tell me everything."

I did.

When I finished, he leaned forward, taking my hands in his. "Are you sure you're all right? That would be an upsetting experience for anyone, but after all you've been through ..."

"I'm fine. Really."

Why *shouldn't* I be fine? I'd had three months to recover. My family, along with Dave and Erin, had even gone to Hawaii and lolled on the beach for two weeks.

Dave regarded me, clearly unconvinced. Sudden longing surged in me, and for a crazy moment I wanted to throw myself into his arms and cry. Wanted to tell him how weak I felt some days, and how much I'd begun to need him. And I wanted to hear that he accepted me, even if sometimes I still wondered if I accepted myself ...

Annie, stop it. I swallowed hard and forced a tiny smile.

Dave inhaled slowly. He held my gaze, his eyes clouding with ... what? Frustration? Disappointment? "You know I'm here for you. Please believe that. Don't keep anything bottled up. It's not healthy."

"Okay. Thank you." How formal I sounded.

When I left, he walked me to his front door and kissed me, long and gently.

Heart flip-flopping, I descended his porch steps and headed across our double-wide street. The large log home Jenna and I had inherited from our father spread before me with gracious elegance. One of twenty-four homes in Grove Landing sky park, our house nestles at the end of Barrister Court and is edged in the back and one side by forest. Grove Landing is a dignified and quiet neighborhood—except for the noise of airplanes on the private runway, or taxiing into hangars built into the houses. Now, in the peaceful afternoon, a crow cawed from the woods on my right. The faint scent of newly cut grass wafted from a neighbor's home. I slowed my steps, drinking in the sensations, inviting them to flow through me, quiet my spirit.

God, why do I always hold back with Dave? Why can't I just let him care for me?

Jenna had left the garage door open for my return. I made sure to shut it. These days, our house was always closed up and locked tight.

In the great room, I sank into the oversized couch facing the circular wooden staircase. The room stretches forty feet long, with a twenty-five-foot ceiling. Banisters run along the hallways of the upper floor on both sides, connected by a walkway toward the back of the great room that is supported by massive log posts. I looked up to my left, toward Kelly's and my bedrooms — and a memory flashed in my brain. I stood

at that banister, gun pointed down at the head of a strange man, hulking over my daughter as she lies on the couch ...

I shuddered. *No.* That was three months ago. This was now. We *would not* face such danger again.

An hour later I heard the unique ring tone of my business line. I hurried from the kitchen toward my office, footsteps echoing over the great room's hardwood floor.

"Annie, it's Tim Blanche." He sounded pushed, irritated. "Bad news. The security camera at the 7-Eleven was broken. Turns out the owner knew it and was just about to have it fixed. Murphy's Law and all that. We're going to need you to draw a composite of the shooter."

My heart sank. I carried the receiver around my desk and sank into my chair. "From what I heard, none of the people in the store saw him clearly except for the boy who was shot."

"Right. Toby Brown. Looked right into the guy's face."

What a terrifying second that must have been. "How is he?"

"They've removed the bullet. He's lucky it didn't hit anything major. They've stabilized him, although there's some problem with bleeding, so he's staying in the hospital a day or two. Doped up on medication for the pain. He's in no shape to be interviewed now, but tomorrow should be fine."

"Okay." The sooner the interview took place, the better Toby's memory would be. I ran a hand through my hair. "Any word on the identity of the man who died?"

"Yeah. Name's Mike Winger. Twenty-two. One of our men met his parents at the morgue. They had to cover up that mangled side of his face. I hear the mother nearly collapsed."

My eyes closed. I could not begin to imagine her grief.

"Annie, you got a pen and paper? I'll give you Toby's hospital room number."

"Yeah." I jotted the note — *Room 287.* "I'll see him tomorrow. And Tim?" Righteous indignation surged through me. How could *anyone* stick a gun in someone's face and pull the trigger? "We're gonna get this guy."

Tim grunted. "It's my case. You bet I'll get him."

Chapter 3

That night I couldn't sleep. I lay on my back, blinking at the grim play of light from a streetlamp across the log beams of my ceiling. The projector in my head replayed the shooting with the jerky motions of a handheld camera. Flash! and

I glance into the SUV's rearview mirror, see the shooter, running . . .

Toby's expression, wrenched in pain . . .

The bloodied pulp of a half-missing face . . .

I fisted my bedcovers, willing the pictures to stop.

When I finally fell into a tossed and troubled ocean of sleep, my mind swelled with taunting dreams. Dreams of darkness . . .

And the tangy smell of dirt. Staleness.

A light turned on.

I found myself

sitting in a courtroom, sketchpad on my lap, colored pencils in hand. A petite young woman takes the witness stand. With a start I recognize her. Tracey Wilagher. Her shoulders are bony, drawn inward. She runs a nervous hand through her brown hair.

An attorney asks her questions about the night her mother died. As I draw her face, I visualize everything she relates. Her fear and denial that night, when her mother's panicked call pulled weak, flu-stricken Tracey out of bed to drive to the beach and rescue her mom from the rage of a drunken, abusive husband.

By the time she reaches the edge of the beach, Tracey says, her head pounds. Her body feels heavy and dull. She forces herself from her car, a sliver of a moon doing little to lighten her way. Where is her mom? She should be here, waiting. Down toward the water a fire flickers, casting light on a form sprawled in the sand. Her stepfather, passed out. "Mom?" Tracey whispers in the darkness. "Where are you?"

No response.

Her knees tremble. She swallows hard, wincing at pain in her throat. Where could her mother be? The last thing she wants is to wake a drunken Darren Welk. She whispers louder, muscles tense. "Mom!" Still no answer.

Tracey tells the court that her next memories jumble. She finds herself stumbling around the edge of the beach, calling her mother's name louder, louder, a rising flood of fear sweeping away all caution. Her chest grows heavy, her knees turn weak. Then she is raking open the doors of Darren Welk's car, searching the front seat, the back. On the floor of the front seat she sees her mother's small evening purse. A horrifying, black thought mushrooms in her brain, and she fumbles for the latch to pop open the trunk. Tears scalding her face, she stumbles to the back of the car to check the trunk—and sways with relief when she sees it's empty.

Tracey can stand it no more. She makes her way back to her car and drives forward as far as she can, stopping at an angle so her headlights wash the length of the beach. The figure of Darren Welk lights up but he does not move. Tracey lurches out

*of her car, searching the beach up and down, forcing her fogged
brain to process. "Mom, please, where are you?"*

The sizzle-hiss of waves upon land is the only sound.

*Something on the sand catches her eye. Something glistening,
not far from the fire's embers. A block of ice falls into Tracey's
stomach as she stares. She forces her leaden legs forward. As she
nears the glimmering dot, she sees others like it. She stops above
them, unwilling to bend down and add undeniable senses to the
terrifying shadows ghosting her mind. Slowly she reaches out a
trembling finger and touches the disfigured surface of the sand.
Granules stick to her skin. She raises her finger, turns it toward
the car's headlights. The granules are dark red ...*

A strangled cry in my windpipe awoke me. My heart
churned.

What ...

Where ...

No ... No. It's okay. My room, my bed.

My throat convulsed in a swallow. A dream. Just a
dream.

But so vivid. So *real*. Almost as real as that day I sat in
the Redwood City courtroom, sketching Tracey Wilagher's
face as she testified.

A chill brushed my shoulders. The air around my bed
hung heavy. I pulled the covers tightly around me, breathing, shivering. Why had I dreamed about this now? That
case was three years ago. I shivered again, more violently.
What was going on? First the shooting, now this.

Whatever was happening, I needed to pray. Now. Pray
against ... something. Something I could almost feel, but
not quite touch ...

Dear Jesus, help. Why did I dream this? What am I sensing? I feel like ... almost like I did this past summer, when the serial killer roamed the streets. Oh, God, please tell me something that frightening isn't happening now. I can't go through anything like that again ...

Prayers and fears swirled like chilled fog in my mind. Until slowly the fog weighted ... settled ... blanketed me with a restless sleep.

Friday, September 23

Chapter 4

I awoke slowly, still haunted by the dream. Tracey Wilagher on the stand ... the drop of blood on her finger ...

With bleary eyes I checked the digital clock by my bed. Six forty-five. Time to get up, shake off the night. Make sure the kids were moving. By seven thirty Stephen and the girls would need to be driving to school—

Wait, what day was this?

Friday. That meant it was Dave's turn to pick up the girls in the afternoon. Good. I was supposed to be at the hospital then, interviewing Toby Brown, and Jenna needed to work on her computer software project all day.

The dream gnawed at me. I forced it from my mind.

In the shower I talked to God. Prayer had become a consistent, reliable force in my life, soothing raindrops upon the thirsty ground of my soul. First I simply praised Him for all He'd done for me. Then I asked for a calmer spirit. And for justice in the shooting I witnessed, that God would heal Toby Brown's leg, and that He'd be with us during our interview. As always, I sought God's protection and His mercy upon my children and Jenna.

And Lord, help me with Dave. Why do I want him yet push him away? Why can't I just enjoy what's happening between us?

Seven thirty. With the kids gone, Jenna and I headed for the kitchen and our coffee. I hoped the routine would settle my nerves. But nearing the kitchen table, I was jolted with a reminder of yesterday. Today's *Record Searchlight* lay upon it. The front page blared news of the latest homicide in Redding, accompanied by a photo of Toby Brown being loaded into the ambulance.

I sighed and walked to a cabinet for a mug. Poured myself some coffee. Sinking into a chair at the table, I pushed the newspaper away. I would deal with it later.

Jenna settled into a seat across from me and pursed her lips. "You don't look so good."

"Thanks."

"What's up? I mean, is it more than what happened yesterday?"

The dream nibbled at my nerves. "Forget me, what about *you*? Did you and Eric patch up your argument last night?"

She made a little *tsking* sound. "I'm not patching up anything. He lied to me. End of story."

"Oh. Okay." I wondered how long the argument would last. Jenna was crazy about Eric.

"So." She tapped a fingernail against the table. "What's wrong?"

I regarded my sister for a moment. Should I tell her? Jenna had grown mighty protective of me—with good reason. What if she read too much into my premonition, got all antsy about things? She'd go into overdrive bossing me. That I didn't need.

"It's nothing." I focused on my coffee cup. "Just a dream I had."

"Really. Not usual for you to be bothered by such a thing. Better tell me about it."

I made a face. "What are you, Miss Dream Interpreter all of a sudden?"

"Annie. Tell me."

I am no match for my sister. I poured out everything. How real it was. How unsettling.

She drew a breath and sat back, gaze drifting out the window. "What was the name of that woman on the jury? You know, the one who made all the headlines the year before?"

"Chelsea Adams."

"Oh yeah. Chelsea Adams." She rubbed a finger on the table, brows knit. "Well." She looked me straight in the eye. "If you're thinking that dream's telling you to move back to Redwood City, you can think again. I'm just beginning to like it here."

Yeah, like I'd want to go back there. Jenna had finally taken the plunge a year and a half ago to leave the "civilization" of her Bay Area town house and now worked as a software consultant from Grove Landing. She flew back to the Bay Area to meet with clients, staying in her town house in Redwood Shores.

I smiled lopsidedly. "Thanks for the warning."

"That's what sisters are for."

We drank our coffee in silence.

The newspaper beckoned. Against my will I drew it toward me. "You read this yet?"

"No, just brought it in. Thought I'd give you the honors."

"Wonderful." I began reading, paraphrasing for Jenna. "Mike Winger was the victim, twenty-two years old—Blanche told me that much yesterday. His parents live in Redding. His dad works construction, and his mom's—oh wow. His mom is assistant to the principal at Foothill High School."

Jenna's coffee cup stopped halfway to her lips. "Oh, how sad. I wonder if the kids know her."

"Well, maybe Stephen. I don't know that Kelly's spent much time in the principal's office." Mike's half-blown-away face flashed in my head. I focused on the wood grain of the table. Was his mother sitting in her own kitchen right now, staring at nothing, just trying to survive? I took a slow drink of coffee and turned back to the article. "It talks about the kid who was shot. Toby. He has three younger siblings. No father. Toby was working at 7-Eleven to help support the family. Oh, Jenna." I leaned back in my chair. "Can you imagine him going back to his job after this?"

She shook her head. "If I were his mom, I wouldn't let him."

"But sounds like they're pretty short on money. And now they're going to have hospital bills."

"Yeah." Jenna tucked a strand of hair behind her ear. "That would be tough."

I stared at the newspaper, thinking about Toby and his family. It took a minute for me to register the article's final words. "This says I'm going to interview Toby today and draw a composite of the shooter. Good grief. Whoever in the Police Department told the reporter that should have kept his mouth shut."

"True, but no surprise. Somebody always talks too much." Jenna pushed back her chair. "Okay, time for breakfast. I'll put a bagel in the toaster for you."

As usual, she hadn't asked. "And if I don't want one?"

She snorted. "Since when do I ever listen to you?"

The phone rang. Jenna answered it, then handed the receiver to me. "It's Chetterling."

I raised my eyebrows. The sheriff's detective and I hadn't worked together since the serial killer case. We'd had little reason to talk since then. "Hi, Ralph, how are you?"

"Hi, Annie. I'm doing fine. Busy as usual. I see you've got some work to do for the Police Department today."

"Oh, you read the papers too, huh."

"Great, aren't they?" He paused. "So, Annie. I have an unusual request for you."

Jenna turned from the toaster, two bagels in hand, to watch me. Chetterling's phone calls never tended to bring good news. I gave her a shrug—*Who knows?* "Okay. Shoot."

"I got a call this morning from a woman down in the Bay Area. Says she needs to talk to you. She couldn't get your phone number since it's unlisted, but she's read about the cases you've worked on with me, so she called the Sheriff's Department. Asked if I'd pass on the message."

What now? The hundredth journalist wanting an interview? Another author writing a true-crime book? "Who is she?"

"That's just it. I'll bet you recognize her name. A few years ago she gained almost as much notoriety as you."

Poor woman. "Great. We ought to make a smashing team."

"That's what I'm afraid of."

"Well, come on, Chetterling, cut the drama. Who is she?"

"Her name's Chelsea Adams."

My jaw slacked. I widened my eyes at Jenna. "You're kidding."

"Nope."

A shiver raked across my shoulders. I dropped my gaze to study the kitchen's hardwood floor, searching for some semblance of reason in this unlikely coincidence.

"Know who she is?"

Did I. Last night's dream rushed over me. The *realness* of it—the feel of colored pencils in my hand, the musty smell of the courtroom, the *thump-thump* of the pacing attorney's feet. "Yeah, I do."

"Thought so. Were you a courtroom artist on the cases she was involved in?"

"Yes. Both of them." I still couldn't believe this. What were the chances of my dream and Ms. Adams's phone call happening within the space of six hours? A queasy premonition slithered through my stomach. "What does she want with me?"

"Don't know. She just says it's very important. So here's her phone number."

Half in a daze, I crossed the kitchen to pull pen and paper from a drawer. Jenna surveyed me suspiciously. When the bagels bounced up in the toaster, she flung open a cupboard and pulled out two plates as if annoyed at the distraction.

"Okay, Ralph." I tossed the pen back in its drawer. "Got it. Thanks."

"So if you call her, you going to tell me what she says?"

"Maybe. But don't you know curiosity killed the cat?"

"Well, can you blame me? Put you and Chelsea Adams together, and my heart goes flip-flop. I just hope if this has anything to do with what she's famous for, the havoc wreaked was in her neck of the woods, not ours."

That makes two of us, Ralph.

By the time I hung up the phone, my bagel sat on a plate, spread with cream cheese. Jenna leaned against the table like a wary soldier, arms crossed. "All right. What's going on?"

I eyed my breakfast, biting my lip. The uneasiness in my stomach would not go away. "I don't know, Jenna. But I have a phone call to make."

Chapter 5

Murder always made the front-page news. He read the article —twice.

And the voices started in.

The Bible says thou shalt not kill. Thou shalt not kill ...

He pushed the newspaper away, shoved a bite of eggs into his mouth. Chewed fast and hard.

Thou shalt not kill ...

No, he did *not* hear them. He was *fine.*

Abruptly the voices shut up.

He sniffed, ran a hand under his nose. His gaze strayed across the kitchen and into the backyard. What a place this was. Nobody was going to drag him from it. Ever.

He stared at the article's first sentence until his eyeballs burned. *Yesterday in the 7-Eleven store on Delworth Street, an unidentified man shot and killed ...*

What kind of time was he looking at? It would be first-degree murder. Plus attempted murder on the kid.

Man. You're talking years in jail.

Better than death, the voices taunted. *They find out you killed more than one person, it's death penalty for sure.*

"Shut up!" He rattled his head—hard. No good. Memories of the bodies surfaced.

Pop ...

Pop ...

A picture of a corpse. And another. Clothes gone. Screaming at him ...

Death penalty ... Murder is a sin.

"Go away!"

He thrust more eggs and bacon into his mouth. Ground them between his teeth, tasting the salty flavor with manic concentration.

They'll kill you, like you killed us.

"Shut *up!*" He shoved away from the table, jumped to his feet.

The taunts whiplashed through his head.

He pressed palms to his ears. Paced a circle, humming. "Mm, mm, mm. Can't hear you!"

You killed us, and they'll find you. They'll shove you in a cell. And we'll laugh, laugh, laugh, 'cause you deserve it, deserve it, deserve it!

"Stop!" He wheeled around, lashed a fist at the air, then stumbled into the counter like a drunken man. Yeah, that's what he needed—a drink. He flung himself toward a cabinet, yanked out a bottle of gin. Poured some into a glass.

"Cheers!" He guzzled it down. The gin pinched his cheeks, tingle-tangled his throat.

You killed us ... you killed us ...

He banged down the glass.

The dirt came next, the dank, biting smell of burial. Pieces of it stuck to his feet like worms. The worms started to crawl—up his heels, over his ankles—their slimy bodies sucking at his skin.

"Ah!" He scrubbed both legs with his hands, but still they crawled.

He fled to the bathroom to scour them off.

In the shower he sucked steam deep into his lungs. Watched the wormy dirt particles nudge across the tile, disappear down the drain.

"Hah, good riddance!"

Droplets splashed and pounded, clearing his head, cleansing his soul.

He turned off the water, braced himself, and listened.

No voices.

He exhaled in relief. His skin glowed red, fresh as he stepped out of the shower, reached for a towel, raised one leg.

Wait, was that dirt on his ankle? How had it stayed there, after all that *water*?

He cursed, rubbing it away with the towel.

More dirt on the other foot. He gasped, smacked at it two, three times.

When he stepped into a pair of pants, new whispers echoed in his brain. *Thou shalt not kill, kill, kill ... Murder is a sin, sin, sin ...*

Dirt crawled onto his big toe. An ant this time. A big, black dirt ant.

"No!"

He threw off his pants. Ran back to the shower and yanked on the water, shoving his body under it, trying to drown out the voices with the sizzle, hiss, pound.

Where are you going to hide when they know everything you've done? When we scream at them that you killed us?

Where are you going to hide ...

Chapter 6

Chelsea Adams huddled on the couch in her family room, frowning at her Bible. The verses ran together in a mindless stream. She couldn't concentrate on anything but the horrifying picture pulsing in her brain: the dim, claustrophobic room in her vision.

Who were those people? *Where* were they? When would it happen?

The memories taunted her. That earthy, dusty smell. The rasping whisper of some demented man holding two people against their will. One of them was the crouching figure on the floor—a female. And the second captive ... Through whose eyes had Chelsea viewed the scene? A man? Woman?

After the vision of that room passed, Chelsea had seen a face. She could close her eyes now and see those features clearly in her mind.

She flopped her Bible closed and tossed it on the couch. *God, this is too confusing. Why can't You tell me everything so I don't have to guess?*

Last night her husband had sensed her terror. One look at her expression when she emerged from the kitchen, and Paul's face went slack. "What's wrong?"

"I had another vision." Tears bit her eyes.

He pulled in a breath. "A bad one?"

"The worst yet."

He held his arms out to her and she pressed against his chest. Wishing she could hide her fear, wishing she didn't have to tell him. Before Paul became a Christian, he tried to deny the visions. Now he knew God sent them, but couldn't understand why his wife had to be the conduit. Why not somebody else for once?

Chelsea stared without seeing at the coffee table. *God, I need Your help. Please lead Annie Kingston to call.*

The phone rang and Chelsea jumped. She jerked her head toward the receiver. It rang once more before she picked it up. "Hello?"

"Hi. I'm trying to reach Chelsea Adams. This is Annie Kingston, returning her call."

Chelsea almost laughed at the timing. *Thank You, God!* She clutched the phone, her heart turning over. "Oh, I'm so glad you called. I didn't expect to hear from you so soon. In fact, I wasn't sure if you'd call at all."

Annie Kingston's laugh was nervous. "Well, Ms. Adams, I have to admit I was rather curious."

"Oh, please call me Chelsea."

"Okay. And I'm Annie."

An awkward pause followed.

"I was in the courtroom, you know," Annie ventured. "For those two cases. As an artist."

Those two cases. No explanation was needed. "I know. I recognized your face the first time I saw you on the news. Then those magazine features mentioned that you'd been in Redwood City. And of course I've heard about you numerous times since." Chelsea paused. She shouldn't have said all that. Maybe Annie didn't like making the news any more than she did. "Anyway, thank you so much for calling back. I've been praying that you would." She stopped. "I ... that is, the most recent stories I read about you mentioned your faith. I understand you're a Christian?"

"Yes."

"Oh, good." Chelsea hesitated. Here came the hard part. *Lord, give me the right words.* "Look, when this kind of thing happens—and fortunately it's not often—it isn't easy for me. I never know how a person's going to respond. But I want you to know I'm clear on one thing. God impressed upon me very strongly to call you."

Silence. Chelsea held her breath.

"Okay."

The word came slowly, wrapped in wariness. "I hear the caution in your voice, Annie, and I don't blame you. I mean, you and I are both—how shall I say it?—known for finding ourselves in the midst of trouble. I can understand why receiving a phone call from me might be rather ... startling."

Tension crept across Chelsea's shoulders. Was she being too candid?

"I just might startle *you*," Annie replied. "Fact is, I had a dream about you last night."

Chelsea blinked. "About *me?*"

"Well, not really about you. But about the Salad King trial—and that story can't be told without your part in it. I dreamed about Tracey Wilagher's testimony, just like it happened. I woke up feeling strange and unsettled. Heavy with premonition. So when I heard you wanted to talk to me ..."

"Oh, thank You, God." Chelsea closed her eyes, relief flooding her chest. "Isn't that just like Him—merciful enough to give us both a confirmation. Your dream certainly wasn't a coincidence."

"You don't think so?"

"Not at all. See, last night was ... memorable for me too. God sent me a vision. I have to admit it was terrifying. Then when it faded, I saw a face. Clearly. A few hours later I felt the strong impression that I was to meet with you, tell you everything. Describe the face so you could draw it."

Silence again. Chelsea could imagine Annie's thoughts —*How do I end this phone call in a hurry?* The woman had been through a lot in the last few years. Why should she allow herself to become tangled in Chelsea's problems?

God, if this is right, please help her hear.

Chelsea waited. Still no answer. "Annie?"

"Yes. I'm ... listening."

Chelsea sighed. "You didn't like what I just said, did you? You're thinking, 'Keep me out of this.'" She laughed self-consciously. "I know how obnoxious I must sound. Plus you're busy, and I have no right to demand your time. I don't expect you to answer right now. Maybe the best thing to do is just let you pray about it. You can call me back ... maybe tonight?"

Annie cleared her throat. "I'm not sure. First of all, I couldn't complete a composite by hearing a description over the phone. I'd have to show it to the person. There's usually a give-and-take as the drawing is refined."

"I know. I would need to come see you." Chelsea winced. How demanding she must sound. "Believe me, I know I'm asking a lot—"

"Are you still in the Bay Area? That's almost four hours away."

"Yes, I am. And it's hard for me to leave. I have two boys in high school. But tomorrow's Saturday, so I could take the day to drive up and see you. I mean, *if* you're available. Which is a lot to expect with such little notice, I know."

Chelsea's words faded. What more to say? She pictured herself in Annie's shoes—hearing a perfect stranger claim her huge request was some message from God.

"Chelsea, thank you for calling. I really appreciate your trust in me. I do need time to think and pray about this, okay? It's just that we had a murder here yesterday, and I'm already needed to work on that case."

Oh no, another murder in Redding? Chelsea closed her eyes. "I'm so sorry to hear that. I understand you'll be busy. Plus you have family, and tomorrow's supposed to be a day off. So . . . I'll just wait to hear from you."

"Okay. I'll get back to you by tonight."

"Thank you, Annie. Very much."

Chelsea hung up and pressed back against the couch, wrung out. *Well, that didn't go very well.* The day stretched before her, oppressive and foreboding. If only she could clear the horrible memories from her head. Now she'd done all she could, and there was nothing to do but wait. God could send messages, but He would not force anyone to act against their will.

Lord, what am I going to do if I never hear from Annie Kingston again?

Chapter 7

One o'clock. My mind ran along dual tracks as I pulled into the parking lot of Shasta Regional Medical Center. For the sake of Toby Brown and Mike Winger, I needed to concentrate on the task at hand. But I couldn't shake Chelsea Adams's call from my mind. For some masochistic reason I'd stuck her phone number in my purse, and now it practically burned a hole through the leather.

After Chelsea's phone call, Jenna pounced me with questions. I kept nothing from her, but I cringed upon relating the "God-told-me-to-call-you" part. As a loving sister, Jenna tries not to denigrate my increasingly vocal faith, but she certainly hasn't embraced it either.

"Annie, that's crazy." She frowned. "How can anybody say 'God told me' when they don't hear a thing? And how are you supposed to respond to that? She's really put you on the spot."

I know very well how God can talk to people. The way He led me—and other Christians, including Dave—to pray while the Poison Killer was still on the Redding streets had been undeniable. "Jenna, I hear you. But remember the news stories from Redwood City. You have to admit Chelsea Adams knows what she's talking about."

Jenna folded her arms. "Fine, but why drag *you* into it? There are plenty of forensic artists in the Bay Area."

My mouth opened, then closed. She had a point.

She jabbed a finger at me. "Don't you go getting mixed up with her, Annie. That would be all you need. All *we* need."

So much for help from my sister. She was all gut reaction with no Christian wisdom. I'd headed out the door to talk to Dave about the phone call. As I crossed the street, I registered the distant rumble of tractors beginning work at the Grove Landing airstrip. At least *that* would make Jenna happy.

In Dave's kitchen I told my tale once again. He listened with an expression of wariness and intrigue. When I finished, he laid a hand at the back of his neck and stared out the window. Vestiges of my past narrow escapes haunted his expression. "Well. I don't know what this is all about." The words came reluctantly. "But yes, I'll pray about it today. Sounds like it might be something important that God needs you to do."

Now, as I drove into the medical center parking lot, it struck me we were all being a little silly. So Chelsea Adams wanted me to draw a composite. Big deal. I did that on a regular basis. And most of the time it was a normal project, no danger involved.

Most of the time.

Annie, stop now. You've got other things to think about.

I pulled into a parking space, climbed out of the SUV, and opened the back door to retrieve my drawing kit. The sun beat through my knit shirt as I crossed the lot. Suddenly a car pulled out of a space right in front of me. I jerked to a halt, then drifted backward, giving him room. A middle-aged man. He didn't even see me.

Hospitals. I'd never felt comfortable around them. People inside and out wrapped up in their pain. Two and a half years ago, after my father's death from a heart attack, I'd crossed this same parking lot, head down, arms hugging my chest, barely noticing the rain or cars. I could only imagine how Toby's mother must have felt yesterday as she hurried into the hospital to see her son.

Justice, Toby. We're going to find who did this to you.

A few minutes later I entered the young man's room. He occupied the first bed, the curtains drawn back. The second bed was empty. *Good.* We'd have some privacy during the interview.

A woman sat beside Toby, both of them staring blank-faced at an old movie on TV. Her brown hair was uncombed, her posture slumped. Seeing me, she clicked off the show and pushed to her feet, questions in her weary brown eyes. She was a few inches shorter than my five-foot-five frame. Worry lines jagged across her forehead, and her mouth drooped. My heart ached for her. Had she been here all night?

"Mrs. Brown?" I held out my hand to her. "I'm Annie Kingston."

"Yes." She gave me a weak handshake and tried to smile. "I recognize you. Can't tell you how glad I am you're the one going to draw the picture. I know we'll find the man who did this to my boy, with your help."

I managed to smile back. If she only knew what kind of pressure those words heaped upon me. The more tragedy I'd seen, the more I hated crime. Every victim deserved justice, *every one.* But all too often it proved elusive. "Those of us working on this case will do the best we can, Mrs. Brown, I promise you that."

"Yes. Thank you." She laced and unlaced her fingers. "And please, call me Sheila."

I nodded, holding her gaze with all the warmth I could muster. She looked so nervous, and my heart went out to her. "Okay. Sheila."

Setting down my portfolio of art supplies, I turned toward Toby. He lay with the covers pulled midchest, hands resting on his stomach, fingers interlaced. His thumbs batted at each other. The bed had been cranked up to elevate his head, numerous pillows used to cushion. I could imagine his mother fussing with those pillows, trying to do what little she could to ease his discomfort. Even now her hand hovered over him, seeking something to do — any small act that could afford some sense of control over her son's fate.

"Hi, Toby." I laid a gentle hand on his shoulder, noting the faint color in his face. "You look a lot better now than the last time I saw you."

The sides of his mouth lifted. "That's not saying much."

"I understand they removed the bullet from your leg and got you patched up. And you're going home tomorrow?"

"Praise God," his mother whispered behind me.

"Yeah." Toby shifted his head against the pillows. "They just want to watch me for today, 'cause I was bleeding some. But they said I was lucky. The bullet didn't hit a bone or nerve or anything." He swallowed. "I want to thank you for helping me yesterday. As bad as it was, you helped keep me calm. There was just something about you being there ..."

That was Jesus' presence, Toby, not mine.

I pulled a chair close to the bed. His mother hesitated. "The detective told me I should leave while you do your work."

"Yes." The presence of any face could skew Toby's memory as he tried to recall the suspect's features. Even I would sit at an angle so he would not look directly at me. "But let's just talk for a while first, all right?"

"Okay."

I sat down while Sheila resumed her seat on the other side of the bed. For a good half hour we simply chatted. Although Toby already seemed to trust me, I wanted to put him more at ease. My work would require him to "see" again the face that caused his trauma. He needed to be eased into emotional readiness for the task. I asked him about school, his friends, if he planned to go to college. I told him about my kids, wondering if he'd ever met Kelly or Stephen, perhaps at a football game.

"No, don't think so," Toby said, "but maybe I will sometime."

Sheila told me the names of Toby's younger brother and sisters. Carla was thirteen; Jeremy, ten; and Maria was seven.

"From what I heard, Toby, you help take care of them." I kept my voice light, conversational.

He shrugged. "I do what I can."

I didn't want to stray into the topic of their financial difficulties. Toby had other worries to concentrate on. "And you'll be back at it. Soon."

We fell silent. Toby pulled in a slow breath and his countenance shifted. I've learned to read the signals—resolve steeling across a victim's features, an aura of expectation misting the air. He was ready.

I looked to his mother. Sheila clasped her son's arm, then rose with a final, pleading look at me — *Take care of my boy. Help him remember.* I nodded.

She crossed to the door and closed it softly behind her. I brought her chair over beside mine to use as a place to lay my materials. Reaching into my portfolio, I first pulled out an eleven-by-fourteen-inch Bristol pad with smooth finish. As an artist who tends to draw with as much detail as an interviewee's memory will allow, I use this paper rather than others of a rougher texture. Then came various pencils, both hard lead and soft, some with rounded tips for the initial, proportional drawing of the face, and others sharpened to a point for the finer details. A kneaded rubber eraser for creating highlights, and a harder vinyl one for full erasure.

"All right, Toby." I scooted my chair farther away from the bed. "I'm going to move over here. I'd like you to focus straight ahead, or close your eyes, or do whatever you need to relax. We're going to work together to do the best we can. But I want you to know that composites are not photographs, so don't be disappointed if the drawing doesn't look perfect to you. A composite is an investigative tool. It can be a lot of help to law enforcement even if it doesn't look like a portrait."

"Okay."

I smiled at him and positioned the drawing pad. *Lord, give me the ability to hear, to interpret. Help me draw an effective composite.* "Toby, we're going to focus on the facial description of the man who shot you rather than all the details of what happened."

"You mean I don't have to tell that story for the millionth time?"

"That's right."

He sighed. "Good."

In a purely cognitive interview it would have been necessary for Toby to recount everything, and through his remembering events, I would have extracted memories of the assailant's face. But over the past year I'd settled into using a different technique—the composite-specific interview. As Toby recalled facial features, I would sketch the proportions first, then fine-tune the drawing with the help of photographs from the FBI *Facial Identification Catalog.*

"Okay, Toby. Tell me what you remember about the man who shot you."

Toby began talking and I listened, jotting notes. This was a crucial time in the interview, a time for free recall with no distraction. When Toby fell silent, I waited until he was ready to continue. A general image formed. A man perhaps in his early thirties, around six feet tall ... Dark hair, short and combed back with no part ... A squared face, protruding brown eyes ... Prominent chin ...

I began to sketch.

Time fell away. Noises of the hospital—voices, footsteps, a cart rattling by—faded into the background, a wash of gray on canvas. My concentration honed, my senses alert to Toby's every word. The familiar scent of lead and eraser, the scratches of pencil against paper, absorbed me. I registered every sniff that Toby made, the rustle of sheets when he paused to shift position. I could practically hear his mind churning, churning to remember more. *Come on, Toby, you can do it.* It was like this in every interview—my words and thoughts, the fibers of my being, straining to connect with the person, to shape the shifting sands of memory.

The killer's face began to emerge. But I would need a better sense of its proportions.

In time, Toby's words ran out. "I can't—I don't know any more." He lifted a hand off the sheet, let it fall.

"All right, you're doing great." I perused my sketch, deciding what to ask first. "You said he had a square face. Just how wide would you say his jaw was in comparison to the cheekbones?"

Toby thought for a moment, then described as best he could.

I nodded. "Good. And tell me about his eyes. How far apart were they?"

We continued back and forth, the image refining. I switched from more open-ended questions to those with dual-choice answers. Were the lips thinner or fuller? Was the nose more pointed or flatter? Then I began to select pages in the *Facial Identification Catalog* for Toby to review. One showed various pictures of protruding eyes; another, selections of jutting chins. I changed pencils, erased, concentrated, listened, and drew. Toby became more animated with the process, his eyes widening at flash memories of certain features.

Not once did I look at my watch. An hour had passed, perhaps. Maybe longer.

"Ready to look at the refined drawing, Toby? It's not final yet but I think we're getting closer."

"I'm ready." Toby's mouth hung open, forming a little O. He lifted his head off the pillows, winced, then laid it back down.

"You all right?"

"Yeah. Just moved my leg enough to remind me why I'm here." He swallowed. "Don't worry about it. I want to see the drawing."

"Here goes." I turned the pad around and held it up.

Toby's eyes roved over the page. "Wow. Yeah. That's him ..." He frowned. "I mean, it is, but there's something ... It's not quite right yet. I'm not sure why."

"That's okay; it's what I expected." I moved my chair closer to his bed. "Let's go over the composite point by point now. It's never too late to make changes. You still have the energy to do that?"

He nodded.

We started at the top and worked down. The eyes had a little less upturn at the outer corners, the cheeks a little more fullness. Toby stared at the drawing. "And the mouth looked harder somehow. Maybe less curve at the top. He just looked ... I mean, everything about him was so *cold*."

Sometimes at this point in an interview, when a vague "something" is still missing, I've needed to lead the witness through a context reinstatement, asking the person to close his eyes and replay all the events. Almost always, something new about the features comes up. But it's an emotional and frightening experience, and I only do it if the person is able and willing. I could see Toby was tiring. I didn't want to put him through that ordeal.

Please, God, let this be right.

I held up the pad. "Okay, Toby, look at the face as a whole now. See anything else that needs to be fixed?"

He stared, frowning. His lips tightened, fingers hooking into the sheets. "No, nothing. That's ... You got it."

"You sure?"

He pulled his bottom lip between his teeth, then nodded. "Yeah. I'm sure."

Thank You, God. I put down the pad. Already his expression was flattening with fatigue. "You did a great job, Toby. Thank you. Hope you'll get some rest now."

He gave me that victim's smile I've come to know — one of pained and weary gratitude. My heart swelled at the sight. I squeezed his shoulder, uttering a silent prayer for him, and said good-bye.

When I slid into my car, the clock read three thirty. Dave would have picked up the girls at school by now. They were probably already home. I pulled out of the medical center parking lot and headed toward the Redding Police Station to log in the composite. From there it would be sent immediately to law enforcement agencies in surrounding towns, to the *Record Searchlight*, and local TV. My work on the case was nearly over.

So why did I feel uneasy?

The tape of Chelsea Adams's voice whirred a rewind in my head. *Click.* Press play. *"God sent me a vision. I have to admit it was terrifying. Then when it faded, I saw a face ..."*

Whir. Rewind. The tape played again.

My fingers drummed the steering wheel. Jenna was right. Why did Chelsea call *me*? I should at least have asked what her vision was about. How unthinking of me! Now my overactive brain, fueled with adrenaline from the task I'd just completed, projected wild explanations. What if the vision she saw was about this shooting? Maybe the face she saw was the one I'd just drawn. Or another person who was somehow involved.

More conjectures flowed. What if Chelsea envisioned someone in my family being hurt? What if it was one of my children? Or Erin, or Dave?

Oh, God, please don't let it be that!

Only by sheer will did I rein in the disturbing thoughts. By the time I reached the police station, I'd forced myself into calmness. But I realized one thing. I could not refuse Chelsea Adams based on the scant information I knew.

Lord, why did You tell her to call me?

Chapter 8

The minute I entered the Redding Police Station, sketch-pad in hand, I found myself hustled toward Tim Blanche's office.

"You got the drawing? Good, we've been waiting for you." Rod Houp, a thin, hunched officer with a face like Mr. Burns on *The Simpsons*, prodded me down the hall. He bristled with the energy I'd become all too familiar with — the adrenaline rush of chasing a killer. "We've just gotten some ID leads on the suspect. Here's hoping the composite is a match." He pulled up short outside the detective's office. The door was slightly ajar, voices filtering through — Blanche's, and a young woman's, fraught with tension. "Hang on just a minute." Rod rapped on the door, then stuck his head inside. "Annie's here."

"Great, send her in."

Rod stepped aside, a brisk wave of his hand ushering me inside the office. He dogged my heels into the cramped quarters and closed the door. Tim rose from behind his battered desk, already reaching for the drawing. "Composite done?"

"Yes, but it's still on the sketchpad. I thought I'd prepare it for you here."

"Yeah, fine. Let's see what you got."

My gaze fell on a figure perched in a chair before Tim's desk. She looked to be in her early twenties. Long dark hair with red-pink streaks. Black liner smudged beneath frightened, chocolate eyes. She took one look at me and pulled in her shoulders, arms cradling her chest. I gave her a tentative smile as I flipped back the cover of the sketchpad and held it out to Blanche. The young woman did not respond, her eyes following the drawing as if it were fire in my hand.

Blanche grabbed the sketchpad and stared at the drawing. Plucked a piece of paper from his desk and compared the two. Back and forth, back and forth jerked his eyes. I watched his face as jagged lines smoothed from his forehead. He gave a quick sigh, aimed a meaningful look at me. "Dayna." He spoke to the young woman. "Is this the guy you're talking about?" He turned the sketchpad toward her.

Dayna's eyes widened. She pulled in a breath, held it. Went very still, as if a wall of immobility might defend her against a knowledge she couldn't deny. Then she nodded and her face crumpled. She dropped her head in both hands and sobbed.

My feet carried me to her, one of my hands resting on her shoulder. I focused questioning eyes on Tim. Satisfaction played across his features. The very air around him crackled with sudden energy. He didn't so much as glance at Dayna. With a flick of his wrist, he motioned to Rod to whisk the girl away. "Show her where the bathroom is, will you? Then have her wait in the lobby until I can talk to her a little more. I've got an arrest warrant to issue."

Without a word Rod complied. Dayna's sobs bounced off the walls as he led her away.

Indignation stiffened my back. Break in the case or not, Blanche had no right to be so insensitive. "We should call Gerri Carson." I kept my voice level. "Whatever's happened here, Dayna could obviously use some help."

Blanche sank into his chair, eyes riveted on the drawing. "Yeah, sure, I'll call her." His tone edged with derision.

My jaw clenched. Okay, so Blanche thought Christianity was for the weak and foolish, that much he'd made clear. A comment here and there, particularly after I'd spoken out during the Poison Killer case, and I knew where he stood. He could think less of me if he wanted. Gerri was another matter. Yes, she was "one of those Christians." She also happened to be a very experienced and caring law enforcement chaplain, and right now an apparent key witness needed help.

"Maybe you'll forget, Tim, with all that's on your mind." Despite my efforts, the words sounded judgmental. I worked to soften them. "How about if I call her for you?"

Blanche's eyes rose to mine, one side of his mouth twisting into the familiar curl. "Fine. Whatever." He regarded me for a moment, then flexed his shoulders, as if to say he was a big enough man to shake aside our differences. "Annie, I got a lot to do, but before you make that phone call, let me tell you what I've learned about this guy. Take it as a warning to be careful while he's on the loose. Sounds like we're dealing with a real sicko." He pointed his finger at me. "But *I'll* get him."

The detective's emphasis suddenly clarified everything. His meaning knifed right through me. Why hadn't I seen it before? Blanche's *I* didn't mean himself over others in law enforcement. It meant himself versus *me*. I'd led authorities to the Poison Killer. I had helped in the case against Bill Bland. And I'd stopped Lisa Willit's murderer from going free.

Blanche's attitude toward me, his cynicism against my faith, was all tied to one thing: jealousy.

I stared at him, hoping against hope that he didn't see the stunning realization on my face. And the anger. How could *anyone* be jealous of me, after what I endured? Who could possibly wish that on himself? I'd gladly, a million times over, have handed the breaking of the serial killer case to Blanche, if he'd wanted to be in my shoes. If he'd wanted to nearly die.

I swallowed, feeling the heightened rise and fall of my chest. An awkward pause prickled the air.

"All right. Tell me what you know." I remained standing.

Blanche pierced me with a look, then blinked away. A little too forcefully, he smacked my sketchpad down on his desk. Handed me the piece of paper that he'd compared to my drawing. My eyes fell on a printout of a driver's license. Orwin Robert Neese. Age thirty-two. Five feet, eleven inches tall. Brown hair and eyes. That face—by now I knew all its contours, its proportions. I had just drawn it. *God, thank You for helping me do it right!* I gave the paper back to Tim and waited.

Blanche jerked his chin toward the chair in which Dayna had sat. "This gal, Dayna Edwington, was one of three people who called today. Said she heard on the TV last evening that Mike Winger had been shot. Wednesday night, she was at a birthday party for some friend. One of those parties where there's too much booze and drugs, people with defenses down and tempers waiting to fly. This Orwin Neese was there. A real hotshot. Has quite a bit of money, apparently through a large inheritance, and flaunts it. According to Dayna, the guy's heartless, paranoid, and has a mean streak. She couldn't see what her roommate—named Amy Flyte—saw in him. Maybe the flamboyance and money. Whatever. Amy told Dayna that Orwin made her feel special. Protected. But then he starts showing real jealousy, surprise, surprise. It gets extreme. She can't talk to another guy, barely look one in the eye. That's the context you've got when Mike Winger arrives at the party and starts showing attention to Amy."

As Blanche talked, my thoughts turned from him to the shooting scene. The film in my mind whirred. I remembered staring in my rearview mirror, seeing the pointed gun jerking up and down in the bearer's murderous dash. *Jealous. Heartless, with a mean streak.* Yes. A man like that could kill in broad daylight.

How close he had come to me and Jenna with a loaded weapon. I shuddered. *God, thank You for Your protection.*

Blanche's gaze fell to the composite and he sniffed. "So Orwin and Mike get in a violent argument. Orwin spouts off about how Mike's the second guy that day who's hit on Amy, and both of these men are going to pay. So will Amy. Orwin says he'll kill all three of them, and they'd better believe him 'cause he's done it before." Blanche lifted his eyebrows and paused, emphasizing the information. "Dayna and Amy hightail it away from the party, along with Mike. Which only makes Orwin madder.

"Then, of course, yesterday Mike Winger was shot. This morning Amy leaves the apartment but doesn't show at work. Dayna gets a call around noon—nobody can find the girl. Dayna calls Trend Gear Stereo Systems, which Orwin owns. He hasn't shown up there either. Dayna's terrified that Orwin killed Mike and now her best friend. So she came in to tell us her story."

I stared at a deep scratch on the top of Blanche's desk, assimilating the information, imagining Dayna's fear. I hoped Blanche *did* find this murderer. Tim could have all the glory he wanted. Just get this guy off the streets. "Dayna looked pretty scared. Any chance Neese would go after her, if he knew how much information she was giving?"

Blanche's mouth flattened. "Oh yeah, don't think she hasn't thought of that. We'll have to keep a real eye on her."

Oh, Dayna. I knew the fear all too well.

"What about this third guy?" I asked. "The other one Orwin said he would kill. Anyone know who he is?"

"None so far. Orwin named no names."

A chill blew down my neck. I clenched my upper arms. "So we could have two people missing? Up to *three* people dead? And we have no idea where Orwin Neese is."

Blanche rubbed a hand down his face. "That's about the long and short of it." He pushed to his feet. "Okay. You go make your phone call to that chaplain. I got more important things to do. I *am* going to find Orwin Neese. Before he kills anybody else."

Help him do it, God, I prayed as I walked from his office. *Help him do it soon.*

Before I left the police station, I called Gerri Carson and told her about Dayna. Gerri said she would come right away, and she'd ask another chaplain to follow up with Dayna during the next few days. Gerri was leaving the following day for a much-anticipated Hawaiian vacation with her husband.

"I know you need the rest, Gerri," I told her. "Thanks for doing this while you're trying to pack."

As Dayna and I waited in the reception area, I assured her that the police were doing all they could to find her roommate, that even now they were issuing an arrest warrant for Orwin Neese. No doubt they would also obtain a search warrant for his home, seeking evidence such as a gun that would match the bullets removed from Mike Winger and Toby Brown.

Dayna sat with fidgeting hands in her lap, eyes downcast, as she talked to me about Amy and their friendship. Her voice shook, and after a short while she could speak no more. She took to rubbing her thumb hard over the back of her hand, watching the skin crinkle over her knuckles. I could do little but silently pray for her. And Amy.

"It's my fault." She whispered the words so softly that I almost wasn't sure I'd heard them at all.

I focused on her profile, the curve of her shoulders. "Why would you say that?"

Her throat convulsed. "I'm the one who wanted to go to that party. Amy wanted to break up with Orwin because of ... the way he is, and she knew he'd be there. But I convinced her to go anyway."

Her final words tilted upward, and another sob rattled her chest.

"Dayna." I laid a hand on her bent neck. The bones of her spine jutted into my palm. That physical sense of her framework jolted me, a reminder of the even greater frailty of her soul. Words of solace evaporated from my tongue. Who was I to tell her not to feel responsible, when my own guilt still plagued me? Guilt over my failure to keep Vic, my ex-husband, from straying. Or to keep Stephen away from drugs. The guilt I'd once felt over Lisa Willit's death. Again and again people had told me these things weren't my fault. My head knew they were right. But my heart didn't want to let go.

Oh, God, what do I say to Dayna? What do I say to myself?

Like some heavenly intervener, Gerri Carson stepped through the door. She wore her chaplain uniform, a short strand of her curly gray hair whisked up by a breeze. I rose to confer with her in whispers, then led her to Dayna. The young woman was now in the best of hands.

Before leaving the station, I talked to another officer investigating the shooting, pulling more information from him about Neese. Then I headed for home. During the fifteen-minute drive, I prayed. For Dayna. For Amy. For justice.

And for wisdom in knowing what to do about Chelsea Adams.

Chapter 9

I arrived home to the domestic scene of Erin and Kelly in the kitchen, making chocolate chip cookies. A comforting sight, however messy. It never fails—those two girls spell disaster for a kitchen. Anytime they bake, sugar ends up crunching underfoot, flour spread across the counters. I took one look around the room and shook my head. I could have sworn they'd had a food fight.

"Hey, Mom." Kelly lifted a white-coated palm and swished back her thick brown hair with her other hand.

"Hi, Annie," Erin sang.

"Hello, girls." I lugged my portfolio and purse over to the table and set them down. The smell of blended butter and eggs tickled my nose. "What are the cookies for?"

"For a while." Erin grinned at me, showing perfect white teeth. Her hair was pulled back in a ponytail, a smear of flour on one fair cheek. I gave her an *oh ha-ha* look and sank into a chair. "How did the interview and all that go?" Erin tore open a package of chocolate chips and dumped them in the mixing bowl full of dough.

I took in her profile, the swing of her small hoop earrings as she churned a wooden spoon through the thick mixture. Her concentrated efforts belied the anxiety she faced every time my work involved a homicide. Witnessing her own mother's murder had plummeted Erin to the depths of pain. And the memories still haunted her.

"Fine." I hoped the girls would let the subject drop. "Did you turn on the oven yet?"

Kelly *tsked*. "Mom, we know what we're doing."

"Hm." I made a point of looking around. "Have you told the kitchen that?"

"We'll clean up." My daughter pulled out a cookie sheet, reached for some dough and balled it in her hands. I watched as she placed the large dollop on the sheet and pulled more dough from the mixture. This time it went in her mouth.

"Hey, no fair." Erin gave her a playful smack and ate a large fingerful herself.

Kelly threw me a furtive glance, the casual veneer sliding from her shoulders like a loosened shawl. She pursed her mouth, hands forming another cookie ball. "So are you going to tell us what happened today? And anyway, do you know who that guy *killed*? This woman who works as the principal's secretary—it was her son! Everybody was talking about it. She wasn't at school, but people were leaving all these flowers and cards on her desk, and everyone was really sad."

I rubbed my arms, feeling chilled in the warm room. *Oh, God, to imagine that woman's grief.* I'd seen the lucky mother today—Toby's mom. Whatever financial difficulties the Browns faced, at least she still had her son.

"So, Mom, did you do the drawing? Is that guy going to be caught, like *now*, before he can hurt somebody else?"

In other words—*Before he can hurt you?*

The unspoken question hung in the air. I sighed inwardly. When it came to my safety, Kelly walked the same tightrope as Erin. They both worried about me—but didn't want to show it. A certain amount of denial came with the territory of teenage-hood. "Yes, I interviewed the boy who was shot and did the drawing. By the time I got the composite to the police station, officers already had a good guess who their suspect was. The drawing confirmed it. They're out hunting the guy now."

"Good." Erin pressed a cookie ball flat with the palm of her hand. "Hope they put him away forever."

Kelly grunted her agreement.

I looked out across the great room. "Where's your Aunt Jenna?"

"Still working." Kelly scratched her nose with the side of her palm, leaving a smear of flour. "But she's gonna be done soon. She's taking us to a movie tonight."

"Oh. She's not going out with Eric?"

"Huh-uh. They're still fighting."

I leaned back in the chair, contemplating the news. A Friday night with Jenna and the girls out. Stephen working at the video store until ten o'clock. That left the evening free for Dave and me.

"Dad wants you to call him." Erin's smile was all too knowing as she popped more dough in her mouth.

So now she'd turned mind reader?

"Well, I'll do that." I pushed to my feet. "As for you two, don't you dare leave for any movie until this kitchen's left the way you found it."

"Yes, Sergeant." Kelly barked the words like a faithful soldier, and Erin mock-saluted.

Chapter 10

An hour and a half after I'd arrived home, the kitchen lay clean and sported the sweet, warm scent of cookies. Jenna and the girls had gone into town. Dave and I met to go out for dinner. We chose a small Italian restaurant, asking for a corner table. Dave reached across the white cloth to lace his fingers in mine. The heady scent of garlic and tomatoes hung in the air. Voices of patrons were a low buzz, hushed by the ambiance of diminished light and the faint strains of opera music. For a moment Dave and I merely gazed at each other. The compassion of his touch, his expectant smile soothed me like the taste of warm honey. The tension on my shoulders began to fall away.

"Feel like talking about your day?" Dave asked the inevitable question lightly enough, but like his daughter and my family, he needed to know.

I told him everything I'd learned about the case. "This girl who's missing, Amy Flyte, she's only nineteen. And Orwin Neese, the suspect, has a scary rap sheet. Assault with a deadly weapon, burglary. He's beat up women. He was bold enough to run down Mike Winger in broad daylight. But if he caught Amy alone, what would he do to her? He sounds like the type who'd want to make someone suffer."

Dave shook his head. "And this other guy who Neese threatened ..."

"Well, maybe. But no one even knows who he is, so that's just speculation. We'll have to see if someone else is reported missing."

The waiter appeared, bearing glasses of water and news of the evening's specials. A timely arrival. Maybe Dave and I could change the subject. Dave ordered a calamari appetizer, and we laid our menus down for the moment.

He took a drink of water. "What are you going to do about Chelsea Adams?"

I focused on a bead of moisture running down my glass. "I need to call her back tonight. I should at least ask what her vision was about. I mean, just on the off chance it has anything to do with this case."

He raised his eyebrows. "Any reason you think it should?"

"I have no idea; it's just that her visions always seem to be ... relevant. Know what I mean?"

He flexed his jaw, thinking. "I only remember two stories about her."

"Yes, but those two stories made national headlines."

He gave me a rueful smile. "Kind of like you. Only last count, you've got three to your name."

"Uh-huh, thanks for reminding me." I sat back, ran a hand through my hair. "What do you think I should do?"

"Have you prayed about it?"

"Most of the way home."

"And?"

"And what? I'm asking for *your* opinion."

"My opinion is that you should do what God leads you to do."

I gave him a look. "Sometimes I don't *know* what God wants me to do, Dave—that's just the problem. Sometimes I need a little help."

"Okay, sorry." He held up a hand, palm out. "Sounds like you feel the need to talk to her some more before you make your decision. I agree with that."

Our calamari arrived, smelling heavenly. My stomach grumbled. I reached for a bite and dipped it into tartar sauce. The tangy, salted flavor exploded in my mouth. I stared at a wall sconce as I chewed, thinking. Why was I making such a big deal of this anyway? All Chelsea Adams wanted was an hour or two of my time on a Saturday. A simple composite. Was that so much to ask?

My mental projector clicked on, running the film of Jenna and her wagging finger. *"Don't you go getting mixed up with her, Annie ..."*

Suddenly I thought of the time. Checked my watch. Almost seven thirty. What had I been thinking? This was unfair to Chelsea. While I sat here waffling about what to do, she waited, not knowing whether or not she would be getting up early the next morning to drive four hours— because of a vision she felt God had given her. She at least deserved my answer.

"Dave, I should call her soon." I leaned back from our table, the intensity in my voice surprising me. "She's just waiting to hear ..."

He nodded with an almost weary acquiescence. "You have her number with you?"

I focused on my plate, thinking back to that afternoon. What had I done with that piece of paper?

"Yes. It's in my purse."

Dave gazed across the room. Conflicting emotions battled upon his features. When it came right down to it, I knew he didn't like this. And I couldn't blame him. Too much in his life had been consumed in the bonfire of tragedy. Anything unknown, any potential trouble for someone dear to him, he would see as spark against tinder. I reached out, laid my hand on his arm. "It's going to be okay. If I do this—all she wants is for me to draw a face. It's no big deal; I do it all the time."

"Sure, I know." He smiled with one side of his mouth.

I squeezed his arm, then reached into my purse to pull out Chelsea's number and my cell phone. A man answered the call. Chelsea's husband? "Oh yes," he said when I identified myself. "I'll get her for you." Simple words, polite words. But I heard in them the same reticence I saw on Dave's face.

Almost by rote, Dave forked another piece of calamari and ate it, watching me intently.

Chelsea's greeting drifted over the line. I got right to the point. "Can you please tell me a little about your vision?"

She hesitated. I could feel her reluctance. Despite her past experiences—or maybe because of them—this was no more comfortable for her than for me. "Yes, but I ..." She gave a nervous laugh. "I hope I don't scare you away."

Oh boy. Not a good lead-in.

She drew an audible breath. "I saw a small, dim room. Two people were shut up in it. A man was talking—obviously their captor."

My eyes fastened on a small pull in the fabric of our tablecloth. All sense of zesty aromas and warm restaurant ambiance faded away. *Two people.* "Who were they?"

"The captives, you mean? I only saw one—barely. A female, in shadows. She was sitting on the floor, head on her knees. I can't even tell you how old she was."

My brain scrambled for relevant explanation. "Was the second a male?"

"I don't know."

"*Could* it be?"

"I guess, but really ... I'm sorry, I just don't know."

I closed my eyes, replaying our earlier conversation. "You said you saw one face clearly."

"Yes, but only after the scene faded. The face of a young man. I don't know who he's supposed to be, or what tie he has to the room."

I brought a hand to my forehead, thoughts churning.

"Annie?" Chelsea's tone wavered. "The thing you should know is, there was a real sense of urgency. I mean, I don't know when all this is supposed to happen, but when it does ... those two people? They're going to die unless they're rescued. And their death isn't going to be pretty."

I straightened, my eyes locking with Dave's. *Two people ... A female ... The face of a young man.* A shiver coiled up my spine.

"Chelsea, how soon can you get here tomorrow?"

Chapter 11

Mike Winger's murder had stirred up the ghost voices. Now they wouldn't leave him alone. They whispered at him incessantly.

They will find you. You murderer ...

He stood staring at the TV screen, gripping the remote, one leg jiggling. Desperately he tried to listen to the news story. Regardless of the voices, he had to know what was going on. The reporter was talking about the killing, how they already had a suspect—

He froze.

They showed a detailed drawing by Annie Kingston.

Annie Kingston. That woman always nailed it.

She could help them find you—

"Shut up!"

He started to pace, then jerked to a stop. No. He couldn't let the voices bug him like this. So what if they wouldn't stop ranting? They were *dead*, and he'd gotten what he wanted. So who was the winner here, huh?

There was only one thing to do when they got this bad. Keep busy. Keep focused. Those voices thought they'd stop him from doing whatever was necessary? No way. They only pushed him to control things all the more.

The reporter rattled on about the killing. And Amy Flyte, the missing girl. They showed her picture. Maybe a young man was missing too, although no one knew who he was.

Now *that* sounded intelligent.

The story ended. He snapped off the TV. Glanced outside. The sun was setting.

Duty called.

The voices were silent. He smiled.

He turned to clomp down the stairs into the basement, mouthing a rap tune. A few delicate chores awaited.

Saturday, September 24

Chapter 12

For the second night in a row I drifted in and out of sleep, a battered vessel on dream-troubled waters. Faces and snatches of scenes ghosted my slumber, from Toby's features cinched with pain, to Dayna sobbing over her missing roommate, to the shrouded room in Chelsea's vision. Dawn finally seeped through my curtains, spilling light on the bedcovers. I opened heavy eyes, prayers filtering through my mind.

Whatever this day brings, Lord, help me know what I should do. Be with Chelsea and me as we meet. Show us what You want us to see.

Chelsea would arrive around eleven.

Jenna had displayed an unusual turn of attitude when I told her what was planned. Whether her reaction was due to my prayers or her feisty protection of the right to change her mind, I would never know. I do think on some level she was intrigued with the possible connection between Chelsea's vision and the murder we witnessed. Whatever my sister's reasoning, I left her to it. I was simply glad I didn't have to argue with her.

At nine o'clock I wandered down our porch steps to pick the paper off the sidewalk. I couldn't deny the game I played with myself in slowing each movement. Maybe if I sauntered, maybe if I tipped my head back to view cerulean sky, the fluttering in my veins would cease. Yesterday's events, bookended by two nights' poor sleep, left me feeling off-kilter and wary. All the same, I chided myself. Why was I so nervous about meeting Chelsea Adams? My only task was to hear her story, draw a composite. Nothing more.

Still, I sensed ... something ...

I stood on the sidewalk, breathing fresh morning air. The temperature was already in the seventies and would climb another ten degrees. Indian summer showed no sign of retreat. The *beep-beep* warning of heavy machinery in reverse sifted through the trees beyond our street. Apparently, the runway crew was working on a Saturday. I gazed across the width of Barrister Court at Dave and Erin's house, their sidewalk lined with multicolored flowers attesting to the care of Dave's hands. Something about that sight jolted my heart.

In the kitchen I poured coffee and settled at the table. Drew the newspaper toward me. The front page sported another article about the murder, this one displaying my composite of Orwin Neese and asking anyone with information about his whereabouts to contact the Redding Police Department. The story also included information about the disappearance of Amy Flyte, accompanied by her photo. I stared at her picture, my chest contracting. She was a pretty girl, with large, round eyes in an oval face. A smile that somehow looked sad. Brown shoulder-length hair.

Oh, God, is this girl locked up in a small, dark room? If so, please help us save her.

The door to our lower level opened and closed. Stephen wandered in, sweatpants low on his hips, chest bare. His blond hair, usually gelled and sticking straight up, was matted from sleep. "Hey." He headed for the refrigerator and opened it. I heard the *thump-slide* of moving containers.

"Good morning. You're up early. You have to go to work?" I turned the newspaper over and pushed it away.

"Yeah, at ten. Where's Aunt Jenna?"

"Working at her computer already, I think."

"Mm." Stephen withdrew a half gallon of milk and headed to the pantry for cereal. Plunking these on the table, he fetched a bowl and spoon and planted himself in a chair.

I watched him with quiet, weary gratitude. So much about Stephen was different—the confidence in his movements, his mellow nature, the way he talked to me. How naïve I had been in the past few years, not realizing the amount of drugs he was taking. I'd become so used to seeing my son under their influence that I'd forgotten how pleasant he could be. *Oh, God, now just help him turn to You.*

"That woman still coming today?" He crunched a large bite of cereal.

"Yes. In a few hours."

"Man. She's something else. Wish I could be here."

I tilted my head. "You remember that much about her?"

"Sure." *Crunch, crunch.* "She was in all the papers and everything when we were in Redwood City. She's this psychic. Knows the future and who did stuff. Wouldn't want her on your bad side."

"She's not a psychic."

He frowned at me, jaws moving. Swallowed. "What would you call her then?"

How to explain this to someone who had little concept of God's power? "She's a Christian. And sometimes God chooses to send her a vision about something. Like some of the stories you read in the Bible."

Stephen sniffed, considering, then shoved in another bite. "I don't see the difference." The words garbled around a mouthful of cereal and milk.

"The difference is that God will do what He chooses to do. If He wants someone to know something so certain actions can be taken, He'll tell that person. But the Bible clearly says that people aren't supposed to consult psychics for supernatural knowledge."

Even as I said the words, I realized how illogical they must sound. Four years ago when I first heard of Chelsea Adams, they'd have sounded crazy to *me*. But what amazing things I'd learned since becoming a Christian. The sound of God's voice. His myriad ways of leading. His power over evil, released through prayer.

Stephen screwed up his face. "Mom, that makes no sense at all."

I managed a smile. "Maybe not now, Stephen. But someday it will." I took a drink of coffee, using the time to form my words. "Just remember, there are two forces at work in this world. If something supernatural doesn't come from God, you'd best stay clear of it."

"Uh-huh." Milk dribbled down his chin and he swiped it with the back of his hand. He shot me a faintly amused look, like a father to an imaginative child. "Well, gotta go take a shower. Watch out for those psychics, Mom." He waggled a finger at me.

As Stephen placed his dishes in the sink, my thoughts drifted back to the newspaper article and Amy Flyte. *Was she the girl Chelsea saw?* I reached out, pulled the newspaper toward me. Turned it over and stared at Amy's photo.

What if she was out there right now, shivering in some dark room, while I sat here in my warm, bright kitchen?

My throat constricted at the mere idea.

I sipped my coffee, but it had gone tepid. From the great room, the grandfather clock chimed nine thirty. An hour and a half before Chelsea came. Why hadn't I insisted she arrive sooner?

I stared at Amy's picture until I could look no more.

At a quarter after eleven the doorbell rang.

Chapter 13

More bad stuff going down everywhere. Last night the TV, this morning the newspaper. Not cool at all. It made his nerves itch.

He bent over the kitchen table, heart thumping. His thoughts scurried like rats. Killers were always found out. Like they should be. Killing was evil.

What was that Bible verse his grandmother used to recite? Something about everything done in darkness would come to light?

He pulled out a kitchen chair, its legs stuttering over the tile floor. Sank into it and stared at the paper.

A speckle of dirt crawled up his right heel.

"Go away!" He brushed at it with his other foot, but it didn't help. Little dirt legs, creeping up toward his ankle. He cursed and batted them off.

The voices started in. *They'll find you, they'll find you . . .*

Taunting little ant feet now marched up both legs in rhythm to the words. He scratched and beat them away, then jumped up to run for the shower.

They'll find you.

Under hot water he scrubbed his feet and hummed. Loudly. By the time he stepped from the shower, he was panting.

This *had* to stop. Ever since Mike Winger's death, the voices and ants had been driving him crazy. He had to find a way to make them disappear—for good. One way or another, he had to show them who was boss.

Chapter 14

My nerves thrummed as I crossed the great room. I heard Jenna's bedroom door open, knew her curiosity would pull her out to meet Chelsea. At least the girls wouldn't be underfoot. Kelly was already over at Erin's house.

With a fixed smile, I pulled open the door. Chelsea stood on my porch, dressed in beige slacks and a tucked-in silk shirt. A purse in one hand and a yellow pad of paper in the other. She looked as striking as I remembered, although her cinnamon hair was cut shorter, not quite to her shoulders. Those amazing eyes rested upon me, their cinnamon color complementing the red-gold tones of her hair. Chelsea's delicately molded face had been wonderful to draw, her jawline and cheekbones sculpted like a model's. But I'd only seen her across the courtroom. Now as she greeted me, mere feet away, I could feel a power in her presence, a sense of stability and confidence. Strange, how in that aura I felt both assured and discomfited. This was a woman I couldn't begin to match, not in appearance, not in faith.

"Chelsea, glad you found us." I stepped back to usher her inside.

She smiled with genuine warmth and reached out to squeeze my hand. "Annie, it's so good to meet you. Thank you for letting me come." She stepped into our great room and, like all who see it for the first time, tipped her head back to admire its vastness. "Wow, that's quite a staircase." She gazed at the custom-built curved stairs. "You have a beautiful place. You are so gracious to open your house to me."

"Thank you. And you're welcome."

We looked at each other. Suddenly I couldn't quite figure what to say. My sister saved me, appearing from the side hallway. From her easy stride, I knew Jenna would be at no loss for words.

"Chelsea, this is my sister, Jenna."

Jenna held out her hand. "Hello, and welcome." She chatted for a few minutes, allowing herself ample time to form a judgment about Chelsea. Finally, and not a moment too soon, she excused herself. "Annie, I'm going to work awhile longer. Then I want to head over to the runway. Time to see how the project is going." She looked to Chelsea. "We have a private airstrip here for homeowners' airplanes. It's being lengthened right now, so the whole thing's closed down."

"Oh." Chelsea looked empathetic. "Bet you want that fixed in a hurry."

"No kidding she does." I shook my head at Jenna. "Poor crew members. The project's just begun, and already she's starting to bug them about their progress."

Jenna threw me one of her looks, then retreated to her bedroom.

I offered Chelsea something to eat. She refused, asking only for ice water. I poured her a glass and we headed for my office. Pulling up a seat for her on the other side of my desk, I invited her to sit, then settled into my chair. Earlier that morning I'd set out my drawing materials. Chelsea surveyed them, her expression tightening.

She folded her hands on her lap and took a deep breath. "You know, I think we should pray first."

"Please, go ahead."

She nodded, resolve firming her mouth. I closed my eyes.

"Father God, Annie and I sit in awe before You. In Your mercy and in Your will, You have brought us together. We don't fully know why and we are anxious. But we do know that You will lead us. We seek that leading; we *claim* it. We ask that You open our ears and our spirits to hear You. Lead us, Jesus. Protect us. Give us wisdom." Her voice rose. "We stand on Your power over evil, and we walk in Your strength …"

The words pelted me like hard rain. By the time Chelsea finished, I felt almost tremulous. Did her intensity flow from frightening details of her vision?

"All right." Tightness squeezed my shoulders. I sought the familiar veneer of a forensic artist conducting an interview. *Just relax, Annie. You've done this many times.* "Since you've assured me you remember the face very well, let's put that aside for a minute. First I want you to tell me everything about your vision."

Chapter 15

Here goes, God.

Chelsea picked up the yellow pad she'd placed on Annie's desk. Not that she needed it to remember every detail of what she'd seen. But the paper provided something to focus on, something to hold.

"I've got notes here." She tried to keep her voice factual. Would Annie think she was crazy? Kick her out of the house after hearing what she had to say? "After I saw this, I wrote everything down." She looked at Annie, then back to her writing. "It started when I was in the kitchen, doing dishes. The boys were in their bedrooms, busy with homework. Paul was ... I don't know where." She drew a breath. "I always know when a vision is coming. The world starts to go black, sort of like when you're about to faint. Fear usually comes with it, just because I ... I don't like the experience. It would be fine with me if I never had another vision in my entire life." She aimed a rueful smile at Annie. "And I've told God so."

Annie shook her head. "I can imagine. I'd do the same."

Chelsea nodded, grateful for the understanding. Annie seemed so warm and kind. Even through her reticence.

"Okay." Chelsea focused on the yellow paper, looking through it. "The first thing I saw was an oval window. Then the picture widened into a shot of a small darkened room. The window was high on the wall, almost near the ceiling. Then I find myself *there*—in the room. Watching through someone else's eyes—someone who's there, like I've crawled inside this person's skin." She paused. "This has happened to me before. Remember the Trent Park case? When I had a vision of that murder, I was *inside* the body of the girl who was killed. I even felt the blows. I felt myself dying."

Annie drew in her shoulders. Chelsea blinked away the older memory. "So now I'm inside this person, though I have no idea who it is. Don't even know if it's a man or woman. But he—she—seems to sense that something shocking and chaotic is going to happen. I realize my feet are bare, and the concrete floor is chilly. I'm struggling to see, because the room is dark. I can barely make out someone else, a figure a few feet away, huddling on the floor. Then on my left, a voice starts talking in a scratchy whisper. A man, but I don't see him—"

A sudden shiver gripped her. She squeezed her eyes closed and tumbled into her story. Heard that hate-filled voice, saying

"Little-known fact about spiders. Some can't even bite humans. Their jaws are too weak. And then there are the deadly ones ..." A low chuckle. "The trick is telling them apart."

The figure on the floor shudders.

"Hey, don't be moving down there." The whisper again, chilling in its feigned empathy. "They're all around you."

Something clicks, and a red light filters through the grayness. Chelsea's heart pounds, blood coursing through her fear-constricted veins. Her eyes pan across the cowering figure—a female, head bent, hugging both knees. The female's feet are

bare. Chelsea's gaze rises, to a shelf built into the wall. Her focus sharpens.

The wood is crawling.

On it, under it, upon its sides — spiders. Small ones, others big and bulbous; some with long, long legs. Myriad webs hang underneath the ledge.

Chelsea's eyes widen in terror. Her gaze flicks away.

Spiders on the wall. Lurking in the corners of the eight-by-ten room. Scuttling across the floor. More boxlike shelves around the room, more and more, creating nooks for weaving, creeping bodies.

"They won't hurt you if you leave them alone." The whisper sounds oh, so casual.

Scuffling noises upon the floor. Chelsea's eyes fix on the man's shoe. It slides forward, avoiding scurrying bodies.

"Most of 'em aren't out to get you. In fact, some are pretty shy. But if you scare one, like put your hand down on him, well, what do you expect?"

The female says nothing. She will not look up. Chelsea sucks a ragged breath.

"The harmless ones bite, and you may not even feel it." The man takes another step. "Others sting like crazy, but their venom isn't toxic. I have quite a few in here, though — " he chuckles — "whose bites are something else. After a while your skin swells and feels real tender. The wound fills with pus, and you end up with a gaping hole. You'll need a doctor. Unfortunately — " sarcasm drips — "I won't be bringing you one."

A rustle of clothes. The man's hand reaches toward the floor, one finger caressing the narrow back of a large brown creature.

"This is a hobo spider. Lots of people mistake them for the brown recluse."

Chelsea's skin begins to crinkle and crawl.

"Only problem—" the man's foot shifts direction—"the poor hobos get trapped in other spiders' webs and are gobbled up, 'cause their own webs aren't sticky. They can't walk on that stuff. So I have to keep replacing them."

He pulls a small jar from his pocket. Inside is a black spider the size of a half dollar. It fills the width of the jar. "Now this one—see that pile of sand in the corner? It belongs to him. Cool-looking dude, huh? Like I said, one of the world's deadliest. The funnel web, from Australia. Atrax Robustus, if you want to get technical. When he bites, he rears way up on his hind legs 'cause his fangs only strike down. Things are seven millimeters long. Look at the venom oozing off of 'em."

He holds the bottle before Chelsea's face. Unscrews the lid, bends down, and shakes out the spider. It scuttles across the floor.

Chelsea shudders violently. Dozens of little legs pinprick across her skin. On an arm. Aaah! She swipes it away. On her neck. On her leg . . . elbow . . . knee . . .

No, no, *she screams to herself,* they're not real, they're not real.

The man laughs. "Imagining 'em already, huh? Just wait. I haven't even locked you in here yet. But since you're enjoying this so much, let me introduce a few more of your roomies. I got some special ones from Africa, called six-eyed crab spiders. They're as bad as the Australian dudes." He sighs with satisfaction. "It'll be more interesting if I don't tell you what they look like."

His foot moves again, comes closer.

"Did you know when a spider bites a bug, it injects a liquid that dissolves its internal organs? Then it just sucks everything

*up, predigested. The African crab spider is so poisonous, that's
kind of what it does to humans. The venom eats up body tissue.
Causes massive internal bleeding."*

Chelsea's lungs congeal. Every nerve comes alive, skittering.

*"Poor thing, you look pale." The man's voice drips with false
empathy. "Too bad I have to do this."*

*Silence. Chelsea's throat closes. She opens her mouth, wheez-
ing in air. The person on the floor hugs herself, trembling.*

*"This is your fault, you know." The man's tone turns hard.
He waves a hand at the female. "She'd have lived. You both
would, if you hadn't started it." He glares at Chelsea. Then suddenly turns and scoops a long-legged black spider off the floor.
Chelsea recoils. He grabs her arm, jerks it straight out. Her legs
start to shake.*

*"What do you think?" His words are measured, taunting.
Any minute now, Chelsea is going to faint. "Is this one poisonous ... or not?"*

*He turns his hand over, opens his fingers. The spider drops
onto Chelsea's wrist.*

And begins to crawl.

Chapter 16

I listened to Chelsea, horrified, muscles tight. My visual brain conjured every detail of her recounting as she spoke. At the end of her vision, the man was about to shut up his two captives in the room. Neither of them fought or tried to run away. Why? They were barefoot, with only the clothes on their backs. They had nothing but their bare hands to kill the spiders with, and they didn't know which were poisonous.

Chelsea's words finally ran out, pulling the plug on the projector in my head. I found myself staring at my desk, holding my body very still. A shard of thought pierced my mind. Chelsea Adams's visions must be *terrifying* for her. The vividness of my own imagination could be all-consuming, but to actually feel present in such a torturous place . . .

For a frozen beat, neither of us spoke.

Slowly I inhaled. Then strained to pull my thoughts away from the scene. *God, couldn't this vision have been about* anything *but spiders?*

But I couldn't dwell on that fact, couldn't allow myself to feel too much. By sheer will, I sought the stabilizing force of analysis. "Okay." What to ask first? "The girl you saw. What color hair did she have?"

Chelsea swallowed. "Brown."

Brown. Like Amy Flyte. "You're sure of that?"

"Yes."

"How long was it?"

She pondered her lap. "I don't know. Because her head was ducked, the hair could have gone down her back and I wouldn't have seen it."

I rubbed my temple. "And you didn't hear her say anything?"

"No. She didn't talk."

I nodded. "About the man. You said he grabbed the arm of the person whose body you were in. He dropped a spider on that person's wrist. Do you remember looking at that wrist?"

Chelsea thought a moment. "Yes. But I was focused on the spider crawling."

The film in my head threatened to whir into motion again. I concentrated on my logic. "That wrist you saw. Was it a man's or woman's?"

Chelsea's expression flattened, as if she'd been down this road before and seen its dead end. "I don't ... My attention was on the spider. I just can't tell you."

"So there's no way for you to know anything about this person?"

Her cinnamon eyes met mine. In them I saw both frustration and steadfastness. "Annie, I have to tell you something. I've learned the hard way not to assume *anything* from my visions. Because of that, I will be very careful to tell you only what I absolutely know to be right. That's why I wrote all these notes." She tapped the yellow pad. "This is what I know for certain that God told me. Anything else is merely conjecture. It's not *wrong* to guess, understand. But I don't dare mix guesses with the truth. What He tells me will not be wrong. What I guess can be very wrong indeed."

I shifted, stalling for time as I absorbed her words. I knew they were true, could understand, after what she'd been through, why she would be so adamant. "I hear what you're saying. I just wondered because we're working on this homicide right now in Redding . . ."

Briefly I told Chelsea about the shooting I'd witnessed and the possibility of two missing people—Amy Flyte and a young man not yet identified. "Amy has brown hair. She might be the girl in your vision. And I'm wondering if the person whose body you were in is the young man." I studied Chelsea's expression for the slightest hint of recognition. If God had given her this vision—and I believed He had —He could continue talking to her, right? Give her new impressions?

She focused on my words, her body still. When I finished, she eased back in the chair, gaze drifting to my desk. For a moment her eyes closed, as if she were praying. It struck me then—the deep level of her caution. This woman would not be swayed to believe one iota more than what God showed her. If anything, her fear of doing so might lead her to err on the side of being *too* cautious.

Chelsea shook her head. "Annie, I know you hope my vision can shed light on your case. But I *don't know*." She spread her hands. "I don't feel anything one way or another. Logic tells me that, with the timing of all this, the vision *is* relevant. But again, that's just *my* logic, not a knowledge God has given me."

Disappointment pulled at my mouth. I worked to keep my expression placid. *So what am I supposed to do, God? If*

You're going to send somebody a vision, why don't You fill in the details that count?

Chelsea tilted her head and shrugged—a gesture that looked almost childlike. "I know you're frustrated. I wish I could tell you more, I really do." She pushed to her feet and wandered aimless steps away from me, one hand rising to her neck.

I watched with a half-wary silence. This woman's ability to read me was on a par with Jenna's. More than a little disconcerting, considering we'd just met. Yet she was candid enough to voice her perceptions and she responded with understanding. Had to admit, that was better than Jenna's arguments.

Chelsea turned back to me, her voice thickening. "My problem is the same as yours. Always has been. I wish God would tell me everything. Sometimes He does. I've had visions where I saw enough to know exactly what I was supposed to do and why. Other times, I know what to do, but *nothing* about why. I'm left with more questions than answers. And I tell you, every time it's like—" she brought her palms together, moving them up and down—"like stepping off a cliff. I *know* God will bring me to safety. He's never failed me yet. But I'm like you, Annie. I just wish I knew everything from the beginning."

Something inside me shifted. Watching Chelsea struggle, I felt resolve flow through my own limbs. Then, *bam*, memories from the Poison Killer case hit. I leaned forward, fists pressed against my legs. "If we knew everything up front, Chelsea—" my voice was low—"we'd be too scared to walk off that cliff."

She dropped her hands. "I know. You're so right." She returned to her chair, sank into it. Summoned the ghost of a smile. "Okay. So. Now that I've got that out of my system, maybe I should describe the face I saw after the vision?"

Yes, the composite. Back on familiar ground. As I reached for my drawing pad and pencil, a new thought wafted into my brain. What if this face was the face of the *captor*, not the second captive? What if that face belonged to Orwin Neese?

I looked at Chelsea expectantly. "Ready if you are."

Chapter 17

For a week now he hadn't seen the second spider.

Thing had to be dead. Probably eaten by the female.

He stroked the side of the terrarium with a finger. Good reason these babies were sometimes called widow spiders. After mating, she'd just gobbled him up.

See? Murder happened even in nature. No big thing. Besides, who cared? The female was bigger and more interesting to watch.

He drew his mouth down, idly wondering how many males would hatch from the sac. Would their sisters mate with them, then eat them up too?

Women were plain deadly.

He squinted through the glass, looking for the spider. Most of his specimens were in the basement, but he'd brought this terrarium up for a few days. Soon he'd exchange it for another. Kept the fascination fresh that way.

Yeah. There was the female. He could barely see her under those twigs in the corner. Sleeping. Button spiders were nocturnal.

He tilted his head, studying the messy web. He could see the egg sac, full of promise. *Can't wait till those little buggers pop.* But as for stored food in the web—nada. Lazy little mama, eating and sleeping her life away. She'd soon need the fly he'd trapped in a jar. He glanced at the insect buzzing against the glass and laughed low in his throat. *You're about to come to a bad end, pal.*

He reached for the jar, remembering a story he'd read about the black button spider. The reason he just had to have a pair. They weren't usually deadly, but their bite was bad news. Nausea, headaches, muscle cramps, banging pulse, mucho pain, and local nerve damage. In South Africa, where they were found, a young boy had been bitten on the arm while helping his daddy with the corn harvest. Kid had screamed himself to death. Literally.

He grated out a laugh.

Wouldn't it be cool to watch something die from this little mama's venom? He scratched his thigh, thinking it over. Some small animal. Like a hamster or a kitten. No, not a hamster. Too quiet. At least a kitten could mew.

Wonder how long it would take ...

He tapped the glass. *Come out, come out, pretty spider. All black and silky, so proud of that red-orange hourglass tattoo.*

The spider slept on.

He sniffed. Wiped his nose. Time to feed the beast. *Sorry, little fly. Your end has come.*

With one hand he held the jar, and with the other, slid the top of the terrarium aside a few inches. Unscrewing the cap, he held it in place and turned the jar over near the open space of the terrarium. Here came the tricky part. *Lose enough flies, you learn to be fast.* He moved aside the cap, thrust the jar into the terrarium, and shook it. The fly tumbled out. Quickly he pulled back the jar and slid the glass top in place. The fly careened into a side of the terrarium, backed up, and buzzed into it again.

Trapped! *Only a matter of time now, buddy.*

His mouth curved in a slow smile as he screwed the cap back on the jar.

Chapter 18

For the next hour Chelsea and I worked on the composite. As anxious as I was to see the face, I had to force myself to concentrate. Would these be the features of Orwin Neese?

As the interview progressed, it became clear the face was not Orwin's. Who then? Perhaps the second captive after all? The young man Orwin had also threatened to kill?

But these questions were pushed aside as a new concern infiltrated my thoughts. Chelsea's description of details was acute. Almost too acute. This vague smear of suspicion began to coagulate, then harden. I tried to battle through it but couldn't deny what my training had taught me. Studies of the interview process have shown that a witness who describes a face extremely well isn't necessarily all that accurate. Some people are simply better with words than others, while their memories may be faulty. A few times in the past I had produced composites that highly confident interviewees swore were right, only to find later that the drawings were less on target than others from more tentative witnesses.

God, has Chelsea fixed details in her mind to a fault? Please don't let her go too far astray.

The worries pulled at me. I worked to keep a poker face, even as my heart picked up speed. We *couldn't* get this wrong. If these features weren't accurate, if they never led to an identification, where would we be then? Always wondering where this person was, what had happened to him ...

On the other hand, if this *was* the man missing along with Amy, authorities already had her picture. That alone may be enough to lead police to both of them.

Then again, if we didn't need this composite, why did God send Chelsea here in the first place?

Minutes ticked by. My palms dampened and I wiped them on my jeans. Chelsea must have noticed my anxiety, but she never let on. She spoke with patience. Calmness. Not once did she waver in her memory or change her mind. After what seemed like a long time, the general essence of the face was complete. I pulled in a breath and studied the drawing.

Small, deep set eyes. Would they alter in the refining process? A somewhat flat nose, thin lips. Narrow jawline and prominent ears. Interesting features. Distinctive.

"Okay." I smiled at Chelsea. "Here's what we have so far. There will probably be things to change, and we can do that one feature at a time." I handed the drawing pad to her.

She looked at it, slow satisfaction planing across her face. "Wow. It's not far, really. Just ... a few details."

"Sure." I flipped to a page in the FBI *Identification Catalog.* "Let's start with the eyes. Any of these closer to the real thing?"

One by one the features took final shape. When the composite was finished, I handed the drawing to Chelsea once more. "Does everything look right now?"

With one glance Chelsea pulled her head back, as if shocked to see the face fully translated from memory to paper. "Yes, absolutely. That's him." She stared at the drawing, lips parted. "I don't know how you do it. This is just ... it's *right*."

Oh, Chelsea, I hope so.

She handed the drawing pad back and I laid it on the desk. Whatever my lingering doubts, I would not voice them. Together we had done the best we could.

Now what?

The composite beckoned me, humming for attention. I found myself looking through it until the features blurred. The projector in my head kicked on, throwing out imagined pictures of

Amy and this man, huddled in the middle of a concrete floor. He is talking to her, trying to keep her calm. Amy's shoulders are drawn in, hands fisted at her waist. She whimpers, afraid to move, afraid to lift her head. A large black spider creeps toward her ankle. Tests her skin with one leg, then crawls upward. Amy screams, smacks it off ...

I pressed my eyes shut.

"Annie?" Chelsea's voice pulled me back. "You okay?"

I shook my head. "Yes. Sorry. I just ... I'm thinking all kinds of things. If this *is* the man we believe is missing, and if he's with Amy Flyte, this drawing could help save them. Amy's picture is being distributed in the media, but if it produces no leads as to her whereabouts, maybe this one will."

If it's on target.

Chelsea nodded. "But we don't know for sure. So what do we do?"

There was only one answer, but I didn't want to admit it. Not at all. I thought of Tim Blanche, his attitude toward me. *Lord, I don't want to do this.* Leaning my head back, I swiveled my chair a slow quarter turn to gaze out the window. Dave was outside, kneeling by his front sidewalk, pulling weeds. At the unexpected sight, my heart tumbled. Suddenly I longed to run across the street, feel his arms around me, beg him to tell me what to do.

"We should pray about it," Chelsea said.

I turned back to her. "Yes, but we can't sit around waiting for a definitive answer, because we both know God doesn't always give them. In the meantime, if this—" I gestured at the composite—"is who I think he is, the scene in your vision has already happened. And we've got two people who need to be found *now*."

Chelsea inhaled slowly. "You think we should go see the detective working the case, don't you." It wasn't a question.

Mentally I thrashed about for a denial. Tried to imagine shoving this composite in my desk drawer, doing nothing. Why couldn't I do that? We didn't know for sure that it had anything to do with Amy Flyte. But if it did? If she and this young man were shut up in that room, praying for help ...

"Yes, I do."

Chelsea ran a hand across her forehead. "Thing is, I've been down that road in the past. And the police didn't believe me."

"I know." I said the words gently, hoping she would hear the empathy behind them. "And *this* detective ... I have to warn you about him. He's not exactly fond of Christians in general—or me, in particular."

Chelsea drew herself up with a weary sigh. The dejection in her face surely mirrored my own. "Great. Then we'd *really* better pray."

We bowed our heads and Chelsea began. "Lord, we've come this far and now we need guidance from You."

Vaguely I registered the sound of the front door closing hard. Swift footfalls across the great room floor. Probably Kelly, on some critical teenage mission to fetch something from her bedroom.

" ... so, Lord, I ask that You lead us. You've brought us together, and we trust ..."

The feet grew closer, then muted. Whoever it was had hit the carpet of the hallway.

" ... open our ears so we can hear ..."

My office door burst open. I jerked up my head. Chelsea swung around in her chair.

Jenna stood in the threshold, hair windblown, breath in puffs. "You'd better get over to the runway." She twisted her mouth. "You're not going to believe this. The digging crew just uncovered a skull."

Chapter 19

Chelsea perched in the backseat of Annie's SUV, mind whirling as Annie hurriedly backed out of the garage. A skull discovered—*now*? Was this why God called her here?

But if that was the reason, her vision happened long ago . . .

"You call the Sheriff's Department?" Annie asked her sister. Jenna sat in the front passenger seat.

"Yeah." Jenna heaved a sigh. Her fingers drummed against the dashboard. "Why does this have to happen *here*? Now? They'll close the area as a crime scene, and the runway will *never* get fixed."

Annie flicked Chelsea an anxious look through the rearview mirror, as if she were afraid of how her sister might sound. Chelsea gave her a wan smile—*It's okay.*

They made a few turns through the neighborhood and soon were on Grove Landing's taxiway. Up ahead Chelsea could see the confusion that the gruesome discovery had wrought. Three crewmen wandered at the paved end of the airstrip, gesturing with wide arm motions and talking into cell phones. Beyond them lay a large area of newly overturned soil, tree stumps, and brush. A dirt-caked backhoe hulked off to the side, like a pouting warrior told to stand down.

Annie pulled the car to a stop some distance from the work area. "Better leave room for all the folks who are going to descend."

"Yeah, well, they better get here pretty soon," Jenna mumbled. "If I hadn't been here and seen that skull come up, I swear those guys would have kept on working. I practically had to stand in front of them to get them to stop." She folded her arms. "Drat it all."

Annie shook her head.

Jenna glowered at her. "What?"

"Nothing. You're just ... being you."

With a huff Jenna opened her car door. Chelsea pressed her lips in amusement. Jenna was one feisty gal, so different from her quiet sister. Annie turned and smiled at Chelsea almost timidly, as if relieved that she didn't seem to judge Jenna. With that silent exchange, Chelsea caught a glimpse of Annie's soul. The woman cared deeply about what others thought of her and her family.

They clambered out of the car.

At the three women's approach the crewmen clipped off their phone conversations. "Thanks for halting everything," Annie called. She walked to the end of the broken pavement, shading her eyes. Chelsea and Jenna followed.

The skull lay about fifteen feet away. Chelsea scanned the dirt around it. Was that a bone she saw, lying to the right?

"We stopped as soon as we saw it." One of the men, tall and with a big stomach, gestured toward the skull.

Jenna snorted. Annie paid her no attention. "Did you see anything else? Any other bones?"

A second man, with a wiry build and leathery face, pointed. "That's a long bone there. Like maybe an arm."

"I see it," Chelsea said. "And look over there. Something else that's white?" Her thoughts tumbled. Was a whole skeleton out there, scattered? How long would it take a body in this environment to degrade to bone?

They milled around, waiting for the arrival of a detective from the Sheriff's Department named Ralph Chetterling —the same man Chelsea had talked to yesterday. After a long fifteen minutes he pulled up in an unmarked vehicle. He climbed out, straightening his massive frame, and walked over to meet them.

"Hi, Jenna. Hey, Annie, long time no see." His dark brown eyes searched Annie's face. "Hear you folks found something of interest."

Something of interest? What a way to put it.

"Hi, Ralph. *They* found it." Annie indicated the men, explaining their work on the runway.

He scanned the site. "Anybody been out there since then?"

"No. We've waited for you." Annie introduced Chelsea to the detective. He shook Chelsea's hand, curious eyes lingering upon her. No doubt he wondered why she'd needed to see Annie so badly. Chelsea cringed inside. She knew her reputation preceded her, and now look what had happened. Almost as if her very presence had caused this. *I'm so sorry this is happening,* she wanted to say. Instead she offered the man a weak smile.

Chetterling nodded, then turned away, his demeanor turning all business. "All right. Let's get to this."

The area soon morphed into a full-fledged investigative scene. As more officials arrived, Annie told Chelsea who they were. Matt Stanish, from the coroner's office, appeared first, followed by Jim Cisneros, an investigator with the Shasta County Sheriff's Department. The three men ventured into the dirt-churned area. Annie, Chelsea, and Jenna sidled to the very end of the pavement to watch. Matt Stanish picked up the skull first and examined it. He held it close to his nose and sniffed.

"Ooh." Chelsea brought a fist to her lips.

"No smell." Stanish looked to Chetterling. "Been here at least a year, but could be much longer." He turned it over, looked at the cranium. "Got a piece missing." He touched the back top portion.

Detective Chetterling leaned in for a look and grunted. "Foul play, maybe? Someone hit in the head?"

Oh, God, another murder? And so close to Annie's house?

"Possibly. Or it could be postmortem." Stanish surveyed the nearby soil. "We'll need to find the missing piece, see how it fits. Or pieces—could be more than one. If the pieces fit tightly together, that's an indication the damage occurred here." He held the skull up, pointing to the broken area. "These things become more brittle after death, so any break is a clean one. But in life they have a little expansion. If someone's hit in the head strong enough to crack the skull, it's not going to be as clean of a break."

Jim Cisneros picked his way over to the half-emerged bone Chelsea had spotted. He lifted it for Stanish to see, his fingertips on each end. "From an arm?"

"Yeah. A humerus."

Cisneros rotated the piece between his fingers. "Not an ounce of tissue on it. We could be looking at a difficult ID." He looked meaningfully at Annie and she gave him a reluctant nod.

"If they can't find out who this is," she whispered to Chelsea, "I may have to create a facial reconstruction for the skull."

Chelsea's eyes widened. She couldn't imagine it. How could anyone look at a skull and determine what the person had looked like?

"I've never done the process on a real case before." Annie bit her lip. "Only studied it in a classroom."

A sick feeling oozed through Chelsea's stomach. She surveyed the scene — an ordinary construction site now turned surreal. The upheaval of dirt almost sneered, as if its blatant disturbance had yielded what they deserved. A backdrop of blue sky and bright sun mocked in contrast to the dismal discovery.

Chetterling and Cisneros stopped searching long enough to secure the area with yellow tape sporting bold black letters: "SHERIFF'S LINE, DO NOT CROSS." Stanish lay the skull down with care and returned to his vehicle, pulling out a long white sheet. This he spread out where dirt met pavement, as a makeshift bed for the deceased. The skull and humerus were laid upon it in deference to their placement within a full skeleton.

What a pitiful sight, Chelsea thought. Woeful, wretched, and abandoned. No one deserved to be buried like trash in a shallow grave.

Jenna's obvious irritation had long since vanished. She gripped her arms, a pained expression creasing her face. "This is awful."

Chelsea murmured her assent.

Stanish lifted a bone fragment from the soil. Held it up to consider.

"From the skull?" Chetterling asked.

"Yeah, think so."

Chetterling drew a long breath. "I'm going to call Delching."

"The forensic anthropologist," Annie whispered to Chelsea.

Stanish stepped over to the white sheet. Chelsea bit her lip, watching as he compared the fragment in his hand with the broken cranium. "It's a fit," he told Chetterling as the detective clicked off the phone.

"A tight one?"

Stanish considered the skull. "Doesn't look perfectly tight to me. Maybe this injury did happen before death. But you know it's not my call. I'll leave that up to Fleck."

Chelsea gave Annie a quizzical look. "Harry Fleck's the medical examiner," Annie explained. "He's the guy who determines the cause and manner of death."

"Oh." Chelsea drew her arms across her chest. A shooting in Redding and now this. Why was she here, in the middle of it all? *God, I just want to go home!*

The three men continued their search.

Upon the white sheet, the makeshift skeleton slowly formed.

Chapter 20

Larry Delching arrived within half an hour. By that time rumor, like a crooked finger, had beckoned my wide-eyed neighbors from their homes. They grouped off to the side, watching like hawks, pelting me with questions. Twice I explained what happened, then heard my story told and retold in whispers as more people appeared. Dave was not among them, but I sure didn't want to call him. The last thing he needed was more sights of death in his neighborhood.

I focused on the scene before me. The potential area for finding more bones stretched wide. The three men were combing and picking through it one square foot at a time. The crewmen, told they could not continue work until the scene was officially cleared—and that could be days—had muttered a few expletives and left. So much for their overtime pay.

Minutes ticked by, indecision playing tug-of-war in my head. Chelsea and I had a task to do; we couldn't stand here all day. But neither could I leave, not with more skeleton pieces surfacing by the minute. The sight of those mournful, soil-caked bones rooted me to the pavement.

I watched Delching work. The man had a lean, compact build and moved with precise motions, craning his neck toward the ground, plucking bones with thumb and fore-finger. On the long white sheet the three men continued to piece the body together, one bone at a time. When this onsite work was done, the skeleton would be moved to the morgue. There Harry Fleck would measure certain bones. Shape and size of the pelvis would help determine whether the person was male or female. The skull's eye sockets, nasal cavity, and lower portion together would lead to a determination of racial ancestry.

"Look here." Delching pushed back soil and debris with both hands as Cisneros and Chetterling squatted beside him. I leaned forward, trying to see. "A femur." He pulled the long leg bone out of the dirt and gently brushed it off. Stanish took it from him, crossed to the white sheet and laid it in place.

Delching wiped sweat from his face, leaving a smudge of dirt on his jaw. "My guess is, with us finding pieces this close together, the skeleton was intact. The backhoe broke it apart."

I absorbed the news, questions swirling. Who was this person? Why was the body here? And—was the timing of its discovery significant? I thought over the events of the last two days. The 7-Eleven shooting ... Chelsea's vision ... now this. Suspicion niggled in my gut. Three disturbing events in a row. Something told me that two of them were more than coincidence.

"What do you think?" I asked Chelsea.

A troubled expression flicked across her face. "I have no idea."

"Does it ... I mean, do you *see* anything?"

Annie, what an idiotic question.

Jenna tilted her head, eyebrows raised, as if she indeed expected some supernatural insight. Chelsea hitched her shoulders. "I'm sorry, I don't know any more than you do."

Jenna spread her hands, then dropped them. "Oh well. It was worth a try."

Chelsea offered her a self-conscious smile.

Tires zinged against pavement. I turned to see a beige car cut to a stop. Adam Bendershil bounded out of the driver's seat, notebook in hand. The passenger door opened, spewing a photographer with camera.

Shades of two days ago. "Oh great." My shoulders slumped. "My favorite reporter is here."

Chelsea jerked around. Up swung the camera, straight at us. *Click. Click.* "Oh." She ducked. Too late.

Jenna practically growled and turned a purposeful back to Adam. He made a beeline for me, a man on a mission. His photographer advanced to the end of the runway, snapping photos of the men, the half-pieced skeleton. Anger tightened my shoulders. That was someone's *body* lying there, not some object of fascination. Couldn't he show a little more respect?

"Annie Kingston." Adam drew up before me, pen poised over paper. "What can you tell me about the skull?"

Sure, Adam, what would you like—name, date of birth, social security number? I shot him a withering look. "You know I don't talk to you."

"Oh, come on now, the Bill Bland case was a year and a half ago. How long are you going to hold a petty grudge?"

Jenna whirled on him. "Leave her alone!"

Adam held up a hand, feigning surprise. "Whoa. Aren't we touchy!"

In my pocket my cell phone went off. The incoming number was Dave's. I strode away from the reporter as I answered. "Hi."

"Hey. I just heard some strange news. What's going on?"

I told him. "Are the girls still with you?"

"Yes. So I'll stay here. Not something they need to see."

"True, and now the media's shown up. One more reason to stay away."

"Uh-oh. Are you all right?"

"Yes." I forced a lilt into my tone.

Dave didn't seem to be buying it. "Annie, do you need me to come out there?"

"No, really. I'm fine." I was doing it again—pushing him away.

"Okay." A sort of weary disappointment coated the word. He paused. "Did you meet with Chelsea Adams?"

"Yes. She's here. We were just finishing when we heard about this."

Silence. I knew he wanted to press for details but wouldn't load that on me now. "Dave, thank you for checking on me. I'll talk to you soon as I can. Tell you about everything."

"Okay. See you soon."

I clicked off the line and wandered back to Chelsea and Jenna, sighing at the heat and Adam Bendershil, who was now calling questions to Larry Delching. Tiredness washed over me. My feet ached. Jenna slumped, hands on her hips, eyes still fixed upon the reporter. Chelsea looked a little wilted herself, and definitely unhappy at Bendershil's presence. She stole a glance at her watch and I checked mine. After three. We needed to leave. At this rate she'd get back to the Bay Area much later than she'd intended.

I touched her arm. "It's getting late for you. If we're going to see Officer Blanche, we need to do it now so you can get started home."

She nodded almost distractedly, then turned to stare at the grimed half skeleton.

"See Officer Blanche?" Jenna, still seething over Bendershil, was quick to jump on a new target. "Whatever for?"

I ignored her, focusing on Chelsea. "What is it?" I gestured toward the laid-out bones. "Do you think this has something to do with your vision?"

She placed a hand at the back of her neck. "I really don't *know*. But you have to admit, this timing . . ."

"Wait a minute, wait a minute." Jenna eyed me with her *don't-be-an-idiot-Annie* look. "*Why* would you two go see Officer Blanche?"

"Jenna—"

"To show him the composite of the face I saw." Chelsea's words were firm, unrattled. "In case it's the man who may be missing after that shooting you witnessed."

Jenna's eyes jumped from Chelsea to me. "What makes you think *that*?"

"Look, let's just go." I turned toward the car. "We can talk about it on the way to the house."

Chelsea threw me a glance and tactfully headed for the vehicle. Her slow walk, the sag of her shoulders, spoke volumes. She didn't relish being the cause of any problem between me and my sister.

Jenna opened her mouth. I turned away and called out to Chetterling. "Ralph, we need to get going."

"Annie, you better tell me what's going on," Jenna demanded.

Chetterling pushed up from his kneeling position in the dirt, arched his back, and made his way to me. Sweat shone on his forehead. He swiped at a trickle on his temple. "Don't know yet, but as you can see, we might need you for this one. Are you up to it?"

I gazed at the face I'd come to know so well. Chetterling's combination of large nose, thin lips, and granite-cut features, combined with his aura of authority, used to intimidate the daylights out of me. But time and again he'd proved his heart. He was a good, caring man, and his question spoke to his selflessness. He knew I was still recovering from the events of the past summer.

"Yes, I'm up to it."

"All right." His eyes roved to Chelsea, who was waiting at the car, then back to me. I could see the lingering questions in his eyes. "Talk to you soon."

Thirty minutes later Chelsea and I, despite Jenna's vehement arguments, were on our way to see Tim Blanche. I drove my SUV, my composite in a large folder on the passenger seat. Chelsea followed in her own car. Once we were done with Blanche, she would head home. We'd each eaten a quick sandwich. The roast beef and cheese sat heavily in my stomach. Now that I'd called the detective and said we needed to see him, I couldn't help wondering how I'd gotten myself into this. Like clotted milk, the man's voice had thickened with scorn when I reminded him why Chelsea's name sounded familiar. "Why on earth does she want to see *me*?"

Here it came. Some woman who claimed to have visions from God trying to tell Detective Tim Blanche how to run his investigation? "We may have information for you about Amy Flyte. We're not sure, but we think we should tell you just in case."

He heaved a sigh, betraying his conundrum. How to deny my request without sounding close-minded and controlling?

"Yeah, all right, come on down if you must," he clipped, "but I'm really busy and you'll have to make it quick."

As if we'd want to linger for a friendly chat. Still, Chelsea and I had a story to tell, and I was determined Blanche would hear it. I could only hope that we'd finish before he threw us both out of his office.

Chapter 21

By the time we reached the station, my heart hammered. I shot Chelsea a crooked smile as we opened the door. "Here goes."

When we stepped into the lobby area, I caught sight of Ryan Burns setting up a small table. A makeshift sign was taped to its edge: "Help crime victim Toby Brown. Every dollar you give will be matched with three more." Nearby on the floor sat a clear plastic box with a slit in the top. A few bills already lay in the bottom of the box.

"Annie Kingston, hi!" Ryan's pudgy face creased into a smile.

"Hi, Ryan." I introduced him to Chelsea and they shook hands. "This is great of you to do." I pointed to the sign. "I take it you're the one who's matching the dollars?"

Ryan's gaze dropped and he shrugged. "Don't tell people, okay? I mean, the police know, but . . ."

I smiled. "Okay."

"Who's Toby Brown?" Chelsea asked.

I opened my purse to pull out my wallet. "The boy who was shot on Thursday. He has a single mom who doesn't make much money. His job helped support the family."

Ryan lifted the plastic box onto the table. I dropped in a twenty-dollar bill as Chelsea reached for her own wallet.

"Hey, thanks." Ryan looked pleased.

He must have been close to thirty, but with his shy demeanor and short, stout frame, Ryan struck me more as an awkward school kid. No one would ever guess he was the wealthiest citizen in Redding. Five years ago, as a clerk in a photocopy store, he'd won $56 million in the California state lottery. Much of his newfound money had gone to help local schools, citizens, and law enforcement.

"So." Ryan ran a hand through his thatch of brown hair. "You here to work on the Orwin Neese case? I saw your drawing of him in the paper. I suppose everybody has by now."

No doubt, including Orwin Neese himself. That thought gave me the shivers. I repressed the urge to throw Chelsea a look. "Yes, you could say that."

"Well, keep safe, okay? We don't need a repeat of last time."

"Oh, don't you worry."

Three months ago Ryan had put up a fifty-thousand-dollar reward for the capture of the Poison Killer. In the end he'd tried to write that check out to me. I insisted he give the money to the Shasta County Sheriff's Department instead.

Ryan shifted his feet. "Well, I need to go. I have a lot more boxes to drop off around town."

Chelsea and I bid him good-bye, then turned reluctant footsteps down the hall.

In Tim Blanche's office, I found myself headed for the same corner, same chair, as Dayna Edwington had occupied the day before. Despite the fifty percent chance of that, ghosted implications drew a finger down my spine. The detective would likely treat me no better. A glance around the room didn't elevate my expectations. Folders and papers cluttered Tim's desk, two Styrofoam coffee cups small islands in the sea of files. More cups lay crushed in the wastebasket. A vague smell of sweat and dust tinged the air. Blanche had probably been working nonstop since the murder. Little sleep and frustration would not make him a ready recipient of our story.

He hung up the phone and stood as we entered, his movements brisk, distracted—almost as if by design. "Let's hope this thing doesn't ring for a few minutes." He waved a hand at the receiver.

"Tim, thanks for taking time for us." I introduced him to Chelsea and he stuck out a hand with a swift nod. She shook it, looking straight into his eyes as if fathoming the man.

Blanche stared back, his wariness obvious. "Sit, please." He indicated the chairs and sank into his own behind the desk, leaning forward, fingertips tapping strewn papers.

"Do you have any leads on Orwin Neese?" I asked. "Or on Amy?"

He made a face, as though I'd accused him of not doing his job. "Nothing on Amy. No one's seen her anywhere, which can't be good. As for Orwin, that's why the phone's ringing so much. We're running down leads from acquaintances of his. I just haven't caught up to him yet. But I will."

I again. No teamwork. Just *I*.

"And the identity of the possible missing young man?"

"Nothing there either." Tim buffed his forehead with one hand. "Not sure he exists. If he did, you'd think we'd have a missing persons report by now."

True. My gaze dropped to the chaos of paper before him. Fresh indecision swirled through me. Chelsea and I had no proven basis for being here, and Tim's impatience to get back to work had him chugging like a race car engine.

"Now." Blanche looked to Chelsea, getting down to business. "What can I do for you?"

She clasped her hands in her lap, sitting almost casually, as though removing herself from Blanche's humming energy field. "I know Annie told you a little about why we needed to see you. And you have some knowledge about my involvement in some cases in the Bay Area?"

"Yeah." He rapped his knuckles against the edge of the desk.

"I'd like to tell you about this recent vision I had."

"Does it have anything to do with this murder?"

"I'm not sure. But as Annie mentioned, in case it does, we think you should know."

Blanche eyed her with a piercing look. "You're not *sure*?"

Chelsea nodded.

He leaned back, folded his arms. "Go ahead."

Chelsea told him, with articulation and calmness. She explained all she'd seen and heard ... and what she had not seen. What she knew and what she didn't know. When she was done, I slid the composite out of its folder and handed it to Blanche. This was my original. I'd made a copy and filed it in my office. "Here's the face."

Tim accepted the drawing, eyes scanning over it. He looked up at me and shrugged. Tossed the composite down on his desk. "Never seen him before."

The phone rang. He held up a finger, then answered it. Chelsea and I waited while he listened, posed terse questions, and took a few notes. "All right, thanks. Let me know what you find out." He rattled down the receiver. "Sorry."

He shifted in his seat, aimed a frowning stare at the pen in his hand. Then pushed back his chair. "I need to take care of something. Be right back."

Chelsea and I exchanged doleful looks as he bustled out of the office. A few minutes passed before he returned.

"Okay." He thumped into his chair, pulled up to the desk. "Where were we? Oh yeah, this drawing." He smacked his hand upon it and looked to me.

Okay, Annie, no backing out now. I leaned forward. "What struck me is that the girl Chelsea saw in the vision had brown hair, like Amy Flyte. And she was with another person in that little room. A person who could be male or female. But then Chelsea saw this face. It's possible this is the young man who's missing."

Tim's lips bunched. He cocked his head, then shook it, as if he hardly knew where to start. "Okay. Let's say I believed in this kind of thing in the first place, which I don't. How many women have brown hair, including you?" He raised his brows at me, then focused on Chelsea. "Besides, you said you didn't see the girl's face. If you *had*, and if you'd described a face to Annie that proved to be Amy Flyte, you might have convinced even this skeptical soul. But under the circumstances, what's here to tie to my case?"

God told her to come to me; that's the tie. Words I wanted to say, but what was the point? Blanche would never accept that.

"I agree there's not much." Chelsea raised her chin. "We only have one thing. I am absolutely certain that God told me to tell this vision to Annie. I'd never spoken to her before. I had to drive almost four hours to get here. But for some reason I was supposed to come."

Wow, this woman had more courage than I. Blanche sat in nonplussed silence. I could almost hear his brain thrash about for some logical answer to this lunacy.

He sniffed. Threw Chelsea the impatient look of an officer facing an imbecile witness. "I'm not going to debate the veracity of your religious beliefs, Ms. Adams. And I certainly can appreciate the fact that you've driven a long way to do what you thought was right. But I just don't see that this has anything to do with me. *Or this case.*"

He hammered the last three words like nails in a coffin. But it was his dark, determined expression that gave him away. Blanche's desire for the glory of solving this case left no room for the likes of me or Chelsea Adams. Imagine the sensational headlines if her vision was proved right! Seeing the hardness on Blanche's face, I almost wondered which scenario he'd consider worse—our composite leading him to a dead end, or leading him to Orwin Neese and two captives.

Chelsea remained still, but I could feel the vibrations emanating from her. She saw through Blanche as well as I. "You may be right," she said. "We felt we should tell you what happened. But of course the decisions are up to you."

Tim's eyebrows twitched. He seared her with a look, as though seeking hidden threats in her words. Then turned to me. "Look, Annie, I'm busy. What exactly do you expect me to do with this?" He gestured toward the drawing.

I forced myself to look him in the eye as I stated the obvious. "Run it in the paper, see what leads it turns up. Nobody knows what young man we're looking for, or if he even exists. This might give you some answers."

"Uh-huh. And what am I supposed to say to the media when I ask them to run it? This guy appeared in some woman's dream, and we thought it was worth a try?"

Some woman's dream? I fought to keep my voice even. "Tim, right now you have nothing on this young man. *If* he exists. I don't see what harm it'll do to use this. Tell the media the drawing's a lead, and that's it. You follow leads all the time. Some work out, some don't."

Blanche threw out his hands. "Fine. And how do I explain this composite to my superiors? Because you know they're going to ask."

"Detective Blanche, just tell them the truth." Chelsea gave a little smile and shrugged. "Tell them you think it's bizarre, but you're working so hard on the case, with leads not panning out, that you think *anything* is worth trying. They'll see how much you want to solve this. Then if the lead is a dead end, well, Annie and I were just wrong. It'll be our fault, not yours."

Go, Chelsea. I felt like slapping her a high five. How was Blanche supposed to say no to such logic without revealing his hidden agenda?

He narrowed his eyes, as though deciphering her craftiness. Then abruptly pushed back his chair. "Maybe I'll do that." He stood, calling our meeting to a close. "Annie, Ms. Adams, thank you for coming down." The words were flat, almost antiseptic. He held out a hand to Chelsea. "Have a safe drive back to the Bay Area."

In other words, good riddance. We'd been dismissed.

Chapter 22

Déjà vu, Chelsea thought as she and Annie walked away from Blanche's office. This was so similar to the first time she'd visited a policeman with information from a vision. She'd been slapped down then too. She should have known this man wouldn't listen.

In the hall Chelsea caught the odd stares of two young officers. Annie met their eyes, then looked away, frowning. "Do you know them?" Chelsea whispered when they were out of earshot.

"Yes." Annie's voice sounded tight. "Rex Whitley and Charlie Tranks. You get the feeling they *knew* what our meeting with Blanche was about?"

Chelsea's heart sank. This too she'd experienced in the Trent Park case—the strange looks when she entered the Haverlon Police Department, rumors flying about her vision. It was one thing to place herself in the midst of such controversy. But now she'd dragged Annie into it. Maybe they'd been wrong to come here. What if God hadn't wanted them to tell the detective at all?

They said no more until they hit the parking lot. Annie's shoulders slumped. "My, that went so well."

"I know." Chelsea sighed. "It's just that we had so little to give him."

Annie pulled to a halt. "Then *why* did we come?"

The frustration in her tone cut through Chelsea. No doubt Annie felt like she'd gotten the short end of the stick. Which was true. Chelsea could return to the Bay Area, never to face these people again. But Annie didn't just live here; she had to *work* with these men. Chelsea touched her hand. "You're mad at me."

"No, I'm not."

"Yes, you are. Because I'm leaving and you're staying. Because I pulled you into this."

Annie eyed her with a mixture of wonder and pique, as if surprised at her insight. Chelsea winced. "I'm sorry. Really. I wouldn't have wanted this for you. In fact, I talked to God about it more than once before I ever tried tracking you down." She tipped her head toward the heavens. "You don't know how many times I wished I didn't have this gift. I know that sounds terribly selfish, because God has used it to save people from harm and bring criminals to justice. But most of the time it just makes people think I'm crazy."

"I don't think you're crazy."

"I know." She tossed Annie a grateful look. "Anyway, I shouldn't lay this on you. Because I do understand what you're feeling. If I were you, I'd feel it too."

Annie shook her head. "Don't apologize. Besides, I ... think we did what God wanted us to do. So if things don't go right, we can just blame Him."

They exchanged weary smiles.

Chelsea turned and gazed toward her car. She needed to get home. If only she and Annie could have ended this day on a better note. She blinked at the sunlight reflecting off the passenger door of her blue Lexus. Her eyes dropped to the dull safety of a tire. "Annie, I feel bad about leaving with everything so up in the air."

Wait. Was the bottom side of that tire puddling against the pavement? Chelsea frowned at it. Turned comparing eyes toward its rear mate. Hey, that one also looked ...

"That's okay, I know you—"

"My tires are flat."

Annie's words cut short. "Huh?"

"The two I see are flat, front and back." Chelsea couldn't believe it. *Both* tires? Not here, not now!

Annie turned to look. "Oh *no.*"

They hurried across the lot. At the Lexus, Chelsea bent down to look at the front tire, as if a closer view would somehow change the truth. It was totally flat. The rear one too. Her mouth hung open. "How could they both—"

"Uh-oh. Look at this." Annie set her purse on the pavement and squatted down. She reached to the front part of the rubber—and pointed to a small slice. "Looks to me like it's been cut."

Chelsea sucked in a breath. She moved to the rear tire, peered at it. Ran gingerly hands over the surface. Another cut. *What in the world?* "Both of them have been slashed." Her voice held disbelief. Two vandalized tires—in the police station parking lot? What kind of person had the *nerve?* She straightened. "I'm going to check the other side."

They scuttled around the car. The third and fourth tires were just as bad.

Chelsea hissed air between her teeth. "I can't *believe* this." She stared at the tires, questions crowding her mind. Who? Why? And how was she going to get home now?

"I can't believe it either. What a rotten prank." Annie surveyed the car parked next to Chelsea's. "Look, those tires are fine." She walked around to its other side. "These are okay too."

Chelsea stared at her. "Something's not right here."

"No kidding." Annie's face looked pinched. "I hate to say it, but we'd better check mine."

The SUV was a few spaces farther down. Chelsea noted the other cars' front tires as they passed—one, two, three. All looked normal. They arrived at Annie's car. The tires were fine. Chelsea turned to survey the line of vehicles in the opposite rows. None slashed there either.

"Well." Annie's voice edged. "Terrific. Some idiot chose your Lexus; wasn't that nice of him."

"Oh," Chelsea groaned, "now what do I do?" *God, why did You let this happen? Is this the thanks I get?* And whatever would Paul say? He hadn't wanted her to come in the first place. She swung back to Annie's car, one hand to her cheek. Feeling absolutely sick. Her eyes fell on a piece of paper stuck beneath Annie's windshield wipers.

Wait, what's that?

Her heart tripped over itself. Standing there in the warm sun, in the police station parking lot, she stared at that bit of paper ... and *knew*. "Annie, there's—"

"I see it."

Drawing her top lip between her teeth, Chelsea stared at the paper. *God, what is happening? Why do I feel so petrified?* Slowly they approached. At the windshield Annie reached out with forefinger and thumb. Clasped the very corner of the note and pulled it out. She turned it over. Chelsea leaned in, pulse scudding.

The letters were written in red felt-tip pen. All capitals.

"I KILLED MIKE WINGER. YOU'RE NEXT."

Chapter 23

The next hour sped by, voices, phone calls, and footsteps pelting us like molten drops of lead. Chelsea and I had run into the station, my fingers still clutching the note. A stunned Tim Blanche and two other officers heard our story, gawking at the flaming piece of evidence I dropped on Blanche's desk. One of the officers hurried away to fetch materials for handling it. He returned, pulling on gloves, then picked up the note and dropped it into a small bag. "I only touched the corner," I repeated three times, as if the mantra itself would raise black swirls of useable prints from the paper. Three other men checked outside, making sure Orwin Neese did not lurk in the parking lot or anywhere nearby. When they felt sure of our safety, the rest of us trooped out, the officers examining Chelsea's tires, my windshield.

Blanche looked fit to be tied. One hand found his hip and dug into it. His eyes drilled holes in my car as if it were to blame. "How could he be right here? *Right here*!" His anger was a live and sizzling thing. He'd been spit at, taunted, and he wasn't going to take it lying down.

Ten feet away Chelsea watched in shocked silence, palms pressed together, fingertips at her mouth. Her wide-eyed gaze cruised the scene, seeking a safe place to land.

"How do we know it's him?" My voice shook. I didn't even try to steady it. My brain lay somewhere on hold, my body moving, mouth speaking on some different plane. How could this be happening to me again?

Blanche spun toward me, face hard. "Who *else* would it be? It's practically got his *signature* on it!"

"I know, but ..." Fragments of past terrors collided in my head. Accepting that someone like Orwin Neese wanted to kill me, had been so *close* to me, was more than I could handle. What if my car hadn't been in the police station parking lot? What if he'd had time to stick a bomb in it? I stared at the SUV, air rattling down my throat. How did I know a bomb *hadn't* been hidden under its hood?

I struggled to plan logically. *Think, Annie, think.* I had to call Jenna. And Dave. And where were the kids? Panic surged through me. Was Stephen still at work, Kelly with Erin? I had to talk to them, had to account for everyone. I looked to my purse to pull out my cell phone. *Oh no.* My purse was gone. I whipped my head around, one hand raking through my hair, searching for the bag.

"Chelsea, my purse is gone! What did I do with it?"

She turned to me, her eyes overbright. "You put it down. When you checked the tire." She pointed toward her Lexus. "There."

Before I could reply, she moved to retrieve it for me.

"Thanks." I opened it, jerked out my phone. Blanche was ordering one of the officers to call a technician as I hit the auto-dial button for home. Kelly answered.

Kelly. Suddenly I couldn't talk. I didn't want to tell her a thing. I'd *promised* her this case wouldn't be dangerous. I pulled in air, willing it not to shiver in my lungs. "Hi. What are you doing?"

"Not much."

"Where's Jenna?"

"I don't know; around here somewhere. What's wrong?"

Was I that transparent? "Nothing. I'm just kind of in a hurry here. Would you find her for me?"

"Yeah, okay." I heard muffled footfalls, voices. "Here she is."

My throat closed again. Despite my sister's tendency toward calm in a storm, I didn't want to talk to her either. I'd failed my family. Again.

"Hi, Annie. What's up?"

I saw Chelsea slip her own phone from her purse, start dialing. Wouldn't her husband just love this news. Blanche's forefinger punched air as he loudly demanded answers from nearby officers. *How* could Orwin Neese have been in such close proximity to the police station that he'd seen me and Chelsea arrive?

"Annie?"

"I'm here."

A pause. I could feel it already, that sister connection—the vibration of invisible fiber optics that heralded unpleasant news. "What's wrong?"

I turned away from the scene—Chelsea on her phone, the growing number of officers—and told her.

Stunned silence. I wandered two steps, looked back toward my car. A technician was pulling out his materials, preparing to dust the wipers and windshield for prints. Vaguely I wondered if they would try Chelsea's tires as well. Could body oil show up on rubber? A memory stumbled through my head, something Chetterling once told me: around forty different ways existed to check for fingerprints.

In the meantime Chelsea would need new tires. She wasn't going home in that car anytime soon.

"Okay." Jenna's voice sounded stiff. "All right. We'll ... handle this. Just like before."

"I don't know if I'm going to get my car back right away." It was the first of a dozen details that came to mind. "You might have to come get us."

"That's fine. No problem."

Bradley Clark, chief of police, emerged from the station with his bearlike stride, beefy arms held away from his sides. He headed straight for Tim Blanche. Knowing Clark's reputation for protecting his department, I read plenty from his creased forehead and working jaw. The pressure to find Orwin Neese had just multiplied tenfold. A man stupid enough to kill in broad daylight, whose face appeared on the front page of every newspaper in town, had trespassed onto their own turf to wreak havoc. How embarrassing. Somebody in the department would have to answer for this—and that somebody was Blanche.

"I'm heading over there now." Jenna's voice tugged at me. "You need to demand protection until this thing's over. *Will* you do that? 'Cause if not, I'll demand it for you."

"Yes, you're right. I'll do it." I dug fingers into my scalp. "Jenna, wait. Bring Kelly with you. We can't leave the kids alone."

"Is Stephen still at work?"

"I think so. I'll call him next."

"Look, this isn't going to take too long. Catching Neese, I mean." Jenna's tone rounded into a soothe. "His picture's everywhere and he's obviously right in the area. Where's he going to hide?"

"Yeah." I licked my lips, needing water. "It can't be soon enough for me."

Time burned on. The technician dusted black powder onto my SUV's windshield and wipers but found no prints. On the premises, all four tires were carefully removed from Chelsea's car. Even pulling the Lexus onto a tow truck bed could have disturbed some of the evidence. In the lab they would try to raise fingerprints. Technicians would measure the slashes, determine the size of knife used. Blanche called a tire garage, catching someone just before they closed for the night. The business, out of stock for the size Chelsea needed, brought over four temporaries to place on the car. The man from the garage would change the tires, then drive the Lexus back to his business. He would find the needed tires on Monday. Sundays they were closed.

Meanwhile I talked to Stephen, making sure he was safe at work. He was supposed to get off at eight but insisted on leaving immediately.

"No," I told him, "you don't need to do that. I'm fine."

"Mom, you are *not* fine! Somebody's threatening to kill you again."

"Stephen, I'm okay. I have policemen all around me right now. I'm more worried about you. Stay at work. Then come straight home."

"I don't care about me."

"Well, I do!" I cut off my words, breathing heavily. Pain tightened my throat. "Just … look. Do what I say. Please. There's a lot going on here already, and I don't want to have to worry about you."

Even then he wasn't convinced, but he finally agreed to stay put. "Keep your cell phone on," he demanded. "And let me know when you get home."

I promised I would.

Two phone calls down, one to go. I brought a hand to my forehead, took a minute to pull myself together. Then phoned Dave. The news knocked the breath out of him. Like Stephen, he wanted to come right away, rescue me on a white horse. "No, it's okay," I told him. "Jenna's coming and she'll bring us home."

Like hound dogs with noses to the ground, the media showed up. This time it was Luke Bremington, another crime reporter from the *Record Searchlight*. Bremington was around my age, with intense brown eyes in a square face. No doubt Adam Bendershil was busy writing about the first crime event of the day. Maybe he was still at Grove Landing, crowing over the bone-by-bone building of the skeleton.

God, what is going on?

Just imagining tomorrow morning's paper tied my muscles in knots.

Bremington aimed straight for me, questions spilling from his thin lips. I turned away with my typical "No comment."

"But just one thing, Ms. Kingston." He leaned toward me. "First the finding of the skeleton in your neighborhood, now this threat on your life. Do you think the two are connected?"

Threat on your life. The words made me shudder. How had he heard this so fast, anyway? My eyes wandered to the police station, suspicion coiling through me. Somewhere in that building, Bremington had an inside source. Rex Whitley or Charlie Tranks, one of the two officers who'd given Chelsea and me those curious stares? The thought misted me with fury. And what was this *connection* business? My mind played the scenes of Chetterling and the other men assembling old, dirt-caked bones ... the recent shooting.

"I can't imagine how they could have anything to do with each other." I dismissed Bremington with a tight smile, then turned my back on him. A moment later I spotted him querying the technicians. Then he disappeared inside the station.

Jenna arrived with Kelly, who ran to me, eyes glistening. I clung to my daughter, assuring her that everything would be okay, this crazy man would be caught soon.

"Oh, he'll be caught, all right." Jenna hugged us both fiercely. "He just better hope it's not by *me*."

I didn't bother talking to Blanche. I went straight to Chief Bradley Clark to request protection. Blanche might fume at my audacity in going over his head, but I would take no chances. My family had experienced too much in the past couple years. I'd been threatened, as had my children. No way could I doubt that Orwin Neese meant what he said. Our house sat outside of town, in the Sheriff's Department's jurisdiction, but this case rested with the Police Department. I didn't care who paid for it; I just wanted someone making his presence known outside my house.

Because of my history, Clark granted my request. Twenty-four hour surveillance, he promised me, three cars a day, in eight-hour shifts.

My family under guard. Again. I just wanted to gather them up and run.

Chapter 24

You can't be thinking of staying there!" Paul's voice fairly crackled in Chelsea's ear. "We've got to get you home *now.*"

If only I could leave. The thought of home plucked at Chelsea's heart. Had she really only been gone since this morning? She wanted to sleep in her own bed tonight, safe, secure. Away from all this craziness. But ...

She glanced toward Annie and her family. Jenna paced with indignation, and Kelly and Annie hung on to each other. Poor Kelly looked so frightened. "Paul, think about it. By the time you drive here to pick me up and we get back home again, it'll be two o'clock in the morning. Then we'll just have to leave early Monday to come back for my car. You'll miss a full day's work. Can you do that?"

"Oh, Monday." Air seeped from his throat. "I've got a board meeting. Someone else will have to get you back there."

"See?" Chelsea took a deep breath. Closed her eyes. Her husband wasn't going to like this. "Paul, it's not just the problem of getting back and forth. I just have this feeling I'm *supposed* to stay."

"Oh no, don't give me that. Look, you went all the way up there to meet with that woman; isn't that enough? I don't want you dragged into another bad situation."

"Believe me, I don't want that either. But look at everything that's happened. While I'm here, that skull is found? Now this threat on Annie's life? All this can't be coincidence, Paul. Whether we like it or not, God's got a reason for me to be here."

"Yeah, and I've got a reason to bring you home. I can't leave you in danger."

"*I'm* not in danger. The threat was only toward Annie."

"Then who slashed your tires?"

Chelsea had no response for that. "Paul, please listen. I just ... I can't walk away in the middle of this. God brought me up here. And even if I did go home, I'd have to turn around and come right back. You might as well let me stay."

Paul would not cave easily. He'd always seen Chelsea's visions as a threat. Yes, he'd witnessed all the good that resulted from them and came to believe they were sent from God. But he was Chelsea's protector and sometimes God asked a little too much.

Lord, if I'm really supposed to stay, please convince my husband.

They argued for another ten minutes. In the end Chelsea wore him down with the logistics. What was the point of driving back and forth? She might as well stay in a hotel until Monday. She'd be safe there. Paul finally sighed. "But what about clothes and toiletries? You don't have anything for overnight."

A last-ditch effort, aimed at her womanhood.

"I'll ... manage. The hotel should have emergency packets. And I'll buy a few things."

By the time Chelsea hung up the phone and rejoined Annie's little group, ambivalence roiled within her. Why had

she been so adamant about staying? She *wanted*
and she missed Paul. Still, she sensed God tell
Annie, even with family nearby, was going to ne
And she couldn't ignore that feeling.

Lord, like the Psalms say, You are my streng
Please protect Annie. And lead me in whatever
to do.

Annie would not hear of her staying in a h

"Maybe she doesn't *want* to stay with us, *.*
stood with arms folded, her cheeks flushed.
more angry over her sister's plight than terrifi
this going on, she probably wants to get as far
as possible."

"But we've got police protection! At least
be guarded. That's better than sleeping alc
room."

"Wait." Chelsea held up a hand. "I don't
you any problems."

"You're not causing me problems." Annie
together. For a moment Chelsea thought sh
cry. "Look, it'll be far more of a problem fo
know where you are and that you're safe. F
us. We'll get you back into town on Monday
car."

Annie would not be swayed. They had
rooms, she said, and Chelsea would occup
She could just call her husband and tell
conversation.

"Okay, that's it!" A call behind them cu
sion. Chelsea turned to see the last of the te
place on her car.

Jerry Flagen, a determined-looking officer who stood
well over six feet, arrived to serve as Annie's first shift of
protection. He, Detective Blanche, and Chief Clark hustled
the four of them into a small conference room in the station
to go over plans. First point of agreement—Annie was not
to go anywhere alone. Jenna, Kelly, and Stephen should also
be careful. Although Neese probably knew little about her
family, this was not the time to take chances.

Chelsea watched Kelly's face. The girl listened with
shoulders drawn in, eyes darting from one policeman to
another as if seeking some kind of assurance. Annie sat close
to her, their fingers entwined. The sight tightened Chelsea's
throat. *Lord, let me somehow be a help to them.*

"Can I at least have my car back?" Annie asked. "Please?
You didn't find any evidence on it. And it was locked, so
there can't be anything inside."

Tim Blanche nodded. "I'll check with the techs. If there's
anything left to do, we won't be able to release it."

"All right, everybody on board here?" Chief Clark rose,
signaling the end of the meeting. "Officer Flagen will follow
you home, Annie." He lowered his chin to look Kelly in the
eye. "We're going to protect your mom; I want you to know
that. Nobody's going to come anywhere near her."

Kelly dropped her gaze and nodded. Chelsea could have
hugged the man for his empathy.

Back in the parking lot, Annie received good news: her
car could be released. Chelsea breathed a prayer of gratitude
for the small victory. While the technicians completed their
work, Jenna drove Chelsea to a drugstore to buy some toiletries. By the time they returned and Annie's car was ready,
it was eight thirty. Darkness had fallen. Annie climbed into

the SUV with Kelly. Chelsea stayed with Jenna. Officer Flagen followed in his police car.

"I can't believe this is happening again," Jenna breathed as she drove toward Grove Landing. "I could *kill* this scumbag."

Chelsea tried to keep her hands from fidgeting in her lap. She needed calmness, but that's the last thing she felt. *God, where are You right now?* "I'm so sorry for all of you. I know Annie's terrified, but she's trying to hold it together for Kelly."

"Oh, don't be sorry for *me*. But Kelly—she almost lost her mom three months ago. No wonder she's petrified. After what this household has been through, we can't do anything but assume the worst." Jenna stopped at a red light. She turned to look at Chelsea. "I'm surprised you're still with us. If I were you, I'd *walk* back to the Bay Area if I had to. Just get out of this madness."

Chelsea managed a smile. "Don't think I haven't considered it. And my husband's not exactly thrilled. But I ... God brought me here, Jenna. I don't understand why yet." She sighed. "I wish I did."

Jenna eyed Chelsea as if trying to figure her out. "Well, next time you talk to God, would you let Him know I'm downright ticked? My sister's the best person on earth and she doesn't deserve this. Seems to me He could take better care of her." The light turned green. She drove through the intersection, her mouth firming. "Meanwhile I have my gun."

Chapter 25

Kelly and I rode in silence until we neared the edge of town. My mind spun with events of the day. Chelsea's vision ... the unknown face ... the discovered skeleton ... the threatening note. I hadn't thought to ask Jenna if she'd checked Chetterling's progress at the airstrip. Were he and Stanish and the others finished with their work?

Tiredness surged through me. I sighed, flexed my aching neck.

Kelly shot me a worried look. "You okay, Mom?"

"Yes, sure. Just worn out."

She exhaled slowly. "Are you going to see Dave tonight?"

Dave. From nowhere the guilt I couldn't shake raised its ugly head. *Here we go again—Annie the troublemaker. Always bringing chaos into Dave's life, when he so deserves some peace ...*

"I don't know, it's pretty late. Maybe I'll just talk to him for a minute."

Kelly made a noise of disapproval in her throat. I ignored it. She and Erin were the same—they wanted to push me toward Dave. But on some level Kelly seemed to sense that even though I wanted to be with him, some nagging *thing* held me back.

"Well, anyway, I want to stay over at Erin's house."

Couldn't blame her. "Sure. I'll walk you across the street. And I'll talk to Dave then, okay?"

The promise sounded so placating, as if I would see Dave merely to please my daughter. Kelly surveyed me, mouth tight. "Are you going to marry him?" The question burst from her as if it had been bottled up for some time.

We stopped at a red light. I made a point of checking the rearview mirror for Jenna and Officer Flagen. Anything to keep from looking my daughter in the eye. "Kelly, we've only been dating for a few months."

"So? It's not like you're going to find anyone else like him. Besides, he loves you, you know that."

Loves me. Dave had never uttered the words. Nor could I be sure I wanted him to. "I love you" demands a response, like a lifeline thrown across a chasm. You either catch your end or it will fall. Could I do that to Dave? Watch him coil the rope back up, walk away alone?

The light turned green. We surged forward. "I'm not . . . I don't know what to tell you. Marriage is a huge commitment and we haven't even discussed it. You have to give us time."

Kelly pushed back against her seat with a sigh. Crossed her arms. "Well, for the record, I want you to. So does Erin. We don't see what you're waiting for."

My mental projector kicked on, the worn-out and caustic scene playing upon the walls of my head. Kelly's father, in our bedroom four and a half years ago . . .

"It's time I told you." The words drop like ice cubes. He unknots his tie, slips it from his neck. I stare at it dangling in his hands, somehow knowing that it's a metaphor, that he does not

see this. "I'm leaving the marriage. Yes, there's someone else. I'll be moving in with her ..."

My fingers stiffened against the steering wheel. In quick succession more fractured scenes flashed.

My father when I am eight years old: "You were supposed to be a boy ..."

My mother, crying to me about Dad's affairs. "He doesn't love us!"

Dave's grief-racked face the day after his beloved wife is killed ...

I took a deep breath, struggling to yank out the splintered memories. Why did they still plague me? I was a Christian now. I *knew* God loved me; I should be able to rest in that. Still, deep inside me hulked this thing, this beast that roared my unworthiness. Hadn't I gone through life feeling like I'd let people down? Truth be told, I hadn't felt worthy since the day I was born. Not to my husband, not to my father before him. And certainly not to someone as wonderful as Dave.

Some time passed before I could answer Kelly. When I did, my voice sounded stripped, barren. "Let us handle it, okay? This isn't for you to decide." I glanced at her, registering the puzzlement etching her forehead. My mouth tried to smile, but it came out lopsided.

We spoke no more on the way home.

When we reached Grove Landing, I drove straight toward the house. I had no energy, emotional or otherwise, to check on progress at the airstrip. Most likely they were gone anyway, now that it was dark. Besides, Kelly shouldn't be exposed to that. She had enough to deal with. Good thing she was going to Erin's. Her best friend would be more comfort to her than anyone, including me.

At the house, Officer Flagen took up his post on Barrister Court, parking just before the curve of the cul-de-sac so he faced the length of the street. I did not envy him the job of sitting in his car for hours. Mind on hold, I showed Chelsea her upstairs guest bedroom and bath, and Jenna provided her with a pair of pajamas. The two women wore the same size of clothes. Next stop—the kitchen. We'd eaten little all day. Not that I possessed much appetite. Jenna, God bless her, said she'd throw some dinner together while I went to see Dave.

Kelly bundled up a few belongings, and together we marched across the street under the officer's watchful eye. Kelly and Erin hugged as if they hadn't seen each other in a year. Dave's green eyes fixed upon me with palpable fear as he drew me inside. The girls headed down the hall to Erin's bedroom. There they would face this new problem in their typical teenage way—with lots of talking and music. Within seconds Erin's CD player kicked on to some hip-hop group.

Dave and I wandered into his family room and sank onto the couch. He put his arm around me and pulled me to his chest. The familiar rush swept over me, the warmth, the throat-tightening desire. I could hear his heart beating.

"Annie." He cradled a hand around my head. "It drives me crazy that this is happening to you. I just want to make it all go away."

Thump-thump, went his heart. The feel of him, the very *life* of him soothed me. At that moment I couldn't imagine why I'd ever want to push him away.

"It's okay." My voice half muffled into his shirt. "It's not going to last long. Neese's face is everywhere; they'll find him soon."

No reply. I knew he wanted to believe that as much as I did.

"Anyway." I laid my head on his shoulder. "I promised I'd tell you about Chelsea."

"Yes. I want to hear everything."

While he stroked my hair, I told him. All about her vision, her reaction to the discovery of bones at the airstrip. About *her.*

"She's amazing, really. She has real insight into people, and then she'll *say* what she sees. Not like Jenna would; she's not that blatant. But in this . . . empathetic way. On the other hand, I wouldn't want to go up against her. She's crafty when she has to be. She played Tim Blanche like a fiddle."

Dave chuckled at that. "Good for her."

The cordless phone rang. Dave sighed, then leaned toward an end table to answer it. "Hello?" I watched his expression still. He held the phone out to me. "It's Chetterling."

Oh great. After I'd purposely left my cell phone at home. Reluctantly I reached for the phone. "Hi, Ralph."

"Hi. Sorry about tracking you down. Jenna gave me the number."

"No problem."

"I heard about the note. You all right?"

"Good news travels fast." I leaned forward, focused on the carpet. Dave laid a hand on my back. "I'm okay. Not real happy but okay."

"Yeah, understood." He paused. "They'll get him soon, Annie. Hang in there. The Sheriff's Department is now helping too. Cars are out there everywhere, searching for him."

Wonderful Chetterling—always looking out for me. Why couldn't Blanche lay aside his dislike long enough to call and assure me like this? Too bad the Sheriff's Department didn't have full jurisdiction over the case. "Thanks, Ralph. I'm glad to know."

"Sure." He cleared his throat. "Look, I also wanted to tell you what's happening with the other case. We recovered most of the skeleton and brought it back to the morgue. Larry Delching and Harry Fleck will be looking at it tomorrow morning. Once the gender and age of the deceased has been determined, we'll look through missing persons reports for any possible fit. If we find one, of course, we'll see if we can establish identity through dental charts, which could take a day or two. But if we don't, we'll need you. Probably by sometime in the afternoon we should be ready to turn things over to you."

"Okay." I fought to keep the tiredness from my voice. *Let's just hope they don't need me.*

He hesitated. "Sure you can handle it, after this?"

I pulled in a long breath. "Sure. It'll keep me busy and out of trouble."

Ha-ha.

"Okay. Thanks, Annie; I know you have a lot on your mind. Somebody'll give you a call tomorrow and let you know what's happening." A pause. "I'll let you go now. But sometime you really are going to have to tell me about your visit with Chelsea Adams."

"Ralph, find Orwin Neese for me, and I'll tell you every *word* that passed between us."

He chuckled. "Deal."

I clicked off the line and set the phone aside. Dave placed his hands on my cheeks, questions in his eyes.

"Guess what I might get to do tomorrow?" I laid my hands over his, reveling at the feel of his palms against my skin. "Bring home a skull."

Sunday, September 25 –
Monday, September 26

Chapter 26

Eight o'clock Sunday morning. We would stay home from church. Far safer not to go out any more than I had to. I descended our circular staircase, smelling the coffee Jenna had made. She always wakes up earlier than I do. "Good morning," I called as I crossed the great room.

God, I do thank You for a good morning, despite everything. At least we've made it through the night, safe and sound.

I peeked through the front window toward the cul-de-sac. An officer I didn't recognize sat dutifully in his vehicle. He was sipping coffee from a mug.

"Hi." Jenna's delayed response sounded grim. "You'd better come in here and look at the paper."

Oh no, now what? Heart skipping a beat, I headed for the kitchen.

She sat at the table, front page unfolded. At the sound of my footsteps she raised her head. Her features were taut. I slipped into the chair opposite her, my eyes questioning.

It had become as predictable as heat in a Redding summer—the local media's crucial role during the hunt for a murderer. Almost as if we formed a triangle, I and law enforcement at one point, suspect at another, and reporters at the third. Of course the public needed to be informed; I understood that. And many times we'd used the media for our own purposes, as when a composite needed circulation. As for the reporters, their job was to get the story —first. Problem was, whatever information they tracked down, they'd report, whether it hurt the case or not. It never seemed to occur to them that out there somewhere a killer read the paper as well.

I took a breath. "How bad is it?"

Jenna's expression mixed cold anger, shock, and ... pity? I froze, not wanting to know. She turned the paper around and pushed it toward me. "I'm going to go see if our friendly policeman outside needs more coffee." She rose and left the kitchen.

I drew the paper closer. My gaze fell upon the front page, then bounced from one headline to the next.

Skeleton Found at Grove Landing

The article was accompanied by a photo of Chelsea and me by the site, Chelsea's eyes caught wide, creases in her forehead.

Neese Threatens Forensic Artist
Psychic Says Missing Woman Trapped with Spiders

I gasped. *How ... What ...* Hardly daring to breathe, I bent over the paper and read.

Forensic artist Annie Kingston and friend Chelsea Adams, a nationally known Bay Area woman who sees "visions from God," told police detective Tim Blanche Saturday afternoon that Adams had seen a vision of a woman and a second person imprisoned in a small, dark room stocked with spiders, some of them poisonous.

Adams and Kingston surmised that the two people may be Amy Flyte, missing since Orwin Neese allegedly vowed to kill her, and a second as yet unknown man whose life Neese also allegedly threatened.

Adams claimed the vision included terrifying details of deadly spiders from Africa and Australia, and an exact layout of the prisonlike room — including built-in shelves in whose corners spiders could weave webs, and a dim red bulb.

According to sources within the Redding Police Department, Adams asked Kingston to draw a face associated with the vision. This face may be that of the missing man, the two women told Blanche. The source said Blanche, skeptical of their claims, had not decided if he would release the sketch to the media . . .

By the time I finished the article, my heart sat in my throat. I pressed back in my chair, palms flat on the table, questions and emotions sloshing within me like crosscurrents. A scene flashed in my head — the back of Luke Bremington's crinkled white shirt as he disappeared into the police station yesterday afternoon. But *who* told him? Blanche was busy in the parking lot with the techs and the cars . . .

Still, in the end the blame rested with him.

My mouth twisted as I remembered the odd looks yesterday from officers Rex Whitley and Charlie Tranks. Just as I'd suspected, Blanche must have told them, and perhaps others, the reason for our visit. Then, evidently, filled in all the details as soon as Chelsea and I left his office. I closed my eyes, imagining the snide comments. *"Can you believe what Annie Kingston claims now? Man, those Christians are nutcakes . . ."*

Which one of those officers knew enough to spout all this to the press? My bet was on Tranks. He and Blanche were tight. I wanted to strangle them both.

And by the way, Chelsea was *not* a psychic.

I took a deep breath, trying to relieve my caved lungs. Now what? How was I going to face anybody? Jenna was right —I should never have gotten mixed up with Chelsea Adams. It was one thing to stand up for my faith and call people to pray. But this was different. This was ... *radical*. Seeing the stark black print on white paper made the whole scenario sound so utterly, completely ridiculous—

Annie, stop. How selfish can you get?

Hot remorse flushed through my veins as I realized the story could cause horrible consequences. If the two people in Chelsea's vision *were* Amy and the missing man, when Neese heard of this he might kill them out of fear. Get rid of the evidence, clean up the spider room. The thought sank within me, down to my gut. My gaze sputtered across cabinets, out the window as the projector in my head ran film of an enraged Neese

banging through the door of that cramped room. Amy and the man cower on the floor, welts from spider bites on their bodies. Neese grabs Amy's hair, jerks the girl to her bare feet. She pleads and cries as he drags her outside, slamming the door behind him ...

I pressed both elbows down on the table and dropped my head in my hands. *God, don't let that happen! What am I supposed to do now? What* can *I do?*

Footsteps heralded my sister's return. I did not look up. I heard the chair opposite me slide across wood, the rustle of clothes as Jenna sat down. I sensed her eyes upon me, but I couldn't speak. She waited. I could feel her empathy.

The film in my head clicked, threatened to turn on again. I pulled its plug. *Logic, Annie. Think it through.*

There was only one way I could deal with this news. I had to convince myself that Chelsea's vision had nothing to do with Amy and the missing man—*if* there even was such a person. I could not think that Blanche's stupidity might cost two innocent lives. Better to imagine myself as a scapegoat, the laughingstock of the Police Department. *Let them point fingers and snigger, God. Just don't let two people die because of this.*

Jenna remained silent. I floundered for words.

"Okay, go ahead." I aimed my challenge at the table, voice low. "Tell me you were right. That I'm an idiot for ever letting Chelsea come."

She pulled in a long breath. "Well, there's not much point in talking about that, is there? It's done. Now we get to figure out what to do about this." She smacked a hand on the newspaper.

I emitted a sick laugh. "You tell me. I can't even think straight."

"Actually, it's not like we *can* do much about it. I just ... wonder where it all will lead. You didn't read the other stories yet, did you?"

I shook my head.

She drummed her fingertips against the paper. "In an odd way everything blends together. Neese threatens to kill you. Which makes the police look for him all the harder. When they find him, who knows? Maybe he'll crack and lead police to two captives locked up somewhere ..."

With a bunch of poisonous spiders. She couldn't even say the words, it sounded so insane.

"And the skeleton at the runway?" My voice sounded thick.

"Oh yeah. Guess that's just an added bonus."

My throat felt tight. "Well, at least my work on the skeleton will be with the Sheriff's Department. I sure don't want to see Tim Blanche again anytime soon." I made a face. "But I do want to call and tell him what I think of him."

"Yeah, agreed. I'll be happy to do it for you."

I squeezed my eyes shut. "The way he treated Chelsea and me was bad enough. But he didn't have to snicker about it to his buddies. Obviously, he never intended to give that drawing to the media. Now he *really* won't. He'll think it would make him look the fool. Only thing he can do is distance himself from us."

A door opened above, the sound filtering over the balcony, through the great room. Chelsea was up. *Oh, wonderful.* I wasn't ready to tell her the news. If I felt this humiliated, imagine how she would react. What's worse, she would see right through me and perceive what I was thinking.

"Did that policeman outside want more coffee?" Anything for an excuse to flee. I could take it out, linger and talk to him.

Jenna shook her head. "You're stuck here, Sis."

I leaned back, folded my arms, and waited.

Chelsea appeared, wearing yesterday's clothes and no makeup. Like Jenna, she was gorgeous without it. One look at our faces and she knew something was wrong. She sat at the head of the table. I got up to pour her some coffee. Jenna slid the newspaper in front of her, tapping the offending article with one finger. "Better look at this one first."

No one spoke while Chelsea read. I placed a mug of coffee on the table and resumed my seat, suddenly feeling like an offending student awaiting word from the principal. If I bemoaned letting her come here, surely she'd feel the same about calling me in the first place. Look at how my town was treating her obedience to God.

Chelsea lifted her eyes, her gaze drifting out the window. Her expression held mixed resignation and calm. In time she cleared her throat, looked to me. "How did they know this?"

I shook my head. "It had to be Blanche. He probably laughed about our conversation to another officer. When Bremington, the reporter, showed up because of Neese's threat, he got a bigger story than he bargained for."

The scenario took root within me, sprouted into renewed anger. *God, why did You let this happen? Why should someone like Blanche get the upper hand, when all we did was what You wanted?*

Chelsea cradled her coffee mug, her features placid. Just seeing her lack of reaction diminished my indignation. I focused on the finely sculpted bones of her cheeks, the smooth skin, struck by the disparity between her fragile beauty and inner strength.

"I'm really sorry." Her eyes turned from Jenna back to me. "I shouldn't be surprised at this; the media never let me alone before. You'd think the police would be tight with their information, but ..." She pressed her lips together. "Anyway, I'm most sorry for you, Annie. Like I said, when my car is fixed, I get to go home. But you have to stay here and work with these people."

I couldn't reply. No use denying the truth.

"The only thing I can tell you—" she offered the tiniest of smiles—"is that time will bear you out. I know God sent me this vision. I know I was supposed to come to you. He wouldn't put us through all this without good reason. His vision *will* become evident as the truth."

Jenna looked on, for once too nonplussed to speak. I know she thought the claims outrageous. But she couldn't help seeing Chelsea's humility. Chelsea hadn't grown defensive, hadn't even mentioned herself.

Time would bear me *out;* God's *vision would become evident.*

If I were Chelsea, I'd be explaining myself backward and forward. Talk about feeling like I'd let people down.

"We have to keep praying." Chelsea's voice grew firmer. "I wouldn't be surprised if God does something quickly. I just don't sense I'm going to drive away tomorrow and leave this all hanging. But whatever happens, God's going to teach us something through this. He always does."

Myriad reactions tickertaped through my head. An aching desire for unshakeable faith like Chelsea's. A question of what God wanted to teach me now—hadn't I learned *enough* this year? And a blazing wish for the ability to read my sister's thoughts.

Jenna sat in stillness, then smacked a palm against the table. "Well, time for breakfast." With that she rose and went to the refrigerator. Chelsea and I exchanged a half-amused glance. My sister had reached her limit with all our God talk. Better give her some space.

Refrigerator drawers rolled open and shut. Soon Jenna had the makings of bacon-and-cheese omelets spread across the counter. Chelsea and I got up to help.

We gave ourselves over to the familiar tasks, willing our busyness to lighten the atmosphere. As we cooked, we talked of other things—from Chelsea's teenage sons, to the Scott Peterson trial in Redwood City, to Milt Waking, the ever-in-your-face former Bay Area reporter who'd covered the Trent Park murder and, more audaciously, the trial of "Salad King" Darren Welk. Although I'd never liked Milt Waking, I'd had to work with him. His news channel had consistently chosen my drawings over other artists'.

"Oh, do I remember him." Jenna whipped a fork through egg-and-milk mixture. "He's *gorgeous*."

Yeah, and as conceited as the day was long.

"Really?" Chelsea said dryly. "I never noticed. I was too busy trying to outrun him. He made me furious."

"He's reporting for FOX now; I guess you know that." Jenna rounded her mouth in an O and fanned it with one hand. "That guy is *hot*."

Chelsea and I exchanged a look. I twisted my lips—*Hey, she's my sister; what am I supposed to do?*

The omelets were ready. Now we'd have to eat, while the newspaper sat like an elephant upon the table. With a firm hand I pushed it off, feeling a tinge of vengeance as it rustled to the floor.

Our discussion turned to the day's plans. Stephen, still in bed, would go to work at one. Kelly remained at the Willits' and would be going to church with Dave and Erin. "Maybe Dave can take the girls to a movie this afternoon," I put in. I paused, imagining the day stretching before me, with nothing to do but worry about Neese and the newspaper article. Suddenly the prospect of a facial reconstruction didn't sound so terrible. At least it would keep me occupied for a day or two. And I'd finally be able to use the techniques I'd studied in the classroom. "As for me, I need to do some preparations in case I receive that assignment today."

"Like what?" Chelsea asked.

"Lay out all the materials, like the vinyl erasers I'll need to cut for measuring tissue depth." I spread my hands. "It's a complicated procedure, building a face from a mere skull. Once I learn factors like the race and sex of the person, I have to reconstruct the body tissue using a special mathematical formula—"

"This is a great subject for breakfast." Jenna frowned at me.

"Sorry." She was right. To the average person it was gruesome to think of holding someone's skull—someone who once walked the earth, alive and well, with muscles and skin forming unique features. Before I entered the field of forensic art, I'd never dreamed of doing such a thing. It was far easier working as a courtroom artist, drawing the living.

"Hey." Jenna turned to Chelsea, face brightening. "Wanna go flying?" She blinked. "Oh, what am I thinking. We shouldn't leave you alone, Annie."

I considered that. "I may be working half the day. Besides, I can't expect you two to just sit around here all day because of me. I have police protection, remember?"

"I guess so." My sister inhaled slowly, thinking. "Chelsea, we could go down to the Bay Area. It's less than an hour. If your husband could come to the San Carlos airport with some of your clothes—at least you'd sleep in your own pajamas tonight. Or I could even leave you there and fly back down to pick you up tomorrow when your car's done." She shook her head. "I should have thought of that last night."

Chelsea smiled. "It was pretty late for that. Besides, we all were a little preoccupied. Anyway, I'd love to go flying, just for the ride."

Soon their plans were set. As we cleared the table, Jenna told Chelsea all about her plane, and how they could make a slight detour and fly past the Golden Gate Bridge. "It's an awesome sight, just awesome."

I chimed in my agreement, my eyes drifting to the newspaper sections spilled upon the kitchen floor. Part of the headline glared up at me, taunting.

... Missing Woman Trapped with Spiders

Chapter 27

*O*h *man.*

He paced the kitchen, hands shoving in and out of his pockets. The newspaper's front page screamed at him from the table. A bare glance at one article was all he'd needed.

He couldn't believe it—that woman had shown up. She knew things. God *told* her. Now she was here.

"Don't you know the Lord above sees everything you do?" his grandmother used to say.

He huffed across the floor to the refrigerator. Strode back again. Maybe if he kept pacing, one time he'd hit the table and the paper would be gone. *Poof.* Or at least the front page would be different. All the regular daily boring stuff. The mayor this and that. School district nonsense.

"Uh-uh-uh." He grunted with each step, making noise to fill his ears, his head. Anything to keep the voices away. If they came, the dirt ants would follow ...

Chelsea Adams knew about the spiders. And that little room in his basement. She *saw* it. The shelves, even the red bulb.

How long until God told her everything about him?

That's what happened with her in that Bay Area case. One vision, then another—until she knew it all. That guy would have gotten away with it if it hadn't been for her.

He slid to a halt. How could this be happening? Whole thing was just nuts. Chelsea Adams "sees" his spiders. Goes to Annie Kingston. Somebody finds a skeleton in Grove Landing. All in *one day*? He punched a fist into his palm. What kind of wild coincidence was *that*?

Wait.

Maybe they were playing with him.

That was it. The ghosts were playing. Dirt ants from the grave had been after him for years. Now some skeleton hand out there had rattled to the surface and waved. *Here I am; come find me!*

Oh no. Little ant feet suddenly scurried on his shoes. Up his ankles. Crawling fast. He cursed and kicked off his Nikes, peeled off his socks. Stumbled to the sink and stuck a foot under the water. He scrubbed with a sponge, heart thudding. Changed feet and scrubbed again.

The dirt ants swirled down the drain. He snapped on the garbage disposal, chewed up every last one of them before they crawled out and hunted him down.

Okay. Okay.

He slumped against a counter, breathing hard, feet dripping water on the floor. *Okay. Think.*

Abruptly he pulled a glass from a cabinet, filled it with water and chugged it down. *Okay.*

Now.

He glared across the room at the newspaper. Trudged to stand over the articles. *Think. Take one problem at a time.*

Annie Kingston's death threat was a dumb move. Except that now she'd be all tripped out and scared ...

Could he use that?

The skeleton. Bad, bad news. But incomplete.

Chelsea Adams's vision. Scary as all get-out. But man, it was also *crazy*.

He started pacing again. Maybe they were straight on everything. Maybe all this vision stuff was a hoax. They were just trying to trap him. He thought of recent phone calls, places he'd been. Had they tracked him down?

Man, you're safe. Stop flippin'.

Still ... Look what Chelsea Adams knew already. Any day now she would see it all. It was only a matter of time.

He muttered and paced. Guzzled more water. Gathered all the information in his head and spun it around. He had to do something. Soon.

What he needed was a good diversion.

Chapter 28

Twelve noon. Jenna and Chelsea had left. Kelly had called from Erin's house after returning from the early service at church. She was upset by the articles in the paper, especially the one about people possibly trapped in a room full of spiders. I tried to soothe her, wishing she didn't have to know at all. But better for her to hear it now than tomorrow at school. Now only Stephen remained at home, knocking about the kitchen for something to eat and talking on his cell phone. Earlier I'd gone outside to thank the surveillance officer who'd come on duty at six a.m. Ben Schalt was his name—a boyish-faced policeman who'd been on the force for two years.

Two years. That wasn't very long. Suddenly I was sorry I'd sent the others on their way.

I headed to my office, intent on keeping busy. But within all too short a time, the materials for a facial reconstruction were laid out upon the table, ready to go.

Now what? I folded my arms, glanced around the room. Walked over to sit in my desk chair.

I needed to pray.

During the final horrific days of seeking the Poison Killer, God had taught me to pray as I'd never done before. There were times when oppression so overwhelmed me that all I could do was open my mouth and let the words flow. Later I learned that God had led others to pray in the same way. Evil had descended upon Redding, and God wanted His people to take part in bringing it to its knees. I'd not experienced prayer of that kind since then. But until now circumstances hadn't warranted it. Sitting here in my chair, I wished again for that overwhelming sense of God's power to fill my mouth with words ...

I closed my eyes and waited.

Nothing.

Irritation niggled in my gut. *God, what is going on?* Sometimes He seemed to purposely make circumstances hard. Why couldn't He guide my words the way He did before? And why, when He sent Chelsea that vision, couldn't He have *explained* it? Instead we were left with threatening pieces that may or may not even fit the same puzzle.

I sighed, fingertips tapping my desk.

Okay, Lord. All I can do is pray in my own way, as best I can. Please help me do that.

Bowing my head, I asked God for His protection over me, my family, and Chelsea, and for guidance. For help in finding Orwin Neese before the man killed anyone else. *And God, if Amy and that man are still alive—please be with them. Please help us find them in time. Also, the skeleton that was discovered. Help us find this person's identity. Guide me in the work I may have to do today ...*

Twenty minutes later I raised my head. I felt no particular strengthening. But one truth I could cling to: God's power *is* released through prayer, whether I feel anything or not.

# # # #

One o'clock rolled around. Stephen drove off to work, leaving me alone. I checked that all doors were locked, the alarm on. Outside in his vehicle, the policeman faithfully watched.

I could do little but putter in the house, dusting some furniture, cleaning bathrooms, while I awaited the phone call from the morgue. A dozen times I checked the clock. Minutes ground by, my feeble attempts to separate Chelsea's vision from Neese turning to dust beneath their wheels. If Amy and the young man were trapped in that nightmarish spider room, unable to sleep, unable to so much as put a hand on the floor for fear of being bitten, every second counted. And if the morning's paper had infuriated Neese enough to end their tortured lives now ...

Oh, God, please help Blanche and his men find Neese! I don't care if Blanche gets all the credit and struts his stuff; just keep these people safe!

And keep me safe too.

On the other hand, as long as Neese was spending time and energy tracking *me* down, those two people might continue to live.

My hand stalled midair, holding the dusting cloth. I squinted out the front window, making sure the surveillance officer was in place.

Ring, you stupid phone! At least working on the skull would take my mind off Orwin Neese.

Finally, around one forty-five, the call came.

"Harry Fleck here, Annie." The medical examiner's voice carried its typical slow cadence. "Ready to come see what we've got?"

"You need me, then?" He sounded so matter-of-fact, it almost irritated me. *Knock it off, Annie. He couldn't have known you've been on pins and needles.* "No missing persons record or anything else to help?"

"Afraid not. How soon can you make it?"

"I'll leave right away."

"Okay. We'll be waiting for you."

I grabbed my purse and a notebook and hurried out the door. Ben Schalt lifted a hand in greeting as I approached his car.

I leaned down to speak through his open window. "The morgue called. I need to go in and pick up some work. You think it's better if you just take me, rather than us both driving?"

"Yeah, fine." He grinned, clearly glad for something to do. "I've got a shift change at two anyway. Hop in."

As I slid inside, I spied the morning newspaper tossed in the backseat. Schalt's eyelids flickered as they followed my gaze, but he said nothing. Fresh anger at Blanche pricked my nerves. "Thank you for taking me." I buckled my seat belt.

On the ride into town I entertained myself with my own visions—of telling Tim Blanche just what I thought of him.

At the morgue I greeted Larry Delching and Harry Fleck—the Harry and Larry team, as they're called. But any similarity between them went no further than their names. Larry, with his small frame and quick gestures, resembled a lightweight boxer next to Harry's heavyweight body and almost laborious movements. Larry's hair was brown, his nose sharp and lips thin. Harry was fifteen years older, white-haired and thick-jowled.

They led me to the skeleton, laid out on a slab and missing surprisingly few bones. "Meet John Doe." Larry's statement weighted with the substance of his words. I opened my notebook and began to write. "No doubt a male, by the shape and size of the pelvis. About six feet tall. Average build. And young. I'd place him between seventeen and twenty-three." He pointed to the arm bones. "He was in good shape. Bones are strong. These here are built up somewhat, indicating that he may have either lifted weights or worked in a job that required upper body strength." He stepped toward the feet. "At some point he had a broken ankle, but at time of death it had long healed. See the faint line here?"

I leaned over to look. "Yes."

Larry waved a hand over the table. "We were able to recover most of the bones, as you can see. A few missing parts, which may contribute to John Doe's story; you never know. But we did the best we could. I think the discovery was remarkably clean, considering that the area had been churned by a backhoe. Also, wood rats tend to carry away bones. Before darkness fell, we were able to move a little farther afield and look for wood rat nests. We managed to find one that held two bones. This one." He pointed to the right third finger. "And this one in the foot."

I shook my head. Wood rats. That was a new one to me.

Larry walked back toward the head and picked up the skull, cradling it with both hands. I moved to stand beside him. "He's Caucasian. See the shape of the eye sockets? Also, we can tell by the nasal aperture and jaw."

I nodded, tilting my head one way, then another as I observed the various areas. "Okay."

Larry tipped the skull. "Dentition is in fairly good shape. A few teeth are missing. Those sockets are clean and open, see? Not filled in with any bone. So I believe these losses are postmortem." He paused while I examined the teeth, then scribbled notes. "Overall the dentition points to someone of lower socioeconomic status. Quite a few of the molars have filled cavities, but there are a couple of teeth with cavities that are not filled. Must have hurt." He flattened his mouth. "Also notice the crookedness. This person never had braces. The teeth don't protrude, however, so I don't see the crookedness affecting the profile to a big degree."

I jotted more notes, then took another minute to peruse the dentition. Larry's comments about socioeconomic level, broken bones, and body strength may not have direct bearing on facial appearance, but any understanding I could gain about John Doe would help give me a feel for him. "Okay. Thanks."

Larry looked to the medical examiner. "Your turn."

"Yes." Harry took the skull in his hands, tilting it forward. "Take a look at our repairs of the cranium. I think you know that this was damaged?"

I nodded.

"You'll see how the pieces fit together, but with some wiggle room. See what I mean?" He paused while I looked over the area. "This indicates that cause of death was blunt force to the head. I've ruled the manner of death as homicide."

Blunt force. Homicide. The words stabbed through me, but I merely nodded. This poor young man, with years ahead of him, had been violently killed. Why? And who was he? Who missed him? Somewhere a mother, father, siblings, friends needed closure.

"This skull was out there a number of years." Harry carefully laid it back down. "It's somewhat fragile. Don't know how well it'll handle a lot of clay."

I shook my head. "That's fine. I'm going to do a two-dimensional reconstruction anyway—the one Karen Taylor developed. You familiar with it?"

Taylor, a nationally recognized forensic artist, had combined aspects from various experts' forms of reconstruction. In her two-dimensional, or drawing, approach, she uses tissue depth indicators to help flesh out the face, then draws the features rather than sculpting them directly onto the skull.

Harry nodded slowly. "That's fine. Good. We'll hear back all the more quickly from you then."

I closed my notebook. "Okay, let's get John Doe's head ready to move. And soon." My gaze lingered on the skull, battered and crying out its story. "I hope we can give this young man back his name."

Larry meticulously packed the skull for transporting, while Harry and I completed the paperwork for its release. "I'll begin working right away," I told them. "I don't have anything else going at the moment." *Except that somebody wants to kill me.*

Harry surveyed me, as if reading my thoughts. "Are you all right? I saw the paper this morning. Didn't know you'd been threatened."

Dear Harry Fleck. It just wasn't in him to mention the other article.

I gave him a wan smile. "I'm fine. I have police protection. In fact, the officer brought me here and another one's taking me home."

"Good." Harry nodded his sage head. "You take care of yourself now, Annie. We sure don't want anything to happen to you."

"Thanks. I will."

On the way back home in the police car, I cradled the boxed skull on my lap, questions and imaginings of John Doe's identity spiraling through my mind.

And at every stoplight, I couldn't help but scan the sidewalks and streets for any sign of Orwin Neese.

Chapter 29

Okay, God, here we go. Please help me.

Upon my table, the skull sat in a stabilizing ring of cork. As I touched it, felt the contours of bone, my other worries faded to background. Here, now, I felt a connection to this unknown person. John Doe deserved his identity; he deserved justice for his untimely death. That responsibility sat heavily on my shoulders.

My first task was to glue the skull's mandible to the cranium so the jaw would not move as I worked on it. In a live person the jaw is relaxed, the teeth not clenched. To simulate that positioning, I first layered in a small "spacer" of clay between the condyle and fossa bones—the hinge of the jaw—to replicate the cartilage that had once been present. Next I glued a small cutting from a round toothpick to the surface of the molars, creating a spacing between the teeth. Then I turned the skull upside down on the cork ring and glued the mandible in place.

So far, so good. I was now ready to tackle the challenge of meticulously cutting the small cylindrical eraser strips into tissue depth indicators.

In my facial reconstruction classes, the tissue depth tables had fascinated me from the beginning. The data, developed in the 1980s by Dr. Stanley Rhine and his colleagues at the

University of New Mexico, simulate the thickness of muscle and other tissues, plus the skin, at twenty-one locations on the face. The mathematical tables vary according to race, gender, and build. Based upon the anthropologist's information on John Doe, I would follow the table for a Caucasian male of average weight.

Carefully measuring in millimeters, I used an exacto knife to cut the vinyl erasers to the required lengths. As I cut each length, I turned the piece on its end and used a ballpoint pen to label its number. Locations one through ten, indicating the center of the face from forehead to chin, required one marker each. Locations eleven through twenty-one, marking the sides of the face, required two apiece. With each cutting, I measured and remeasured, holding my breath as I pushed the exacto knife straight down through the eraser material. Mistakes at this crucial point would skew the final results.

Markers cut, I was ready to glue them onto the skull. From there I would position the skull *exactly* in what's called the Frankfort Horizontal Plane for photographing from the front and side views. Facial reconstruction is tricky at every step, including the photography. If the skull was positioned wrong, if I aimed the camera incorrectly, I would distort the picture, making the skull look narrower or wider than in reality. The photos had to be precise, because from them I would begin to draw the face.

I took a moment to lean back and flex my shoulders and neck. Pulling in a deep breath, I studied the two boards I'd set up earlier that day—one for the frontal drawing and one for the lateral, or side. Each was covered with a large sheet of Bristol paper. On top of this paper I would tape the photo of the skull, then cover it with a sheet of vellum for tracing. At that point I would begin to connect the dots, contouring around the tissue depth markers for the general shape of the face.

Vaguely I registered a fifteen-minute chime from the grandfather clock in the great room. It was telling me I needed to get on with my work.

The tissue marker placement chart lay at the end of the table. I reached for it, studying the twenty-one locations. My challenge went further than simply following the chart. The unique features of every skull demand that the procedure be tailored accordingly. Markers five and six, between the nose and upper lip, for example, should be angled a little differently depending upon gender and race. Placement of markers nineteen, twenty, and twenty-one, around the sides of the mouth, varies according to position of the teeth.

Sudden self-doubt flailed in my chest. Who did I think I was, attempting such a project at this stage in my career? What if I couldn't get this part right?

I *had* to get this part right.

I closed my eyes, steadied my breathing. *God, I really need Your help.*

I reached for marker number one and my tube of cement glue. As I started to unscrew the tube's cap, the phone rang. I jumped, dropping the marker. It rolled toward the edge of the table. With a sigh I crossed to my desk. Caller ID read a familiar number: Tim Blanche's direct line at the station.

Oh, terrific. I steeled myself and picked up the receiver. "Annie, hello."

With two words his voice said it all. An awareness that I would be upset with him, balanced by his typical righteous self-defense. I pictured him seated at his desk, impatiently tapping a pen upon strewn papers, that Elvis smirk on his lips.

"Hi, Tim." I couldn't help my guarded tone.

"Look, uh, I needed to call you for a couple of reasons. First to say I'm sorry for that story in today's paper. I have no idea who told all that to the reporter."

Really. And who blathered to the informant in the first place?

"It wasn't even accurate." My fingers tightened on the phone. "We never claimed to know for certain that the vision has to do with Orwin Neese. We only came to you *in case* it did."

"Yeah, I know. The media get things wrong all the time."

So now it was the newspaper's fault. Anger heated my words. "Speaking of the paper, are you going to run that composite I gave you?"

A pause. I could hear the excuse wheels turning in his head.

"Because you still could, you know, even though you don't want to. Let it leak to the media just like the rest of the information. Then you don't have to take the heat for falling for our ridiculous story."

"Look, Annie—"

"The fact is, Tim, Chelsea and I came to you because we thought you could be trusted. I know some supernatural vision isn't the kind of lead you were looking for, but what do you have to lose? If Neese *is* holding those two people, now he's been tipped off. They could end up paying with their lives."

Blanche snorted. "I didn't call to hear you tell me how to handle this case. You're the artist, remember? I'm the detective. I *said* I'm sorry the newspaper thing happened. I think you should accept that."

Only Tim Blanche could apologize for something without accepting one iota of the blame. I would get nowhere with the man. *Face it, Annie, he's not going to give that drawing to the media.*

My gaze slid to the large file drawers across the office and hung there. But I *did* have my own copy.

I licked my lips, pushed down my emotions. I had to admit he was right. I had no business telling him how to do his job. "Fine. Apology accepted." Not that he would believe that from my tone. "So what else did you call about?"

A heavy pause. I envisioned his slitted eyes, the *tap-tap* of his fingers. "This is a courtesy call, really. And not one I had to make, I might add."

Translation: I'd ticked him off royally. Better hold my tongue.

"I wanted to check up on you, see if you're all right."

"I'm okay." My voice softened a little. "I'm very grateful for the officer outside my door."

"Yeah, good. I've also got an update for you. We managed to pry some information from one of Neese's buddies. The guy was with Neese yesterday when he left that note on your car."

I blinked. "What happened? Why was Neese there in the first place?"

"You're not going to believe this. It was a 'random thing,' to quote this guy. Said Neese is crazy and you never know what he's going to do. The guy admitted he was helping

Neese skip town, with Neese ducked down in the front seat. Then they went by the station, at which point Neese sat up straight just to show how macho he is. At that moment you and Chelsea were getting out of your cars. He saw you and decided to leave the note. Chelsea's slashed tires were an added bonus."

I closed my eyes, trying to assimilate the information. A threat on my life—a random thing? What kind of man *was* this? "Are you trying to tell me he's not really out to kill me?"

"Well, I can't say that. He left the note; we can't just ignore it. The man's already killed at least one person, and in broad daylight."

I shook my head. "I don't understand this. Why would he *want* to kill me? It's not like he wants to stop me from doing something. My work on the case is done, so where's the logic?"

"*Logic?* With a guy like that? Where was the logic in threatening to kill his girlfriend because she looked at another man? In running a victim down in front of a store full of witnesses? Or walking onto the police station parking lot when he's a wanted man? This guy doesn't think; he just reacts. He's a lowlife."

I had no argument for that. Threatening me, terrifying me and my children—a haphazard act.

"Did this friend know where Neese was headed?" I asked.

"No. But Neese left the impression he had some place in the area to hole up in for a couple days while he takes care of some 'financial business.'" Blanche sniffed. "We'll lean on this guy some more, see if he remembers anything else.

Anyway, I wanted you to know Neese may still be in the general area. And that he's unpredictable and deadly."

I turned, glanced out the window. The new surveillance officer sat in his car looking bored, one palm hitting the steering wheel. I hoped this one had more than two years' experience on the force. "Don't worry, I'm well aware."

"Okay." Blanche's voice turned brisk. I heard the squeak of his chair. "Gotta go. Just know that I'm on this. I'll find him."

I hung up the phone, frowning. Blanche sure had an unsettling way of settling things.

Forget him, Annie. Just ... move on.

I forced myself to turn toward the work that awaited. But those file drawers on the other side of the office beckoned me. I stepped out from behind my desk, crossed the room. Opened the top drawer and slid out the drawing of the man Chelsea had seen. I stared at it. What if I gave this to the press? After all, it was *my* drawing ...

Yeah, but it's his case.

I checked the clock on my wall. Almost four thirty. If I did give it to the newspaper, I'd have to do it soon for it to run in tomorrow's edition. Once the act was committed, there would be no taking it back. And Blanche would know I'd done it.

The man would probably never speak to me again.

As if I cared.

I stared at the drawing, indecision playing tug-of-war in my head.

Chapter 30

He ran a finger down the terrarium glass. This one held more than one spider.

"Here, little ones. Come out, come out for Daddy."

Button spiders were so shy.

Inside the terrarium lay piles of twigs. And in those twigs, webs. He tapped the glass.

He bent down, cocked his head. Yup. There was one — underneath the bundle in the corner. The brown button that was more of a cream color. On its underside he could see half of the orange hourglass marking. He craned his neck. There was another one — a black button. His lip curled as he watched the spider navigate its web. Above its spinnerets ran the characteristic red stripes.

"I like you even more." He picked up a long, whittled stick and carefully poked its end down toward the creature. Black buttons could cause some real damage. "Think I'll take you to my little room downstairs."

Of course the spider scurried away. They didn't like to be messed with. Sometimes these guys would even drop to the ground and play dead. But if they got trapped or squeezed — watch out.

He pursued it with his stick. Finally the spider crawled upon it. "Hah. Got ya." He pulled up the stick and poked the end of it into a jar. With a fingernail he pushed the spider off, then slipped the lid onto the container without screwing it down.

"Hang in there. I'll have you in your new digs in no time. Just have to get a few of your pals."

He moved to the next terrarium, home to a half dozen delicate violin spiders. They had long, long legs and a violin shape on their heads. "How pretty you are," he crooned.

Down into the terrarium went the stick.

How had the newspaper put that part about the spider room victims? *Amy Flyte and the possible missing man.* He chortled. They thought they knew so much. Possible missing man—dig *that* for a name.

If only those reporters knew a little more. Like where he planned to take his creepy crawly little friends.

Chapter 31

I needed a drink of water. Good excuse to escape the office while I mulled over my decision. Laying the composite down, I headed for the kitchen. As I crossed the great room, my peripheral vision snagged on a car driving up. Jenna and Chelsea.

Thank You, God. They would help me think this through.

I busied myself with pulling a glass from a cabinet, filling it with ice water as I heard the garage door go up. For no reason at all my heart began to beat hard, as if I were a hapless child with a dire request about to face parents. I *wanted* to call Luke Bremington as an "unnamed source" and offer him a copy of the drawing. But I knew I shouldn't.

The door leading from the garage/hangar opened. Chelsea appeared, carrying a green overnight bag. "Hey!" Her face lit up and she raised the suitcase. "I got my stuff."

"Great." I put down the glass and folded my arms. Chelsea toted her suitcase to the edge of the kitchen and set it down. Jenna followed, lugging her heavy pilot bag.

"Annie, hi. Everything okay here?" My sister looked around as if expecting a stalker to jump from the shadows.

"Yeah. It's been quiet."

"Oh, good." She thudded the bag onto the kitchen table. "You should have come with us. It was a gorgeous day for flying."

"Glad you had such a good time. Chelsea, did your husband meet you at San Carlos with your things?"

"Yes." She laughed. "Don't ever try having your husband pack for you. I had to go over every item of makeup on the phone with him this morning, not to mention every piece of clothing."

I smiled. "Are you hungry?"

"No. We ate in the Bay Area with Paul and my sons."

"Speaking of which, you ought to *see* her sons." Jenna bugged her eyes. "Michael's what, sixteen?" She looked to Chelsea, who nodded. "And Scott's fourteen. Great-looking kids. Our girls would go nuts."

No doubt.

Chelsea surveyed me. "How are *you*, Annie? How's your work?"

"Work's fine. I got the skull and I'm progressing along. It's a male and young. He was killed by a blow to the head." They processed the information, expressions sobering. "I need to get back at it soon. But first I need some advice."

We sat around the kitchen table. I told them about my conversation with Tim Blanche and my desire to give the composite to the media. Chelsea listened quietly, concern in her eyes. Meanwhile my animated sister huffed her disdain at Orwin Neese's "random act"—and at Tim Blanche.

"So what are you waiting for?" Jenna spread her hands. "Call the reporter."

"You know it's not that simple. I'd be overstepping my bounds as a forensic artist. Decisions on how to track down suspects and victims aren't mine to make."

"But this drawing is *yours*. You didn't do it as some police assignment. Besides, you're involved personally in the Neese case. You're a witness to the murder, and now the guy's threatened to kill you."

"I know, but—"

"Oh, when I think about it, Blanche just makes me *furious*!" Jenna slapped the table. "He's so worried about his own reputation. Okay, so your vision stuff is a little strange—" she shrugged at Chelsea—"and we don't even know if it's relevant to the case, but still, it's *something*."

I nodded slowly.

Chelsea cleared her throat. "How much time is left to get the drawing in tomorrow's paper?"

"Not much. The paper's already laid out by now. They'd have to pull something and stick this in before going to press. But time is even more important for Amy and that man, if they're in that room. Every minute could count."

"Yes, I just ... I wish God would tell me more." Chelsea rubbed her forehead.

"I say do it," Jenna declared. "So you 'overstep your bounds' and Blanche gets mad at you. Big deal. Or let *me* leak the drawing. Then you can say you had nothing to do with it."

I nailed her with a look. Jenna knew I couldn't tell a half-truth. "Maybe we—"

The phone rang.

Jenna waved her hand at it. "Let it go."

I pushed from my chair. "Better not. It could be important." At the kitchen counter I checked the incoming ID. *Rod Blakely.* My head jerked up. "It's the policeman outside." I spun toward the window, nerves tingling. "He's not in his car."

"Well, answer it!" Jenna jumped from her chair and grabbed the cordless phone. "Hello?"

I angled my line of vision down the street. An unfamiliar vehicle was parked some distance from the house. Who was that behind the wheel? I swung around, eyes searching Jenna's face. Chelsea pushed back from the table, one hand on her heart.

"Yes, okay, thanks." Jenna fluttered a *be calm* gesture and cocked her head, listening. "He told you we'd want to talk to him?" She crossed to the window, pulling back a sheer curtain. "Okay, I see his car. But I don't recognize it. And I can't see his face."

Officer Blakely now stood on the sidewalk next to the car. He reached toward the window, pulled back a driver's license, and spoke into his phone.

"Okay." Jenna covered the mouthpiece and whispered, "He's seeing who—" Her head jerked and she slid her hand away. "Yes, I'm here. *Who?*" Her face slackened. Slowly she lowered the phone.

"You're not going to believe this. That reporter Milt Waking's out front. He wants to see you and Chelsea."

Chapter 32

For a moment none of us moved. A horrified look creased Chelsea's face. "Milt Waking? *Here?*" Like an automaton, she pulled to her feet, skirted the table, and edged toward the window. One of her hands floated up to circle the base of her neck. "I can't believe it. I just can't believe it. How did he *find* me?"

I nudged her away from the glass. "Get back so he won't see you. We don't have to let him in." My mind whirled. Milt Waking, at my door. I'd thought it bad enough dealing with local reporters. And *this* man—talk about arrogance. If Tim Blanche had taken the class, Milt Waking taught it.

Chelsea drew in her shoulders. "I know, but—how does he know I'm here?"

I closed my eyes, trying to remember the last time I'd seen Milt on FOX News. Had he been covering a West Coast story? Maybe somehow he'd seen our local paper this morning ... But even so, how did he get here so fast?

"Jenna," I hissed, "tell the officer to send him away—*now*."

"Wait a minute." Jenna's eyes danced across the kitchen as if seeking an alternative answer. She blinked a few times. Pulled the receiver to her ear. "Officer? We don't know if we want to see him or not. Tell him to cool his heels; we'll call you back."

She clicked off the line.

My mouth hung open. "Are you *crazy?*"

"No, huh-uh." Chelsea held up both hands. "I'm not seeing him; he's nothing but trouble."

"I know, I know." Jenna took her time laying the phone on the table, then faced us, one hand on her hip. *Uh-oh.* I could see the wheels turning in her head. "Hear me out, okay? I think we should let him in, because we need to find out why he's here. That much can't hurt."

"Oh, yes it can." Chelsea's voice bent upward. "That guy can make a story out of anything. You let him near you and the next thing you know—"

"I don't want him here, either." I shot my sister a withering look. "The very fact that he's hunted Chelsea down—that should tell you something."

"O-*kay.*" Jenna gave an exaggerated shrug. "So we hear his story, and if we don't like it, we throw him out. We've got a policeman right outside the door to help us."

Chelsea paced the kitchen, indignation rolling off her shoulders. "He absolutely *hounded* me during the Trent Park murder case. If it weren't for him—"

"If it weren't for him, how would the Salad King trial have gone?" Jenna reminded her.

That brought Chelsea to a halt. I opened my mouth, then closed it. My sister's logic began to seep into my head. Milt Waking was a consummate pain, but he also made things happen.

Chelsea sighed. "Okay, so he has his ... strengths. But if we talk to him, prepare for every word to end up on national news."

"If he wants a story, he's going to get it whether we talk to him or not." Jenna eyed us both, exasperated. "Look, weren't we were just talking about leaking that composite to the press? Now a FOX News correspondent shows up at our door. You gonna tell me that's just coincidence? I'd have guessed you two would see this as an answer to prayer."

Chelsea cast her a beleaguered look. "Oh, please. It wouldn't be the first time God used Milt Waking. But I sure hoped I'd never see that happen again."

Jenna half chuckled. Chelsea made a face, then heaved a martyr's sigh. "Well, it's your house. But can we at least establish some ground rules? Believe me—that give-an-inch-take-a-mile phrase? Milt Waking invented it."

Before we could change our minds, Jenna returned the officer's call. "Could you hand your phone to Mr. Waking for a moment?" She paused. "Hi, this is Jenna Gerralon, Annie Kingston's sister." She pounded out the words like a no-nonsense judge. "We're going to let you in. But if you don't behave yourself, I'm throwing you right back out. Got it?"

She punched off the line and tossed her head. "Here goes. You two better crank up your prayer machines."

Chapter 33

Milt Waking might as well have entered a lions' den. Jenna opened the door, shoulders arched, claws ready if the man made one false move. I hung behind her, glaring and wary. Chelsea lurked off to the side, arms crossed. Milt made eye contact with each of us, surprise flitting across his face, then quickly fading. "Ladies." He dipped his head, and that charm-ridden Waking smile spread across his movie-star features. His thick dark hair was perfectly combed, as if he stood before the camera. "Thank you for seeing me." His gaze wandered back to Jenna and hung there, approval in his brown eyes. She stared up at him, features stern. But her shoulders sank the tiniest bit. Milt's eyes warmed and he smiled wider.

Uh-oh. I saw that spark.

My sister lifted her chin. "I'm Jenna. I suppose you've deduced that."

He inclined his head like a prince to a princess. "Pleasure to meet you."

They gazed at each other.

Jenna swept her arm toward me. "You know my sister, Annie Kingston."

"Yes, of course, nice to see you again. And Ms. Adams. It's been a while."

Chelsea muttered a stiff greeting.

"Have a seat, Mr. Waking." Jenna lifted a hand toward the furniture around the fireplace. "You need something to drink?"

"No, thank you. And call me Milt."

He trod across the hardwood floor, hands clasped, feigned humility blanketing his shoulders. He stood about six one, wearing casual khaki pants and a designer knit shirt. Traveling clothes. I'd never seen him in anything but the suit and tie of his profession. He seated himself on the end of a couch, knees apart. Even in his purposeful casualness a certain power emanated from him. This was a man who knew his own charisma and how to use it. The effect may have held little sway over Chelsea and me, but I could already see the churnings within my sister.

Why had I let this man in my house?

Milt's gaze traveled around the room. "You've got a great-looking place here."

"Thank you." I sat in the armchair between the two couches, Milt on my left. Chelsea chose to sit to my right, as far away from Milt as she could get. Jenna slipped onto the other end of the couch Milt had taken, angling her body slightly toward him.

I took a deep breath. "All right, we have no time for games. Why are you here and what do you want? And we expect the truth."

"Fine, I'm going to lay all my cards on the table." He raised his eyebrows, sincerity his middle name.

Chelsea gave him a look: *That'll be the day.*

"First, let me tell you what's happened to me since the Salad King case." He cleared his throat. "As you can imagine,

I found myself in high demand. First I moved up to anchorman for our San Francisco station, then went to FOX News. I took that job with one quid pro quo, which I'll tell you in a minute." He flashed a little smile at Jenna. "Two years ago, Annie, you made national headlines. Then a second and third time. But I was always on the other side of the country." Milt turned his hands palm up. "So I told my boss the next time you came up in the news, I *had* to be here."

I pressed back in my chair, trying to keep my face impassive. He couldn't possibly understand what his words did to me. Every time I'd ended up in danger, I promised myself it would never happen again. Now to hear from a reporter this was simply a given? Indignation spiraled through me. I was a *person*. A sister and a mother. Not some sensational news story waiting to happen.

Milt laced his fingers. "So I started watching this area. Making some contacts."

Contacts. In other words, sources who'd leak him information.

"I've been covering a story in San Diego. I saw the local article about you witnessing a crime. I checked with my producer, saying I may need to come up here. Then I read this morning's Redding paper. All the stuff about you two." He looked to Chelsea. "Your vision, your photo with Annie. I took the next plane." He spread his hands.

"And the quid pro quo?" Distrust laced Jenna's tone.

Milt looked at Chelsea. "Ms. Adams, you shouldn't find it hard to believe I've been watching for news of you too. My condition for leaving the Bay Area was—" a sheepish expression crossed his face—"if you ever made headlines again, I'd be able to drop everything to pursue the story.

So when I saw *both* of you, together, I knew something was really up."

No doubt. He must have thought he'd died and gone to heaven.

Chelsea eagled-eyed Milt but said nothing. Jenna crossed her arms. "So what do you want from us? You've got your contacts—go talk to them."

"True, but ..." Milt turned to me. "I want to know what *you* need."

Chelsea stared at him in disbelief. "We don't need anything from *you*."

"Yes, you do." Milt looked her in the eye. "I know you don't like me, Ms. Adams. But you let me in here. You wouldn't have done that unless you thought I might help you in some way."

Chelsea dropped her gaze. Jenna's expression showed grudging admiration that Milt had seen through her before he even walked in the door. I sought a zinger, some comment caustic enough to shoot down this man's grandiose notions. But my tongue lay dead.

Milt sought each of our faces. "Have you talked to anybody in the Police Department today after these stories hit? Do you know what's going on?"

Here it came—reining us in with knowledge we were desperate to have. I gave him a slow blink. "I suppose you do."

He scratched his cheek. "Well, I know a few things. Like the findings of the department's handwriting expert? He compared that threatening note to some of Orwin Neese's handwriting. The results are inconclusive. Not surprising, I suppose, with that purposeful block lettering. Still, the police have no reason to think it *wasn't* written by Neese."

An analysis of the note already? Blanche hadn't even bothered to tell me. Not that it mattered; we knew Neese left the note. But how had Milt found this out so soon?

Sudden reality sledgehammered my chest. No matter what we did, Milt Waking was going to get his story. He'd plaster my face and Chelsea's on national news — and there wasn't one thing we could do to stop it.

Oh, God, help.

Milt sighed. "I have to be honest with you. The police aren't going to talk to you much anymore. They've clamped down, particularly after your phone conversation with Blanche this afternoon."

Violation heated my cheeks. "Who told you about that?"

He shrugged. "From what I hear, Tim Blanche is a real controlling guy. He doesn't want people thinking he'll fall for this 'vision from God' stuff." Milt leaned forward. "Which means he's not going to give that drawing to the paper."

"Mr. Waking—" Chelsea sounded cool—"I don't see how you expect to impress us with all this inside knowledge. You're only succeeding in violating our privacy."

He shook his head. "Ms. Adams, I know you believe in that vision of yours. But surprise, surprise, the police aren't listening. So here I am—coming to your rescue." He turned to me. "I know you've got a copy of that drawing. Forget Blanche; give the drawing to me. I'll put it on national TV, where everyone will see it."

My mouth dropped open. What had this man done, bugged our kitchen? "Why in the world would I join forces with *you*?"

Milt spread his hands. "Let's drop the pretenses, shall we? You obviously believe in Ms. Adams's vision. I've seen her in action enough to believe it too. I don't understand it, but I believe it." He leaned toward Chelsea, voice intensifying. "You've been in this position before—when the police wouldn't listen. And what did you do? You took matters into your own hands because you had to. Now you need to again."

Chelsea stared. "Odd, but I hadn't come to that conclusion."

"Yet. But you were headed there."

"Uh, Mr. Know-it-all-reporter," Jenna cut in. "You seem to forget that wouldn't be Chelsea's call. The drawing belongs to Annie."

Milt offered her a hint of a smile, then turned to me.

"She's right." I shook my head. "And I'm afraid my hands are tied. There are ethics in my field, Mr. Waking." *Unlike yours*, my tone implied. "It's not appropriate for a forensic artist to—"

Chelsea's breath hitched. I glanced at her and stilled. Her face had gone slack, eyes glazing. "Chelsea?"

Her mouth opened but no sound came.

"What's wrong?" Jenna started to rise.

Milt laid a hand on her arm. "Wait, I know that look. She's having a vision."

Chapter 34

The dirt ants were back.

Somehow he had to ignore them. Too much work to do.

He stood in his basement, panting. The door to the little room was closed. All his creepy crawly friends were in there now, doing their thing.

Little ant feet pricked up his ankles. He swiped them away. *No, no, you're not here, you're not!*

Quit thinking about 'em. Focus on the future. The truth would die here, that's what mattered. He'd be safe again. He could go back to doing fun stuff. Get himself a steady woman. Start traveling again, maybe leave this town for good. They could end up anywhere—Africa, South America, Timbuktu. She'd have to be loyal. Take real good care of him ...

Tiny legs scurried on his bare feet, like cold needles. "Get *off!*" He doubled over, scrubbed at a foot with both hands. His heart did that funny grind thing, started to pound.

Okay, okay. I can handle this.

He sank down on the floor. Pulled both pant legs up to his knees. See? Nothing there.

Man, he had to beat this thing before he ended up in the loony bin. Fact was, those people deserved to die. They'd gotten in his way, so he took care of them. Big deal. He wasn't some mama's boy. Some haunted soul. He didn't even *have* a soul.

Hey—

His head jerked at a terrible thought.

What if Chelsea Adams could see him *right now*? What if she told everybody about the dirt ants and the long showers? His fingers curled into his palms. People would laugh at him. Think he was psycho.

Anger blazed in his stomach. He arched his back, giving himself room to breathe. *You wanna watch, Chelsea Adams? Fine. I'll show you what I can do.*

"So, uh ... Amy!" He threw the words toward the closed door. "Any poisonous ones get you yet?" He barked out a laugh. It felt so good, he laughed a second time. Silence answered him. "Not talking, I see. So how about you, man-without-a-name? Did you know that's what they're calling you? How many times have *you* been bitten?"

Snickers and guffaws rolled off his lips.

Way to go, man. He felt better already. This was the ticket. Every time those dirt ants came, he'd just show 'em who was boss.

Hey.

His neck straightened. And his spine. He pulled his hands into his lap. Sat still, closed his eyes ...

Feeling ...

Nothing on his feet.

The dirt ants were gone.

He examined his ankles to be sure. Nothing. Not one prickly feeling.

It *worked*.

"Hah!" He scrabbled to his feet, elated. He'd hit on something. He'd really found it!

The power lay in the role, man; it was all in the role. He just had to keep playing it.

Grinning, he slapped off the lights and headed for the stairs.

"Bye now!" he singsonged to the door of the little room. "Bye, Amy; bye, man-without-a-name. Bye-bye till you die-die!"

Hammering the stairwell with a victorious fist, he bounced up the steps toward civilization.

Chapter 35

Chelsea fell headlong into the vision ...

And landed with a sickening *crack*.

What?

Where?

Sensations flooded her. Evil. All around her. *Within* her.

No!

She ventured a terrified gaze—and saw the world through *his* eyes.

The oppression within him enclosed her, wrapped clammy hands around her neck. His mind writhed with paranoia, hatred, malevolence. He would deceive and plan and kill. Anything to protect himself.

Scenes of him formed, flipping from one to the next, like TV channels. He

hunches over a kitchen table, reading the newspaper. Seething, stunned. Forming his next move.

Flip. He

croons at spiders in a glass terrarium, fascinated by them and their ability to wound. Using a stick, he captures them into a jar. They will go down to his basement, into the little room.

Flip.

He is scrubbing at his feet, panic-stricken, mind screaming that he will overcome.

Flash, he's

yelling at Amy and the "man-with-no-name" through the closed door. "How many times have you been bitten?"

The scenes froze.

Disappeared.

A powerful force ripped Chelsea from the man's horrifying mind. She spun ... tumbled ... landed outside on the ground. There she stared at an oval window, then its surroundings ...

Her world undulated.

The vision faded.

Her next sensation was the feel of the couch beneath her legs.

Annie's house?

Chelsea couldn't move. The evil of the man's soul lingered, nibbling at her lungs. *Help me, God, please!*

She opened half-focused eyes.

Navy blue fabric. Her pants.

Hands in a lap. Her own.

Someone called her name. She lifted her head, feeling the return to her own body as if she'd fallen from an alien planet.

"*Chelsea.* Are you all right?"

Annie's voice. Chelsea blinked at her, dazed. Her tongue felt thick. "Yes. Yes, I'm ... here now."

Her gaze pulled to Milt Waking, who ogled her with a half-open mouth. Two words surged into Chelsea's mind, quiet words of thunderous authority.

Tell him.

Chapter 36

I stared at Chelsea, my breath caught. *"I'm here now"*? Where had she gone?

Jenna half rose. "Chelsea! Talk to us!" Milt craned his neck like some jack-in-the-box waiting to spring, bristling with anticipation. I could have punched him.

Chelsea lay a trembling hand across her cheek. Swallowed. "I . . . I saw him. I was *inside* his mind. He was yelling at Amy and the man through a door. *Taunting* them."

She shuddered, drew her arms across her chest. My mind spun. Taunting two captives? Then Orwin Neese *did* have them both. And they were still alive.

"What did you see, what did you see?" Milt could barely contain himself.

Chelsea shivered. "It was the same man. But this time I felt his thoughts. He's so terrified of being caught, and he'll kill to keep that from happening." She focused on me. "Then I saw scenes of him. Sort of like I was in his head and watching him on TV at the same time. He saw the paper this morning and didn't like what he read. People are going to pay." Her eyes grew distant. "I saw him standing before terrariums that held different kinds of spiders. He was taking spiders out of them, putting them into jars. He's going to release them in that little room."

The words hit me like rampant electricity. Jenna and I exchanged a horrified glance.

"Wait, wait—you mean the little room with the shelves?" Milt spoke rapidly, as if to pull everything he could from Chelsea before she clammed up. "Where he's keeping those two people?"

"Chelsea, don't answer." I seared him with a look. "You already got more than you bargained for, Milt. I think it's time you left."

"No." Chelsea's voice firmed. She straightened. "No, Milt, don't go. Annie, he needs to stay."

I gawked at her. *"Why?"*

"Because he's supposed to know. Don't you see the timing? It's God's planning, Annie. I have to tell him."

No, huh-uh. This "timing" was sheer bad luck. Coincidence. And I wanted Milt Waking out of my house. "I don't think—"

"I saw something new, something important." Chelsea raked in a breath. "Remember the oval window? I saw it from the *outside*. The top half is just above ground level, and there's a semicircular well cut out of the dirt at its lower half, with a little stone retaining wall. I was sitting near that well, looking down, so I could see the whole window. At the bottom of the well is cement, with a drain."

"The room must be in a basement," Jenna breathed. "Would you recognize that window if you saw it?"

"Absolutely."

"Unusual shape." Milt spoke half to himself. "Why would a basement window be oval?"

Chelsea shook her head, then looked meaningfully at me. I blinked at her, beginning to understand. The police should be told about the window. It was a solid lead.

And one Blanche would never listen to.

Sickness coiled through my stomach. Now what? Why had God placed us in such an untenable position? The police wouldn't want to hear our story, while here sat Milt Waking, a *reporter*, hanging on Chelsea's every word. If the situation weren't so frightening, I'd laugh.

Almost.

Milt rubbed his chin, as if already spinning the news story. "How many homes in this area have basements? I'd bet not that many."

"Maybe not a total basement, but it could be like ours." Jenna gestured toward the door leading downstairs. "That lower level is a basement in front, but a walk-out in back because the lot slopes. You see only two stories from the front of the house, but three from the back." She pushed to her feet and paced toward the fireplace, energy bristling from her. "The room Chelsea saw could be toward the middle of a basement, where the lot has leveled down some, but not completely."

"Was the ground around the window sloped?" Milt asked.

Chelsea closed her eyes. "I ... don't know. I didn't notice."

I ran a hand through my hair. Everything about this was so warped. But it fit with what Blanche had heard. Neese *was* hiding in some house. Blanche just didn't believe he was nurturing a nightmare in the basement.

The phone rang. I jumped.

"Better get that," Jenna said. "It could be Dave and the kids."

At the mere mention of them, terror seared my chest. Where were they? I wanted them home—*now*. None of us

would go anywhere. We would lock ourselves up until the atrocious killer was caught and the world righted itself on its axis.

I hurried to the kitchen phone. Dave's house number appeared on the ID. I jerked up the receiver. "Dave? Are you home? Is everything okay?"

"Yes." He sounded surprised at my intensity. "Is everything okay with *you*?"

"Yes. No. I mean, we're safe, but . . ."

"But what?"

I pulled out a kitchen chair and sank into it. How to explain it all—Blanche's phone call, Milt, Chelsea's vision? The fear gripping my soul, as if some ravenous monster stormed its way toward my family?

"Annie?"

The story spilled out of me. Dave listened with no interruption. "Now what do we do?" I said. "The police don't want to hear from us, and Chelsea's done this one-eighty, thinking God sent Milt here. But why should we trust him?" Tears bit my eyes and I stiffened my back. This was not the time to lose it.

"Hang on, I'm coming over right now."

"But the girls. They can't be left alone and I don't want them to know—"

"Stop it, Annie." Frustration weighted his words. "I am *going* to help you figure this out; don't you dare find excuses to pull away."

My mouth opened. I hadn't pulled away—for once. I was too petrified. "Dave, I do want you here. Please come."

"I'm on my way." His words were brusque. "I'll bring the girls so they won't be alone. We can send them up to

Kelly's room. They'll want explanations, but we'll handle that later."

"Okay." Relief trickled through my veins. "Thank you." I clicked off the line and headed back to the great room. Three questioning faces turned toward me.

"It was Dave." I halted at the back of the armchair. "He's coming over to help us talk this through. We'll send Kelly and Erin upstairs."

Curiosity creased Milt's features. "Dave?"

"Willit. My neighbor."

He surveyed me. Only then did I realize what I'd done. Milt would remember Dave's name from the news stories about Lisa's death. Now he would see us together. He was a reporter; he would *know*. I stared at him, feeling my face harden. Sending a signal — *Subject closed, and don't you go there, buddy.*

I veered to the front door and opened it. Dave and the girls were crossing the street. Our guarding policeman stood outside his vehicle, watching them. "Hi!" I hurled a brightness into the word that fooled no one. "How was the movie?" Kelly and Erin stepped inside, their faces leery. "Hey, girls." I hugged Kelly, smelling her flower-scented shampoo, put an arm around Erin's shoulder. I did not look at Dave. If I did, my facade might crumble.

Kelly pressed her lips. "Dave says we need to go upstairs." Underneath the statement raged a thousand fearful questions.

I smiled at her lopsidedly. "We're just discussing things. Figuring out the best way to help the police." *Boy, Annie, talk about a spin.*

Chelsea and Jenna called out greetings. Milt Waking rose, and I introduced him to the girls and Dave. Words and actions, all surface level, while underneath every expression flowed anxiety and fright. Well, except for Milt. I could practically hear the reporter calculating his Neilson ratings when this whole thing was over and done.

The girls tromped upstairs, mildly soothed. Our expanded group resumed their seats. Dave eased onto the couch at my right with Chelsea. I wanted to sit close to him, but didn't dare with Milt in the house. Dave's presence shifted the dynamics. Another male—and one who cared for *us*, not some national television career.

The two men sized each other up.

The girls' steps muted as they hit the upstairs carpet. Kelly's bedroom door clicked shut.

"So." Milt raised his hands with ill-muted expectation. "Let me sum up where we are. We have a spider-crazed idiot out there. Who has also threatened to kill you, Annie. With Chelsea's visions, we now know more than the police. Problem is, the police won't listen." He cocked his head. "Which leads us to the question of the day: *Will* you let me help you catch this guy? Hopefully before these two people die?"

Chapter 37

Milt's challenge slapped me in the face. How *dare* he state the situation like that! As if the two captives' deaths could possibly be our fault.

Still, could I sit back, knowing what I did, and do nothing?

Jenna bristled too. "You are a jerk, Milt Waking."

"Why should we trust you in the first place?" Dave demanded.

Milt shrugged. "We'll set ground rules and I'll follow them. For one thing, I'll never reveal you as my sources."

Jenna snorted. "Oh, *that* makes me feel better."

"Hey." Milt turned to her, defensiveness twisting his face. "I do come with some credentials, you know. You can't be where I am in my business without trustworthiness. I protect more sources than you'd ever guess."

Jenna glared at him. But I could have sworn I saw another spark. Almost as if on some level they enjoyed the spat.

"Mr. Waking," Chelsea said, "what are you going to do if we don't give you the drawing?"

He eased back against the couch. "Honestly? I have plenty enough information to start on-site reporting. A cameraman and rented microwave truck are here and ready to go. We'll break the story on the air tomorrow morning.

Plus, the producer for *On the Record*, Greta Van Susteren's show, is very interested in featuring it tomorrow night. I'll talk about the skeleton that was found. And your visions, Ms. Adams—*both* of them. I'll talk about the two of you." He waved a hand between Chelsea and me. "How the police refuse to run your drawing, even though it could help their case." He paused, as if reveling in the thought. "That ought to turn up the heat on them. Public outcry might force the police to use it."

A rock sank in my stomach. "So what do you need us for, Milt? You have what you want; go file your story."

"No, I don't have everything. I want the drawing."

"You just told us your story would force Blanche to release it to the media."

"But I want it now. *I* want to be the one to release it."

Okay, this was *too* blatantly honest. There had to be major manipulation in here somewhere. "So get a copy from your 'inside sources.'"

He sighed. "I can't. Blanche has it locked up tight."

Ah, there it was.

Jenna watched Milt, arms crossed and mouth firm. Dave focused in the distance, his businessman's mind clearly calculating. Chelsea sat stiffly, cheeks flushed. "You are as devious as you ever were, Milt Waking," she said. "I see where you're headed. You mentioned *both* of my visions. You want a bargain, don't you? If we give you the drawing, you'll hold back the information about the oval window—a lead for the police that this evil man shouldn't know about."

I stared at Milt. "Is that what you're thinking? You'd threaten to release crucial information that might tip off a murderer? That could save two lives?"

Jenna heaved toward him and punched his shoulder. "I ought to strangle you right now! We're not—"

"Wait a minute." Dave's hand shot up. He gave my sister a firm look. "Let's just calm down. There may be two lives at stake." He glanced around our group. "Milt, is Chelsea right about this? If Annie gives you the drawing, you'll keep quiet about the window?"

The reporter's head wagged. "I hadn't thought of that, but now that you mention it . . ."

I could have kicked him. Jenna rolled a disgusted look toward the ceiling.

Dave's jaw worked. He locked eyes with Milt. "You would compromise the safety of two innocent people just to get an exclusive?"

Milt held up both hands, all innocence. "The whole point of getting the drawing to the media is to *find* those two people. Think of the coverage you'll get on national television! You give me the drawing, not only will I keep quiet about the window, I'll start researching it myself. Believe me, I *will* find that house. I'll tell you everything I discover, including inside information from the Police Department." He cast me a meaningful look. "It's got to drive you crazy that they're not telling you much. Especially with your own life on the line."

If I never saw this man again, it would be too soon. "I think you are despicable."

"I agree." Chelsea glared at him. "But there's something far more important than our opinions." She drew herself up with a sigh. "I don't like this so-called bargain of yours at all. Fact is, Mr. Waking, you're not the one in control. We don't need to strike any deal with you just because it's what you want." She looked to me. "But Annie, I sense this is what *God* wants. I don't know why, and as far as I'm concerned, He could have chosen anyone other than Mr. Waking to help us. But there you have it. I think we all need to work together from here on out."

We all began talking at once. At first we could only argue. Then, over the next forty minutes—amid Jenna's temper, Dave's protectiveness, and Milt's infuriating self-certainty —we somehow managed to forge a path toward wary agreement. I still could hardly believe what we were doing. I could only trust it was God's leading. It *had* to be.

Technical details followed. Exchanging phone numbers. Copying the drawing for Milt. The minute it was in his hands, he veered toward the door.

"Wait a minute." Chelsea motioned to him. "Sit back down. We're going to pray before you leave."

Milt gave her a leary stare, then shrugged. He lowered himself back to the couch.

We bowed our heads.

"Dear God," Chelsea began, "thank You for bringing us together. Even if we don't quite trust one another. Thank You for sending Milt here. Even if he is a royal pain."

Jenna tittered.

"And for sending me another vision, terrifying as it was. Now we give our information and Annie's drawing into Milt's hands. Use him, Lord, as You did before, even if he doesn't believe You're doing so. Speak through him, guide his actions, and lead us to the answers. For You are the God of justice and truth, and we claim justice for these murders, and for all victims involved. Please protect us now, and Annie's children. In Jesus' name. Amen."

Milt pushed immediately to his feet, raring to leave. "Great. See you soon."

At the door he promised to call in the morning and tell us when the story would air. With a final lingering glance at Jenna, he escaped, victorious, into the night.

I closed and bolted the door behind him, then slumped against it. Dave walked over and held out his arms. I pressed myself against his chest, wondering what on earth we'd done and what would happen now.

Most of all, I begged God that our actions would save two lives.

Chapter 38

Seven fifteen. The sun had set, pulling an oppressive dusk over Grove Landing. Soon we would face another night with Orwin Neese on the loose. In the great room, I glanced at the large array of rear windows looking out over glooming forest and shivered.

Erin and Kelly still hung out upstairs. I'd gone up after Milt left, asking them to turn down their music. Dave stayed, too worried to leave. He and I retreated into the TV room and shut the door. I huddled next to him on the leather couch, my brain squalling that we made the wrong decision. He tried to calm me, keep me focused on prayer. And pray we did.

When Dave left with Erin, I wandered into the kitchen, vaguely thinking I needed to make dinner. My mind still wouldn't focus. Jenna shooed me out, announcing she'd cook something. Chelsea volunteered to help. Stephen arrived home from work, insisting that I tell him in detail what happened. Denying his request would only have belittled him. In his seventeen-year-old maleness, he saw himself as defender of our family. I told him everything.

He mulled over the information. "I want that reporter's cell phone number."

"Why?"

"Just in case, that's why. You have it, Jenna has it. I'll bet Dave even has it." He paused, daring me to deny the fact.

I gave him the number.

Dinner tasted like sawdust. I ate by rote, ill-concealing my distraction. "Annie," Jenna nudged me when I pushed back my plate, "go work on your project. It'll get your mind off things."

I didn't argue. Besides, my office had only front windows, and out on the street a policeman watched.

Minutes later I stood before the skull, struggling to remember where I had left off—was it only three to four hours ago? It seemed like days. I gazed at the cut vinyl markers, remembering I'd dropped one when the phone rang.

There it lay.

Breathing a prayer for accuracy, I began gluing the markers onto the skull. Formal names of the points whispered in my head, remnants from my days of extra studying. *One—the supraglabella, center forehead ... Two—glabella, center forehead between the eyes ... Three—nasion, center top of nose* ... With each marker I consulted a chart, then checked and rechecked its placement, taking care not to rush. Mistakes at this stage would throw off the entire drawing.

Time narrowed into a focused stream of concentration. Not once did I look up from my task.

When I finished the gluing, it was nearly ten. Neck muscles aching, I leaned back and observed my progress. Numbered markers protruded from the skull like the blunt ends of rubber arrows. The two eye sockets glared at me in violation.

Who are you, John Doe? What will you look like?

Hours of work remained. Positioning the skull, photographing, then the actual phase of drawing. With the day's events still rattling in my head, I knew I wouldn't sleep. Even the thought of trying frightened me—lying in the dark, my mind conjuring gruesome scenes.

Better to keep working.

As the night hours wore on, this forlorn skull would slowly morph into a definable face.

I stopped long enough to bid Chelsea and Jenna good night, telling them I planned to work late. Then I eased into Kelly's room and sat beside her on the bed. She leaned her head on my shoulder. "Tomorrow's Mike Winger's funeral at one o'clock," she said. "Remember, his mom works in the principal's office? That's gonna be real sad."

"Yes, it will." I stroked her hair.

"I wish I could go."

"Why? You didn't know him."

"Yeah, but I know his mom a little. I'd do it for her ..." She raised her head. "Do you really think the man who shot Mike has that girl and guy in some room with a bunch of spiders?"

I thought of Chelsea's second vision. "I'm afraid so. But we're doing everything we can to find them."

Kelly shuddered. "I just can't imagine it."

Neither could I. But I clung to the belief that Neese would be caught soon. I had to believe Chelsea was right—God brought Milt here for a reason. God *was* in control, even in these terrible circumstances.

Lord, thank You for this assurance. Help me lean on it as I work tonight.

Back in my office I turned my attention fully to work, resting in the hope that tomorrow this nightmare would be over.

Chapter 39

*P*oom, *poom, puh-poom-poom, chaka-laka-laka.*

He jerked his neck to a rap tune.

Poom-puh-chek-chek.

Adrenaline flowed through his limbs. He felt *good.* Channeling the power, feelin' it. No more dirt ants. No more voices from the past.

He was *free.*

Puh-puh-poom—

He halted, midrock, hand hovering over the terrarium. Better rein in the kick now, steady those fingers.

A bunch of hobo spiders hung out down in the glass crib. Big suckers, with long legs. A jar sat nearby, its vented top off. The jar stood about three inches high. Small enough to fit in his pocket.

"Here, itsy, bitsy spider." Carefully he edged aside a damp wood pile in the terrarium. There sat one, hiding in a funnel web. With one finger he peeled back the top of the web. The spider scurried for cover.

He scooped it into a measuring cup. "Gotcha!"

He carried the cup out and over, like a helicopter airlifting a victim, and dropped the spider into the jar. Then sat back to consider it. How many should he collect? Five? Ten?

No need to cover the jar while he caught the rest. Hobo spiders were poor climbers.

Poo-puh-poom-poom.

His neck chicken-stretched a few more beats before he resumed his task. Spider number two—spotted, caught, air-lifted, and dumped in the jar. Spider number three. And four. Five, six, seven.

Perfect.

Puh-puh-poom.

He screwed down the jar lid, placed the top back on the terrarium. Picked up the jar and held it close to his face. The spiders scuttled and tumbled over each other, cramped in their close quarters. Poor things didn't like the light.

"Don't you worry." He ran a finger down the glass. "Darkness is coming soon."

The rap CD ended. In the sudden silence he could hear his heart pump. A good, strong beat, without fear.

He glanced out the window. Night had fallen.

Time to shimmy.

Jar in hand, he stepped into the garage. Sliding into his car, he punched the automatic door opener. The garage door whirred open. A satisfying sound, exciting. Could it be heard from the prison room in the basement? Would his captives' heads raise at the vague noise that signaled freedom, even as their spider walls closed in around them?

He snickered at the thought.

Minutes later he drove a back road toward eastern Redding, headed for the highway that would take him to Grove Landing. No need for a map; he knew the way.

He'd been there before.

Chapter 40

By midnight I'd positioned the skull and photographed it from front and side, using a digital camera. My printer spat out the eight-by-tens, its *click, whir* loud in the still house. I peeked out the drawn window blinds, peering up the cul-de-sac. I could see the vague shape of the policeman sitting in his car. I hoped he managed to stay awake.

It's Monday. What will the day bring? Will they find you, Orwin Neese?

Carrying the two photographs to my dual boards, I taped one picture to each, lining them up so I could look from one to the other on a level plane. Then I covered each photograph with a sheet of vellum, taping it at the top only. In this way I could create my drawing on the see-through paper while still able to lift the vellum and reexamine the picture as needed. The skull sat nearby for further reference.

Time to begin drawing.

You can do this, Annie. Forget that you've never done it for a real case.

First up—facial contouring, a light connect-the-dots line from one tissue depth marker to the next. Marker number sixteen, the zygomatic arch, lying back from the cheekbones and close to the ears, is the widest area on the face. I began there and worked my way down the skull. Due to John Doe's youth, I would draw all the contours as firm rather than soft and sagging.

A shape of one cheek formed, heading toward the mouth. Markers nineteen and twenty-one, above and below the second molars, would be good indicators for shading the cheek planes—to an extent. John Doe's weight would also be a factor. The second cheek formed. The temples, and forehead.

Soon the frontal view outline was complete. I stared at it, biting my lip. Not too bad.

Now, over to the lateral board. Working back and forth would afford a better way of checking my work as it progressed. When I finished the outline, I plunged into the next challenge: the eyes.

Back to the frontal view. Carefully I positioned the eyeballs in the centers of their sockets. Switching to the profile board, I made sure the eyeballs showed the right amount of protrusion. Back and forth between the two perspectives I looked, drew, studied, drew some more. My concentration laser-focused, my worries about Neese and spiders and death threats fading. The eyes slowly formed, their skull cavity visible from the photo underneath. They were deep set and small. Almost beady.

I needed to add a sense of color, but there was no way to tell what hue John Doe's eyes had been. I went for ambiguity, shading the irises more at the top near the lid, and less at the bottom in a reflected-light effect. That done, I turned to the brows. They were tricky. There were some structural indications as to their placement, but no hair had been found with the skull, so I couldn't know their thickness and texture. I could only follow the general patterns of male eyebrows, making them heavier than a female's, with less of an arch.

I stopped for a breather. Flexed my shoulders and neck. John Doe's eyes, all the more compelling without the rest of his features, locked onto me with beseeching vengeance. *Look at us. We represent a name, an identity. Give us justice.*

With God's help I would.

Wait a minute. I stared at them, entranced. These eyes were almost ...

Oh no. Had I done this wrong? Had my work been influenced by memory?

I tore my gaze away. *Annie, don't go there.* I could not think of that possibility, not now. I needed to draw with a fresh mind, creating based on what I saw.

I glanced at the time. Almost two in the morning.

I needed a drink.

Padding softly through the great room, I was aware of the grandfather clock ticking, the play of shadows from the single lit lamp. In the kitchen, water hissed into my glass. I turned toward the windows, uncomfortable with their empty stare upon my back. Still wondering about those eyes I'd just drawn. A streetlight illuminated the pavement between my house and Dave's, the police car outside its umbra. I could see the vague outline of the officer inside. He wasn't moving. Did he wonder at the lights so late in my office? Odd, but I didn't even feel tired. No doubt I'd pay for the lack of sleep tomorrow.

Back in the office I prayed I would draw John Doe's face right. I didn't like my uneasiness about those eyes. Determined, I began work on the nose.

God, help me regain my focus.

The nasal cavity at its broadest point determines a nose's width. From its bony contours, I sketched the general shape. For the soft tissue on top of bone, I consulted a formula. I drew, lifted the vellum sheets up to check the photographs, frowned at the skull, sketched some more. Time fuzzed as I concentrated. I heard nothing, felt nothing. Knew only the paper in front of me, and the nose that emerged. I didn't dare look at other sections of the drawing except as indicators of how to complete this part. By the time I finished the nose, my fingers cramped from gripping the pencil. Sweat trickled under my armpits. Afraid to survey what I'd done, fearful of what the half face might tell me, I moved immediately to the mouth, calculating the approach I'd take.

Although John Doe's teeth were crooked, he didn't have unusual enough dentition to affect his profile, so the teeth didn't need to show. I would draw the lips closed.

First, the frontal view. *Focus, Annie; just remember what you've learned.* The width is determined by measuring the six front teeth ... the height, by noting the upper and lower teeth enamel. I worked on the profile, the front view, the profile again. Determining size, shape, lift of the lip corners. Back and forth, back and forth, sketching, erasing, redrawing.

Sometime during that process, a tiny voice within me began to whisper the truth.

I ignored it.

My work continued, the lips adopting a thin shape. After this would come the ears. Then the hair, although I would have to downplay its style, since I had no clue to go on.

Yes, you do, Annie. You know.

No, I don't.

The whisper intensified. I pushed it aside. It nagged at me, daring me to stop, to look at John Doe's face as a whole. *You'll know when you see it all. You just don't want to admit it.*

I finished the mouth. Went straight to the ears. They would not look as I suspected. They *wouldn't.* For a time I occupied my brain with recitation of my studies. *The ear sits behind the angle of the jaw … It's usually at a backward angle of about fifteen degrees … Be careful not to draw them like they're glued to the head … An ear is roughly equal in length to the nose …*

I spoke under my breath, eyes glancing back and forth between the two drawing boards, my hand fashioning, shaping. With every ounce of will I considered the ears only, and the part of the skull that defined them. I would not look at the whole, because if I did … If I did, I would begin to draw from memory, from another face, another day and interview—

The ears birthed beneath my hand. I couldn't help but notice their size. With each line of the pencil, the whispers echoed. My denials fell away. Abruptly I stepped back, staring at the finished face. I took in the lateral view first, putting off the inevitable. Then my eyes snapped to the frontal drawing.

It was him. *Exactly* him.

I dropped the pencil. Stood staring, breathing hard, a thousand questions ricocheting through my head. What did this mean? What about the drawing I'd given Milt? What about our reason for letting him take it? It didn't fit anymore. Everything was wrong, all wrong, and I couldn't make head nor tails of it.

If I'd known this twelve hours ago, I'd *never* have given that drawing to Milt Waking.

"Oh, God, what do I *do?*"

I turned toward my closed office door, heart skipping. I had to wake Jenna and Chelsea, no matter that it was four a.m. They'd have to know; we had to *talk*. I walked to the door, grabbed the knob —

My business line rang.

I turned to stare at the phone as if it were some UFO landed upon my desk.

A second ring.

Who ... I hurried to answer it, not bothering to check the ID. Even as I picked it up, I knew my voice would shake.

"H–hello?"

"Annie Kingston."

The way he spoke my name. Grated, in a rough whisper, like Chelsea had described it. Every muscle in my throat clamped down.

"I know you're listening, whether you answer or not." He snickered. "This is Orwin Neese. I have a little surprise for you."

Chapter 41

No response. He could feel her fear creeping over the telephone wire. Like the dirt ants used to creep on his feet, scuffling over nerve endings. Now they were *her* nerves.

He gripped the phone, breathing open-mouthed in silent jubilation. "Still won't talk, huh?"

Man, shut up and get on with it. What if they could somehow trace the call?

"Look out on your back deck. There's a little jar sitting there."

She gasped, sending a tremor of excitement up his spine. "A j–jar?" Her voice was reed-thin and hollow. "What ..."

"Don't worry, it's not a bomb." He poured out the words like syrup. "Nothing like that. Just a few hobo pals to keep you company."

Silence.

"Orwin, why are you doing this to me? You need to turn yourself—"

He slammed down the phone.

Swiveling around, he checked in all directions. Nobody in sight of the phone booth. Who would be way out here this time of night?

Pa-pa-pum-pum. He mouthed a beat, slapping his legs as he hustled back to his car.

All the way home he sang loudly with the radio.

Chapter 42

The receiver clattered onto my desk. I bent over, pulling in breaths, heart thwacking. My mind yanked in multiple directions. I should snatch up the phone, call the policeman outside—

What if he was *dead?*

No, I needed to run to the back deck. What if Neese *had* left a bomb? Stephen's bedroom was down there—

But what if Neese lurked in the shadows, waiting for me to slip outside? That would be stupid, Annie, *stupid.*

Seconds blurred. I fumbled for the phone. *Where's the officer's phone number, Annie? Where did you put it?* I flailed around the desk, pushing aside paper and stacked mail, rattling my penholder to the floor. *There!* I snatched up the small yellow sheet and punched in the number.

"Officer Shelton."

In one breathless sentence I told the man what happened. He responded calmly, in control. I was to wait for him near the front door. He would call for backup. For all we knew, Neese was still in the area. I slammed down the receiver and darted through the great room, throwing back the door at the policeman's swift rap. Meantime the household began to awaken amid the noise of my pounding feet. Jenna rushed from the hall and Chelsea appeared on the staircase. Shelton strode through the house and down the stairs to the rec room. I followed. Gun drawn, he ventured out the sliding door to the deck.

The commotion brought Stephen stumbling from his bedroom, clad only in boxer shorts, blinking in the light. One hand gripped his cell phone, ready to dial 911.

I huddled in the rec room, pulse skidding. Chelsea hung back, pinching the fabric of her pajama top, eyes wide. My sister grasped her own gun, ready for action. "Just let me at him! I find Neese around here, he'll die young."

The policeman stuck his head in the door. "I need a rag of some kind."

I ran to fetch a washcloth from Stephen's bathroom and thrust it into Shelton's hand.

The policeman slipped inside, holding a small jar, the cloth protecting it from his fingerprints. He stopped to lock the sliding door. I wedged our sawed-off broom handle behind it.

Jenna took one look at the jar and hissed through her teeth. Stephen's face twisted. "Oh *man.*"

Shelton held up Neese's "present." I frowned at it, fingers clenching, already knowing what I would see.

Spiders. Big ones. Their appendages almost rivaled the size of a daddy longlegs'. They scrambled and tumbled and rolled over each other in one nauseating, horrifying heap.

"Oh." Shudder-fingers clamped onto my body and shook it. I wheeled away from the sight, brain screaming. *It's all real, it's real!* Not that I'd doubted Chelsea, but seeing the creatures here, bottled up and left for me, rocketed her visions into hard reality. If Neese left these spiders here, then he did have them, did collect them. The horror room *did* exist—

But what about the drawing I just finished?

Wait. I stilled, hands at my cheeks, breath catching. *Hobos.* The projector in my head kicked on to the scene from Chelsea's vision. The man

bending toward the floor. He caresses the narrow back of a large brown spider.

"This is a hobo spider. Lots of people mistake them for the brown recluse ..."

"Chelsea." I whirled to face her. "This morning, did the newspaper article say anything about what kind of spiders you saw in your vision?"

She swallowed hard, then shook her head.

I closed my eyes. "Then I don't get it. This just doesn't fit."

"What doesn't—wait!" Jenna hurled the word at Officer Shelton's back as he headed for the stairs. "Don't leave us down here!"

Just seeing my sister so rattled shook me all the more. Shelton hit the steps as he barked into his radio, replies squawking. We clambered after him. In the great room our erratic footfalls bounced around like pinballs against flippers.

"Police cars are on the way." Shelton held the jar out from his body, as if spider jaws could bite through the glass. "They'll be searching the forest back there. Neese clearly didn't come by way of the street, which means he trekked in through the woods. Probably long gone, but we've got to make sure."

How did Neese even know where I lived?

Jenna grabbed my arm. "Annie, what were you trying to say down there?"

"I—"

"Mom!" Kelly's voice tumbled from the landing above us. I looked up to see her grabbing a banister, face full of fear. "What's happening?"

Oh, God, why did she have to wake up?

I hurried up the circular stairs, knowing I would have to tell her. Refusing her questions would only scare her more. I pulled her close, easing hair from her eyes, and related the sordid tale as gently as I could. Only then—as I said the words—did the steel-fisted truth fully seize me. Forget swirling questions, the enigma of John Doe's face. All that mattered was that Neese had been *here*. At my house. Close to me.

Close to my children.

Rage and panic clotted my throat. "Honey, go get dressed." I turned away before Kelly could see my expression contort. *God, help!* We had to get out of the house, out of Grove Landing. *Now.* I would not face death again. And I surely wouldn't leave my son and daughter in harm's way.

Red and blue lights flashed through the tall front windows. I peered outside, seeing police cars skid to a stop in front of the house. At least their sirens were off. Still, the rotating beams alone were enough to pull half-wakened neighbors from bed.

Dave. What if he spotted the all-too-familiar sight outside my house? He'd be petrified.

I trotted down the steps and toward the kitchen phone. Chelsea passed me, grim-faced. "I'm going to get dressed." I barely registered her words. Jenna was not in sight, probably throwing on some clothes as well. In the kitchen I dialed Dave's number with trembling fingers. He answered on the third ring, voice groggy. "Annie?"

A third relating of the story—Neese's phone call, spiders in the night. Police searching the forest. If I hadn't been so terrified, I'd have laughed. What had we done, fallen into some warped nightmare?

Within ten minutes Dave materialized at my door, a shaking Erin at his side. Kelly let loose a sob and pulled to her like a magnet. Together they sank down on a couch, hugging, murmuring soothing phrases neither of them believed.

Dave wrapped his arms around me. "You all right?"

I nodded, unable to speak.

More cars in the street, these from the Sheriff's Department. Chetterling was not among the deputies. I was glad he was off duty. At least somebody I knew was sleeping through the night. Teams quickly coordinated, heavy-beamed flashlights turned on. The search through the forest was launched.

"Kelly." From behind the couch, I leaned over to nudge her shoulder. "Why don't you and Erin go crawl in your bed? You'll be safe up there."

They looked at each other, then made their way up the stairs without a word.

The rest of us fell onto the furniture around the fireplace to wait, Jenna and Chelsea on one couch, Dave and I on the other. Stephen perched in the middle chair, fingers gripping its arms. His cell phone lay beside him. One leg rocked back and forth, as if his fizzling energy could not be contained. He shot me a look. "Whatever happens, Mom, I want to know about it. I'll tell you right now—I see this guy, I'm killing him. We are *not* going through this again."

Dave opened his mouth, then shut it. I could only nod feebly, as if my son had informed me he intended to go out for a stroll on a sunny afternoon. My brain was already on overload, sorting puzzle pieces.

Jenna paid him no attention. "Annie, tell us what you meant about things not fitting."

"It's my drawing of John Doe." I pulled my arms across my chest, the words tumbling. "You're not going to believe this. It's the face Chelsea saw after the scene in her vision—the man we thought was captured by Orwin Neese. It's the *same drawing* we just gave Milt Waking!"

Shocked silence. Dave pressed my hand and Jenna stared at me. Chelsea's eyes pulled toward the fireplace as if seeking explanation upon its stones. "Then ... what?" she whispered. "My vision was of the past, when John Doe was killed? And Orwin Neese is just playing with us?"

"It can't be." My head wagged. "Did you look closely at the jar Neese left? It's full of hobo spiders. He told me on the phone. He couldn't know that, Chelsea, no way. Not unless he was the one in that room, in your vision."

Chelsea brought a hand to her forehead. "I need to ... I have to think about it. Maybe you're ... Because remember, I saw that room, then it disappeared, and I saw that young man's face afterward. Like it was two separate entities." She bit her lip. "You think the vision's about two completely different crimes?"

"It must be." Dave frowned. "Think about it. We have two murder cases going on. God sent you one vision—about both of them."

"Oh, I can't believe—! This is why I told you I can't assume anything." Chelsea's tone pulsed. "I should only have relied on what I saw for sure."

"It's not your fault." I leaned toward her. "If anything, *I* led us all to assume. And the more that happened, the more our assumption seemed to fit."

"But what now?" Jenna raised a hand and let it drop. "Milt's going on the air this morning with the wrong information. He has to know both drawings tie to the skeleton at the runway. They have nothing to do with Neese."

"Call him," Stephen declared. "Right now. He should know about what just happened, anyway."

"But don't you see?" I slumped against the couch. "The whole point of giving him that drawing was in hopes that identifying the man would lead police to that horrible room. Now it doesn't even apply. Meanwhile Amy Flyte's still missing, plus maybe some *other* man. And we know the spider room exists, but we've got no leads for finding it."

Dave squeezed my shoulder. "We've got the oval window."

"Yeah, we got that." Stephen picked up his cell phone, beeped through its menu. "It has to be right. If she knew about the exact kind of spiders—" he jerked his head toward Chelsea—"then she's gotta be right about the window. I'm calling the reporter."

"Wait!" I started to rise. "I should do it."

Dave caught my arm. "It's okay, Annie; let him."

If Milt was asleep when his phone rang, he apparently woke in a hurry. Stephen introduced himself and launched into his story. Then held the phone out to me. "He wants to talk to you."

I ended up pressing the speaker phone button so we all could hear. Questions and worries batted back and forth, but Milt remained adamant. He wasn't canceling his story. In fact, he had even more of one now, with information on two murders instead of one. "We'll film as a breaking news story, with updates during the day. Your drawing will get lots of national exposure, which could help solve John Doe's ID. Meanwhile I'll be investigating the recent murder. Neese's threats have grown more serious, and we still have at least one missing person. We need to find her."

I clicked off the line, feeling battered and sleep deprived. Questions and worries sludged through my brain. Two new realizations hit. One, Blanche had been right about my drawing after all. It had nothing to do with his case. Therefore, two: In giving the composite to Milt, I'd ended up meddling in *Chetterling's* murder investigation, not Blanche's. Now John Doe's face would be released on national news—before Chetterling had even seen it.

I sat on the couch, Dave's arm around me. Jenna and Stephen batted questions and conjectures back and forth. Chelsea stared at the floor, deep in thought. Then, as if hearing the same inner voice, our eyes pulled to each other. I took a deep breath. "We need to pray."

Chelsea nodded. Rose to go to her bedroom and returned with a Bible in hand. Neither Jenna nor Stephen protested. "I'm going to pray some psalms for us." Chelsea opened her Bible. "Psalm 56 is a good place to start."

I lay back against Dave's shoulder, closed my eyes.

" 'When I am afraid,' " Chelsea read, " 'I will trust in you. In God, whose word I praise, in God I trust; I will not be afraid. What can mortal man do to me? All day long they—'" She paused. "I'll substitute *he*. 'All day long he twists my words ... he conspires, he lurks, he watches my steps, eager to take my life. On no account let him escape; in your anger, O God—'" her voice rose—"'bring *him* down ... For you have delivered me from death and my feet from stumbling, that I may walk before God in the light of life.'"

Psalm 91 followed, and other passages Chelsea had marked. I was too tired to read, but every fiber of my being prayed silently with her.

The sun rose.

The officers and deputies called off their forest search for Neese, declaring the area clear. Extra surveillance was placed on our house. Orwin remained out there, somewhere, "eager to take my life."

Please, God, let this end today.

Chapter 43

Six thirty a.m.

Earlier Dave had awakened Erin and the two returned home. Erin needed to get ready for school. Jenna clattered about the kitchen, making coffee and breakfast. *As if I wanted to eat.* Chelsea was taking a shower and Stephen was getting dressed.

A vise slid around my chest. So much at stake, so many variables, none of which I could control. As if fear of Neese and concern for his captives wasn't enough, I paced the great room, worrying about Milt's report. No doubt he'd sensationalize to the max. Not that he needed to. Chelsea's visions, a room full of spiders, missing people, threats on my life, and two different murder investigations—the convoluted tale had all the makings of the country's next macabre fascination. In no time we could have the media masses camped out on my doorstep.

God, why did You want Milt Waking here?

I dialed the reporter's cell phone, heart thumping. "You were supposed to call. When's your story running?"

"Around seven fifteen." He sounded distracted. "Prime time while people are getting ready for work."

Seven fifteen. Only forty minutes away. "Milt, you'd better keep your promises."

"I'll keep them. Look, gotta go." He clicked off.

I stared daggers at the phone, then threw it on the couch. A new worry lasered through my head, and I snatched the receiver up again, punched in Chetterling's home number. No way he was going to hear everything on the news. It had to come from me.

He answered on the first ring. "Annie! I just heard what happened last night. You okay over there?"

"We're fine, Ralph, but you need to know ... I have to tell you something important."

Explanations poured in a torrent, my feet slapping against the hardwood floor as I paced. "I'd *never* have released the drawing, Ralph, if I knew it was about your case. Blanche wasn't listening to us, and I was so worried about the two missing people ..."

"Okay." Chetterling sighed. "We'll talk about your decision making later. Right now we've got other things to worry about. At least John Doe will get more exposure—and more quickly—than I expected. Meanwhile you need to keep yourself safe. The manhunt for Neese is huge now, Annie. I just got off a conference call that included the sheriff and the chief of police. With Neese's picture on national news, we'll find him."

Gratitude welled in my chest. Chetterling could have come at me with both barrels, and he'd have been entitled. "Thank you so much, Ralph, for not strangling me."

At seven a.m. we turned on FOX News. Chelsea had called her husband to tell him what was happening. Jenna had made eggs and bacon, and we took our plates into the TV room, gathering nervously on the leather couch and chairs. I called Stephen up from his bedroom, mindful of his need to know. Fortunately, Kelly had not yet appeared.

The "breaking news" story catapulted onto the screen at seven twenty, the anchor setting the stage for "two bizarre murders in Redding, California."

Milt stood at the end of the Grove Landing runway, churned ground behind him and yellow crime-scene tape shuddering in a breeze. The moment seemed so surreal. While we watched on national television, he filmed not half a mile away.

"This story is indeed strange and is growing more so by the hour." Milt gestured toward the construction site. "This is a private runway at Grove Landing, a sky park outside Redding. Here on Saturday a skeleton was discovered by the crew who'd been hired to lengthen the airstrip. Two days previously, in a seemingly unrelated incident, thirty-two-year-old Orwin Neese allegedly chased Mike Winger, twenty-two, into a convenience store and fatally shot him, also wounding a clerk." The scene switched to the exterior of the 7-Eleven. "What is the connection between these crimes? Much is yet unknown, but they begin with two women who've gained notoriety through other highly watched cases—Annie Kingston, a local forensic artist, and Chelsea Adams, a woman whose 'visions from God' were proved true through the so-called Trent Park and Salad King murder trials in the California Bay Area a few years ago."

Oh boy, here goes.

With a balance of professional detachment and personal dismay, Milt laid out details. He began with reminders of the famous cases I'd worked on and that I was considered a "local hero." Jenna nodded with satisfaction. The way she leaned toward the screen in rapt attention—there was more to her body language than concern about the story. Was she really attracted to that jerk?

Milt turned to current information: Mike Winger's death and my composite of suspect Orwin Neese. Chelsea's vision of the spider room and an unknown man's face, which I had also drawn—the same face that my forensic work had now proven to belong to the discovered skeleton. Missing Amy Flyte, and perhaps a second person—another young man. Neese's alleged threats on my life, including a jar of spiders with a serious bite—a lesser-known species that Chelsea Adams had seen in her vision. And most important, long close-ups of two drawings. Anyone knowing the whereabouts of Orwin Neese should call the Redding Police Department at the number on the screen. Anyone recognizing John Doe should contact the Shasta County Sheriff's Department, number also displayed.

"Meanwhile Annie Kingston remains in an undisclosed location, protected by authorities. Redding Police and the Shasta County Sheriff's Department are working together on the manhunt for Orwin Neese ..."

When the report ended, I sighed my relief. No promises broken, and my whereabouts kept private. *Thank You, God.*

Grimly the news anchor promised to keep watchers advised of new developments in the story.

Jenna muted the TV. "Whew. He did great!"

Chelsea's eyes closed. "I can breathe now. Thank You, Lord."

Stephen stared at the television, jaw working. "You did the right thing, Mom, talking to him. I'll bet he knows more than the policemen. I mean, what have *they* done? This guy shows up and things start to happen."

I made no comment. Likely, Stephen's opinion lay as much in his lingering contempt of police as in his trust of Milt Waking. In my son's drug days—which weren't that long ago—the police had been his enemies.

Kelly appeared in the doorway, fully dressed. "What are you all watching? Stephen, aren't you going to school?"

School. The thought hadn't crossed my mind. Dave had already said he'd take Erin, assuming that Kelly and Stephen wouldn't be going. "No, he's not," I announced, "and you're not going either."

"Why?"

Chelsea rose and began to stack our breakfast plates.

"Because you should stay here with me. Because ..." I looked to my sister for help.

"Annie—"

"But I want to *go*." Kelly's voice turned almost panicky. "What am I going to do here all day, sit around and wait for some crazy man to show up?"

"No, Kelly, no." I hurried to her side. "He's not coming back; we're too protected here. We've got four officers out there now instead of one, on all sides of the house."

"But there's nothing for me to *do* here." Tears filled my daughter's eyes. "Am I supposed to stay home every day until he's caught? I just want to get on with my life."

I searched for a reply. My fear cried, *Don't let her out of your sight.* But I could understand how she wanted the normalcy of school and friends. If I were her age, I'd want the same thing.

Dishes in hand, Chelsea headed for the sink.

Jenna caught my eye and gave a small nod. *Let her go*, she mouthed.

Stephen saw our wordless exchange. "I'm staying right here." He jabbed a finger at the floor.

"I know you planned to, Stephen." Jenna layered gratitude into her tone. "But we've got police outside and we're not going anywhere. Why don't you go to school, where you can be with Kelly? She and Erin will be safe driving there and back with you."

He shrugged, unconvinced. "But I don't even see her much during the day. We're in totally different classes."

"At least you're *there*. And she'll feel better, being with her friends."

The phone rang. I checked the ID. *Oh great.* "I need to answer this," I told the kids. "It's Detective Blanche. But I'm not through talking to you yet." I pushed the talk button. "Hi, Tim."

Blanche made no preamble. "Just wanted to update you while I had a minute. I'll be busy, and you probably won't hear from me again for a while." His terse words held the cutting edge of smugness. Apparently, he'd heard about the news story—vindication that he'd been right to doubt that the drawing Chelsea and I brought him had anything to do with his case.

"Thank you," I clipped, struck even more by what he didn't say. No "How are you?" No personal concern for me and my family. A rogue voice in my brain whispered that this horrific day had actually afforded the self-aggrandizing Blanche two favors—Neese's latest trick and Milt Waking's national newscast. Imagine the greater coverage for Blanche when he captured his quarry.

Annie, knock it off. You should apologize to him, admit he was right.

Blanche informed me that a massive manhunt was under-way, calls were coming into the station, leads being followed. No earthshaking revelations there. "And after hearing what happened last night, Ryan Burns called to say he'll cover all expenses for your protection, no matter the cost. He didn't really want me to tell you, but I thought you should know."

"Oh, wow, that's incredible of him."

Kelly waved a furious hand, signaling me to hurry. I nod-ded to her—*I know.*

"Yeah, it is. He did ask me to give you a message. Says to tell you please don't put your life on the line this time."

I managed a smile. "He can count on that."

"All right, that's it." Blanche suddenly sounded pressed.

Kelly glared at me impatiently. "Wait, Tim," I blurted. "Before you go—my daughter wants to go to school. Do you think that's okay?"

He pulled in a breath. "I think so. She's safe there. Lots of people around. Just tell her to stay alert, and you should make sure the principal is fully apprised of the situation. But who knows if Neese is even aware of your kids? He's never mentioned them. It's you he's after."

Thanks a lot, Blanche. I hung up the phone, not sure whether to feel better or not.

Ten minutes later Stephen and Kelly left for school. Since he didn't work Mondays, Stephen could bring her and Erin home. "I'll leave my cell phone on vibrate," he said, sounding none too happy about going. "Call if you need me."

I promised I would.

In my office I phoned the school and talked to the principal. He assured me he would check on Kelly throughout the day. Then I headed for the kitchen, feeling the slow tick of time. This day would seem an eternity.

Chelsea and Jenna sat at the table, nursing cups of coffee. Sometime soon Chelsea should hear from the tire shop as to when her car would be ready. Then she'd be gone, away from this madness. If I were her, I'd be itching to leave. But she seemed more concerned about me than herself.

I felt too antsy to sit with her and Jenna. I headed back to my office, intent on spending some much-needed time with God. Outside, policemen watched the property, and people across the country now looked with suspicion on anyone resembling Orwin Neese. Others, I hoped, were calling in leads about John Doe.

Nothing left for me to do but pray.

Chapter 44

He snapped off the car radio. This was it—kickoff, with the stands filled. Time to do or die.

The face he'd seen on TV still throbbed in his brain. That face, come back from the dead. Chelsea Adams had *seen* it—before the skeleton was even discovered. She was getting closer. Anytime now, she would know all.

No way he was facing a multiple murder rap. No. Way.

His fingers beat a tune against the steering wheel. Narrow-eyed, he stared at the building in the distance. This plan had its flaws. One straight line from A to B would have been easier. Less killing.

Oh well, nothing was perfect.

He picked up the cell phone. Sat up straight and cleared his throat. Dialed the number. It was answered on the second ring.

"Foothill High School, principal's office." A young voice.

"This is Detective Tim Blanche with the Redding Police Department." His words came out clipped, tight. "I need to talk to one of your students *immediately*—Kelly Kingston. I'll wait while you bring her to the phone."

"Oh, wow. Okay. But I'm just filling in here. I'll have to find out how to check her schedule—"

"This is an emergency! I don't *care* if you're just filling in; I need you to *hurry*."

"Okay, I'll get her."

Sounds followed—the click of the receiver laid down, the creak of a chair. He waited, seconds creeping.

Come on, come on ...

Chapter 45

Kelly snatched up the phone in the principal's office, her breath hitching. From her classroom she'd run down a flight of stairs and the entire length of the hall, panic choking her throat. What was wrong? Why would a policeman call?

God, please let Mom be all right.

"H–Hello?"

"Kelly, this is Detective Tim Blanche." The voice sounded official. "I've been leading the hunt for Orwin Neese. I talked to your mother just this morning. We have a situation, and I need you to do *exactly* what I say, you hear?"

Detective Blanche. The one who told her mom she could go to school. "Okay."

"Orwin Neese has kidnapped your mother. We—"

Kelly wailed. Her knees gave way and she grabbed the edge of the desk.

"We've just picked your brother up, but now we need to get you to safety. I want you to put down the phone right now, talk to *no one*, and walk straight out the front door. One of our plainclothes detectives is waiting in an unmarked car. He'll show you his badge. You'll be brought straight to the police station."

"But my mom! Is she—"

"We'll answer your questions in the car. Come *now*."

The line went dead.

Kelly dropped the phone. Everything blurred. The girl behind the desk asked her something, but she couldn't hear. Wind and screaming filled her head. *Mom, Mom!* She whirled out of the office and streaked down the hall. Her legs felt like rubber. Was she even moving? Was this a horrible dream?

God, I don't care about me; just let Mom be okay!

She hit the building's door and shoved through it. Stumbled into sunlight. Her head swiveled back and forth, searching for the policeman.

An engine gunned some distance away. A white car surged toward her and punched to a stop. A man leaned over and pushed open the passenger door. "Hurry!"

Kelly blinked at the empty backseat. Something ... "Where's Stephen?"

"He's headed to the station in another car; just get *in*!"

A sob burst from her and she fell into the car, throat closing up. The car jumped forward. "What happened to my mom? Where *is* she —"

"She'll be okay; just calm down. I need to show you my badge."

They turned out of the parking lot. The man reached into his pocket and pulled out something. Not a badge. A cloth. He stuck it in her face. Kelly gasped, yanked her head back. He pressed the rag against her nose. Dizziness swept over her. She raised her hands to fight ... push it away ...

The world went black.

Chapter 46

At ten forty-five the tire shop called. Chelsea's car would be ready at two o'clock. Jenna would drive her into Redding.

Exhaustion lumped in my chest, but no way could I sleep. My emotions bounced all over the place.

We stayed glued to FOX News as it aired updates from Milt Waking. Tips about Orwin Neese were already filtering into the police station. And the Sheriff's Department had received a couple of leads about John Doe. We saw interviews with detectives, sheriff's deputies. Milt interviewed Tim Blanche around nine o'clock, and that footage had already replayed a couple of times.

The scant information didn't console me. I was a caged tiger, hungry for answers. When would Neese be caught? Were Amy Flyte and the unknown man still alive? Who was John Doe? Was he connected to Neese, or did Chelsea's vision indeed link two unrelated crimes?

Milt was supposed to call with whatever information he'd discovered. It was high time he did.

Dave had needed to attend a meeting in town at nine thirty. He phoned when it ended, seeking any news. "I'll be home in twenty minutes. Want me to come over?"

I wandered into the great room, looked through the windows toward his house. "You don't have to take care of other work?"

"Annie, how can I? I keep worrying about *you*."

My gritty eyes closed. "Yes, Dave. Please come."

"Okay. And ... Annie?" His voice caught. "I want you to know something. I couldn't manage without you in my life."

The words seeped into my soul. *Oh, Dave. What we could have ... if I could only cut the strings to all my insecurities.* "I need you too. So much."

There. I'd said it.

For a moment neither of us spoke.

"See you soon, Annie," Dave whispered—and hung up.

I pulled the phone from my ear and stared across the room.

The TV beckoned. "Nothing new." Jenna sighed. "They're airing other stories now."

Frustration curled my fingers. How could the world turn as normal, with all this going on? I headed upstairs for a shower, hoping it would calm me. It didn't. I only succeeded in riling myself up more over the fact that Milt still hadn't called.

By eleven thirty I would wait no longer. That man, what an ingrate! Getting all that airtime and already breaking his promises to us.

I stalked to the kitchen and dialed his cell phone. "Where *are* you?"

"At the Building Services Department." His words were terse.

I heard voices in the background. "What are you doing?"

"Reporting to you, apparently."

"Well, don't sound so put out. You did promise to do that, remember?"

"Sorry, I'm a tad busy here. Do you have any idea how many calls I've fielded this morning? This story's heating up like a wildfire and I'm jumping all over the place."

I wanted to strangle him. "I'm so happy for you."

"Annie." His voice tightened. "I didn't have to answer your call, you know. What do you want?"

What did I *want*? I pushed a fist against the counter. "I want this to be *over*, how's that for starters? I want to know where Neese is! I want to know you're *doing* something in return for the drawing I gave you —"

"I'm doing what I can. And it's not like I can control where Neese goes."

"Did I say that? I just want to know what you're up to."

"I can't talk here."

"Great. When *can* you talk?" Call waiting clicked in my ear. I held out the receiver to check the ID. Erin's cell number. Instant concern stiffened my back. Why would she be phoning? "Milt, I need to go; I'm getting a call from the high school." Without waiting for a reply, I hit the flash button to jump over.

"Erin, hi. Are you okay?"

"Annie!" Her voice sounded breathless. "Please tell me you know. *Where's Kelly?*"

Chapter 47

The girl was still woozy, stumbling around like some Ecstasy-drugged chick. He practically had to carry her inside. She slumped against him as he dragged her through the kitchen, down the basement stairs.

Let the fun begin.

He held her up with one hand, opened the storage room door, and leaned around to flick on the one bulb—a red 40-watt. It glowed the faint color of blood.

He could just make out a few scurrying creatures on the floor.

"Okay, in you go."

The girl tried to fight as he pulled her inside. "Hey, knock it off." He grabbed a waving arm.

"No, lemme 'lone."

Her words slurred. Did she even know what she was doing? He pushed her over to a corner, then slid her to the floor. Her head lolled, hair over her face.

Too bad; it was a pretty face.

He stood up. Watched as a fly landed on her arm. He'd stocked the room with a good number as food for the spiders. Most had probably been caught by now.

Bending down, he unlaced her shoes and pulled them off, then her socks. Just to be nice, he used the socks to sweep the wall and floor around her clear of spiders. That would do—for a little while.

Outside the room, he used a key to lock her in. He wondered how long she'd take to fully wake up.

When she did, she'd be screaming.

Chapter 48

Erin's question pierced me like a poison-tipped arrow. That catch in her voice . . .

"What do you *mean*, where's Kelly? She's at school with you."

Erin dragged in a breath. "She was, but something happened. We have two classes in a row together, and during the first one someone from the principal's office came to get her. Said she had an emergency phone call. Kelly left and never came back. I picked up her backpack and took it to the next class, but she never showed up there either."

The poison leaked across my chest. "Did she leave her cell phone?"

"No, she always keeps it in her back pocket. But I called it like five times and she never answered."

Breath froze in my lungs. I blinked rapidly. *Wait a minute, Annie, just wait; there'll be an explanation.* "Maybe she's with Stephen. Did you try him?"

"Oh no, I should have. I just thought maybe you'd—"

"It's okay, I'll do it. Keep your phone on; I'll call you right back." My heart pumped dreading beats as I punched off the line. First I tried auto-dialing Kelly. Surely Erin was wrong. My daughter would pick up.

One ring. A second. Third, fourth, fifth. "Hey, this is Kelly Kingston. Leave me a message and I'll—"

"Come *on*, Kelly." I jabbed off the line, hit her auto-dial once more. Again her canned voice. The hammer against my ribs kicked into double time. I auto-dialed Stephen, silently pleading. "Do you know where Kelly is?"

Surprised silence. "Why, have you been trying to call her?"

"Stephen, don't answer my question with a question! *Do* you know where she is?"

"Here, as far as I know. What's going on? Why are you asking?"

"Because she's not there! Erin says she was called out from class for an emergency phone call and never came back."

"Wait, Mom." The words congealed. "What are you talking about?"

The tone of my voice brought Jenna to the kitchen threshold, forehead etched. Chelsea was close behind her. Tears clawed my eyes. "Kelly's missing," I blurted to them, then told Stephen what I knew. Jenna's cheeks drained to paste. Chelsea brought her hands to her mouth.

Annie, keep calm. There'll be an explanation.

"Stephen, the principal told me he'd keep an eye on Kelly. Would you go check with his office?"

"Okay, I'm walking there right now." Stephen's voice rode on puffs of air. In the background I could hear the high school hall noises of trudging feet and laughter. I threw a helpless look at Jenna. How dare anyone laugh at a time like this? "Mrs. Winger isn't here today, remember?" Stephen said. "Mike's funeral is this afternoon. So I don't know who told Kelly to come to the office. Hold on, I'm here."

Muffled noises. Stephen, talking to a female. She sounded young. My son's tone sharpened. "I can't believe you—" He cut himself off, his words clearing. "Mom, some idiot junior is filling in at the front desk. She says Kelly got a call from a detective named Tim Branch or something like that. He said there was an emergency and Kelly had to come to the phone right away. The principal wasn't in the office and this girl didn't even think to find him first. She just went and got Kelly."

Tim Blanche?

"Kelly came and talked to the man on the phone, then got real upset and ran out."

My eyes fixated on the floor, brain scrambling to concoct a reason, *any* reason, for Blanche to call my daughter without telling me. And what could he possibly say to make her run —where? Out of the school building? *Alone?*

"I picked up her backpack, but she never showed up at the next class either."

My legs weakened. I sank into a chair.

"What, *what?*" Jenna gripped the table. Chelsea lowered herself into a seat across from me, her eyes never leaving my face.

"Okay, Stephen." I forced calm into my voice. "I'll call Detective Blanche. There has to be a reason for what happened. I'll get back to you."

"Okay. Man, it better be good, scaring us like this. I'm gonna strangle that cop."

I hung up. Quickly told Jenna and Chelsea what I heard. Then with shaking fingers I blipped through incoming calls until I found Blanche's direct number. I hit the send button, barely breathing while the phone rang, my heart twisting up my throat. A voice inside my head whispered the truth, but I would not listen.

Blanche's answering machine picked up. I exhaled in panicked frustration. "He's not in his office! Jenna, would you read me the police station number?"

She strode to the refrigerator and read it off the white magnet that listed the county's emergency numbers. I dialed again.

"Redding Police Department."

"This is Annie Kingston. I need to talk to Detective Tim Blanche right away."

"All right. I'll put you through to his off—"

"No, wait, he's not in his office! Please *find* him." I closed my eyes and waited, desperate prayers filtering through my head.

Blanche came on the line. I told him what happened. "Please, Tim, *please* tell me you called her."

"Annie, I didn't call your daughter out of school. Why would I? I've been out chasing leads on Neese and just got back."

"Somebody else, then. Someone from your department."

"Look, if something like that happened, I'd know about it. Nobody's called her."

My windpipe squeezed shut. *Oh, God, no.* "Whoever called her said he was you. He got her to *leave the school*, Tim."

"All right, just hold on. We'll look for her. I'll send officers to the school. If she's not there, we'll put out an alert."

"Okay." How could I sound so calm? How could my fingers hold the phone? Alerts were for children who'd been kidnapped. Who wound up dead.

He spouted assurances I barely heard. I clicked off the line and locked eyes with my sister, my limbs icing over.

"It'll be okay." Jenna's tone belied her fright. "It's just some big mistake."

Yes, a mistake. That's all. Any minute now we'd straighten it out. I would accept any explanation, even the sick joke of some other student. *Anything.* But deep within I knew. I could feel my daughter out there somewhere, snatched away, terrified and helpless.

Praying for me to save her.

Chapter 49

Kelly swam at the bottom of a thick, dark ocean. Terrifying dreams wrapped around her chest like seaweed—a call at school, a man in a car, a dim little room … Her arms pushed through the mucky water, legs kicking. Slowly she rose. Her body felt heavy, drained. Push, kick … push, kick …

She broke the surface.

Her eyes opened.

Dim red light. Shelves on a wall. A small, dirty oval window. The smell of dust and … something. A close, buggy kind of smell. A concrete floor.

Little things crept on it.

The truth punched her in the stomach. *The spider room.*

Shock kicked through her body. Kelly jerked up straight, head pivoting. No, no, no, she *hated* spiders. Wildly she stared at the floor, the walls, the shelves. They were *everywhere.* Something tickled the back of her hand. A little white one. She screamed, shook it off.

She scrambled to her feet, running both hands up and down her legs, her arms, around her neck. Were they on her head? Her back? She shrieked and swiped herself again and again. Bent over and streaked violent fingers through her hair.

How was she here; what happened? *Oh, please, God*—her feet were bare! What if she stepped on a spider? Kelly's mind exploded. The call, the car, that man ... dragged through a kitchen, down steps, into this room ... that killer with the spiders, and the jar at her house, and those people he kidnapped, and *her mom*!

Did he have Mom too? Where was she? In another room with more spiders? Was she dead? Kelly moaned. What was that man going to *do* to them?

Panic seized her throat. She wailed and threw herself at the door, yanking at the knob. It wouldn't budge, though she rattled and pulled it. *Please, please!* It wouldn't turn, it wouldn't turn. Her nerves singed. She was locked in here; she'd be bitten to death. Her fist thudded against the wood. "Let me out! *Please.* Let me *out!*"

She begged and shrieked. Pounded and pounded and pounded ... until her hand bruised and all energy drained away. Sobbing, she sagged against the wood. This couldn't be real; how could it be happening? What if the man never came back; what if she was in here forever? What if he *did* come back—

Movement on her arm. She gasped, struck at it. A fly buzzed from her skin.

Spiders! Kelly wrenched away from the door. They could be anywhere: the walls, the floor. She couldn't touch anything. She had to stand in the middle of the room and watch her bare feet—

What if they came down from the ceiling?

She threw her head back, squinted up. Saw one crawling straight above her.

Her feet eased one sideways step. Her shoulders drew in. She brought both hands to her mouth, shuddering. She would not move from this spot.

Oh, God, where are You? Please help me! Please send somebody! Where's my mom?

Kelly cried. Cried and sobbed until her chest burned. Her knees shook, but she didn't dare sit down. How long could she stand here?

The door rattled. She sucked in air, froze.

The sound of a key in a lock. The door swung open. The man stepped inside, holding her cell phone. Kelly shrank from him, eyes wide.

He glared at her. "Stop making so much noise."

Her throat closed up. She couldn't even swallow.

His mouth twisted into a slow smile. "Well. Like your new place?"

Kelly's heart beat out of her chest. She clutched her arms, trembling.

"What's the matter, girl? Can't you talk?"

Air shook in her lungs. "Wh–who are you?" Her voice barely worked. "Why did you bring me here?"

"Who *am* I?" He barked out a laugh. "Man, the chloroform must have played with your head. Don't you remember the name Orwin Neese? A little present in a jar, left at your house?"

She stared at him, trying to make sense of it. "Please let me out."

"What's the matter, you scared of spiders?"

She nodded.

More laughter burst from him. "Oh ho, that's funny! But then, you should be. Especially of certain ones in here."

No! She looked frantically around her feet.

"Don't worry, you seem to be safe at the moment. Just watch where you step." He sniggered. "You hear the stories about that girl Amy Flyte being in here? And the man-with-no-name? They got bit by two of the deadly ones. I moved their bodies out this morning."

Kelly's muscles went cold. Any minute now she'd faint. *No, no, I can't be on the floor!* She blinked hard, trying to clear her head.

"Oh, relax, not all of them are poisonous. Some won't hurt much when they bite." He grinned. "Then again, others'll hurt so bad, you'll *wish* you were dead."

Tears spilled out of Kelly's eyes. "Where's my mom?"

"How should I know?"

She was safe? Then everything he said on the phone was a lie. "*Please* let me out; I won't tell anyone. You won't even have to take me anywhere. I'll just run away and you'll never see me again."

He sighed. "Wish I could do that."

The cell phone in his hand rang. Kelly gasped. The ring tone from home! She grabbed for it, but he yanked away. "Nuh-uh. No can do."

"Let me talk to my mom!"

His mouth drew down in fake sympathy. "Aw, you think she's worried about you? She probably doesn't even know you're missing."

Yes, she did. Mom would know. Erin would have called her by now, or Stephen or somebody. Kelly couldn't let herself believe that no one even knew she was gone. The ringing continued. "*Please* let me have it."

"Well. Tell you what." He smirked. "I'll make you a little bargain ..."

Chapter 50

M<small>Y</small> mind had turned to Styrofoam, airy and weightless. Clear thinking vanished; logic fled. In their place a cold, seeping fear. *Please, God, I can't stand this; let Kelly be all right!* Before calling Stephen back, I took a deep breath. I didn't want to sound like I'd fallen into a bottomless chasm.

He answered immediately. I told him of my conversation with Blanche.

Stephen snorted. "Like the police are going to do anything. Forget them; *I'll* find her. The principal's already put out a call over the speaker system. I'll let you know soon as I hear anything."

"Okay." *See, Annie? She's there, at school somewhere.* "Good."

"Mom, I *will* take care of my sister. Call you back soon."

The line silenced. Within half a minute the phone rang. It was the high school principal, telling me he'd checked on Kelly just thirty minutes before she disappeared. She'd been fine. He assured me all would be well. She *had* to be there. They were searching the buildings for her, and the grounds . . .

I thanked him, my voice like steel wire, and hung up.

Milt Waking called, already alerted. I didn't have the energy to talk to him. Jenna took the phone and told him what little we knew. He told her he'd do whatever possible to help.

Chelsea drew her chair close to mine, her hand on my arm. I knew she was praying. Jenna hugged me hard, then paced the kitchen like a caged lion.

Dave arrived, his face a mask of shock and dread. He'd just gotten off the phone with an hysterical Erin, who insisted Kelly wasn't anywhere on school grounds. I pressed against his chest, shaking, seeking strength. He held me, murmuring that everything would be all right.

More empty assurances.

We waited. I sat again in the kitchen chair, Chelsea on one side and Dave on the other. Jenna paced and fretted. *This is what all those parents have gone through,* I thought. Those whose children had vanished. How did they stand it when no word came? How did they *survive?* Every second flattened out, every minute an eternity ...

The projector in my head kicked on. Out spewed scenes of Kelly

pulled out a school building door and forced into a car ...

tied up, duct tape secured over her mouth ...

crying, dazed, praying for help ...

The scenes spit faster, harder, until my eyes burned and a sob rattled up my throat. And riding on that sob—sudden, clutching anger.

How could God let this happen?

I threw an accusing look at Chelsea. "Why doesn't God send you a vision right now? Tell you where Kelly is?"

She drew back, pale-cheeked, eyes full of pity. "I don't know, Annie. I wish He would."

"He *has* to. If ever He needed to show you something, it's now!"

Dave pulled me to him and stroked my hair, muttering soothing words. The anger dissipated as quickly as it came, receding tide from a barren shore.

The phone rang. Then rang again. Each time the sound jerked me up, praying to see my daughter's cell number on the ID. But no Kelly. First Chetterling called. I pleaded with him to find her. "I don't trust Tim. I know he's looking for her, but he doesn't *care* like you do, Ralph; he doesn't even *know* Kelly."

"Annie, we'll do everything, I promise you." Underneath Chetterling's authoritative words I could hear his fear. "We'll bring her back to you."

I tried dialing Kelly again. I had to. If only to hear her recorded voice, sounding well, alive ...

She didn't answer.

Blanche called, checking to see if we'd heard anything. Then Stephen. Cops had shown up at school, he said. They'd searched everywhere. Kelly wasn't there. "I'm leaving, Mom; no point in staying here."

My brain was numb. "Are you coming home?"

"No. I'm hooking up with Milt."

"*Why?*"

"Because he'll *do* something, that's why. Forget the police. He'll help me find Kelly."

"Stephen, no! You can't be running around out there; what if something happens to you too?"

"Nothing's going to happen to me. Look, I've already talked to Milt. I'm almost at the Building Department. I'll call you back as soon as I know anything."

The line went dead. Panic hit me, clear and cold. I could not lose two children at once. I jabbed in Milt's number. "What are you *thinking*? How *dare* you tell my son to leave school!"

"Annie, calm down. I didn't tell him to come; that was his own idea. Besides, I'm on to something and I could use his help. He can keep looking up things while I'm filming."

My fingers clenched the phone. I could not believe what I was hearing. "Forget filming, Milt; who *cares* about your stupid career? Just help me find my daughter!"

Call waiting clicked in my ear. I yanked away the receiver and checked the ID.

Kelly's cell number.

Chapter 51

Kelly trembled before the man, hands fisted at her throat. Her breath came in little spurts. She could feel strands of hair caught on her wet cheeks.

He held up her phone and tilted it back and forth, taunting her. It had stopped ringing. "Here's what you wanted."

She reached for it. He snatched it away. "Not so fast."

Her arm hung midair. She glanced feverishly toward the door. It stood open a few inches. Could she push past him, run for it?

"This is like jail." His voice fell into a rough whisper. "You know, you get one phone call?"

She eyed him.

Something moved on her toe. She gasped, jerked her chin down to see a long-legged spider. She screamed and shook her foot hard. The spider dropped off. Terror kicked up Kelly's throat. She had to get out of there, she had to get *out*! With a strangled cry she rushed the man, fighting like crazy. He cursed and dropped the phone, hands scrambling to capture her arms. She hit and kicked and tried to bite. He caught one of her wrists in a vise grip, then the other. Slammed her back against the door.

His mouth thrust close to hers, breathing hard. His breath stank. "You'll get out of here when I let you out, understand? It *might* help if you do what I *tell* you."

She shuddered, tried to fight again, but he held on tighter. Slowly Kelly's courage trickled away. She sagged and started to cry. "Please help me, Jesus."

His head bounced back. Disgust and blackness rolled across his face. He glared at her and she tensed. Was he going to hit her?

His teeth gritted. "Hope you didn't break your phone." Without taking his eyes from her, he scooped up the cell and flipped it open. Looked down at it. "Well, whaddya know." Kelly slid her arms across her chest. Her back and head throbbed. The man sniffed. "All right, Kelly. You ready to do things my way? Or you want me to go get some more spiders?"

Kelly. He knew her name. She swallowed, tried to find her voice. "What do you want me to do?"

"You're going to call your mom."

Hope flashed before her. "Okay."

"That's more like it. But listen carefully. You're going to say one sentence only. Is that clear?"

She licked her lips. "Please let me just talk to her. I won't tell her where I am."

He scowled. "*One sentence.* And it's going to be what I tell you. Or I'm finding the most poisonous spider in here and pushing it into your face. Got it?"

Dizziness washed over her. She managed a nod.

"Good girl. Okay. I'm going to call her and hold the phone to your ear. Here's what you're going to say." He told her the sentence. "Now. You got an auto-dial for your home number?"

"Hit two."

"Good. You ready?"

"Yes."

"Here goes." He punched the digit.

Chapter 52

I crushed the phone against my ear, hope soaring in my chest. "Kelly, where *are* you?"

"Mom!" Her voice ran raw with terror. "He put me in the spider room!"

Muffled noises. *Click.* The line fell silent.

"No, Kelly, come back. *Kelly!*" I shoved to my feet. *God, please, let me hear her.* "Kelly!"

Frantically I punched in her number, my heart slamming as I heard the rings. One, two, three, four, five. "Hey, this is Kelly Kingston. Leave me a—" I jabbed off the call, tried again. Five more rings. "Hey, this is—"

I threw my head back, cried toward the ceiling, "She's not answering!"

The world spun. *The spider room.* No. It could not be. *Kelly's in the spider room.* My mind shattered into a million pieces.

Dave caught me, lowered me back into the chair. "Annie, tell us what she said."

I bent over, sucking in oxygen. Kelly's words echoed in my ears. "She's ... there. Neese has her."

Jenna gasped. Chelsea choked *no* and murmured prayers. Dave's fingers froze around my arms. "Oh, *God.*"

My lungs crumpled in on themselves. I could not live with this knowledge. Any moment now I would stop breathing.

Kelly trapped with spiders. Kelly hated spiders as much as I did. Had she been bitten? What did Neese want with her? Why hadn't he taken *me*?

God, help her, she's just a kid. You can't let him hurt her!

Horror bubbled up in my stomach. My mental projector spun a scene of Kelly

screaming on the floor of the darkened room, flicking away a brown spider, a black one ...

I crushed my forehead into my hands, fighting to turn the picture *off*.

Jenna grabbed the phone and tried Kelly again. "No answer. We have to call the police." She punched more numbers.

A sudden thought pulled me up straight. "Wait, they can trace where she is, can't they? She called from her cell phone—"

Blanche apparently answered. Jenna spoke to him, then held the receiver out to me. I forced myself to repeat Kelly's words. Those hated, terrifying words. *Are they enough for you, Tim Blanche—you, who wouldn't listen to us? Will you finally admit the spider room exists, now that my daughter is in it?* Blanche asked me questions. Had Kelly said *I* or *we*? Did I hear anyone else's voice? "Tim, I told you everything." My mouth answered, my brain on hold, as if I'd stepped outside my body. "What about the call—can you trace it?"

Yes, eventually. Cell phone calls were connected through cell towers. In time they'd learn her approximate location.

In time? We didn't *have* time!

"We're going to do everything we can, Annie; you just hang on," Blanche clipped. "We've been getting lots of leads on Neese this morning. The Sheriff's Department is helping chase them down. We may close in on him soon."

God, please, You have to keep Kelly safe ...

I hung up the phone, a cry rattling up my throat. Dave held me, Chelsea and Jenna patting my back, my shoulder. Sick remorse washed over me and I gave in to the tears. My daughter was *gone*, and it wasn't Tim Blanche's fault. It wasn't God's fault. It was *mine*. "I should never have let her go to school," I sobbed into Dave's shirt. "I should have known to keep her home."

He soothed that I shouldn't blame myself, but his words drowned in the flood of old guilt. Hadn't I always let people down? Now my daughter would pay the ultimate price for my failure. *Kelly, what have I done to you?* "Dave, I'm an awful mother and you know it! I can't even protect my own children. Stephen and his drugs ... And I couldn't keep my marriage. I *never* measure up, even my own *father* didn't want me."

"Annie, Annie." Dave cradled my head. "You know none of that's true."

I balled the fabric of his shirt. "God, just bring Kelly back to me, *please*. I don't need anything else, ever. Just keep Kelly *safe*."

"He will, Annie." Chelsea's voice sounded hoarse. "We're going to pray for that right now. And we're going to pray for you too. Because everything you've just said is a lie from Satan. It's completely *unacceptable*."

I choked off the tears and straightened. What was I doing, collapsing like this? Kelly needed me to find her. I *had* to be strong.

Chelsea's eyes shone. She squeezed my hand. "Will you let me pray aloud for you and Kelly? Right now?"

What else could we do? I nodded.

She stood, gripped my shoulder. Dave laced his fingers tightly with mine.

"Lord, we come before You in the name of Your precious Son, Jesus, to pray for Kelly's safety. You have given us authority to come before Your throne, and oh, God—" her words cracked—"we cling to that authority now. *Please* protect Kelly. Draw a guarding circle around her to keep her safe from everything in that room. And God, let her feel Your presence. Send Your comfort, Your strengthening power to keep her calm while the police search for her. Lead them to her quickly, God, we beg You. And once she's rescued, please heal all her lingering fears ..."

Jenna choked and started to cry.

Chelsea's fingers tightened on me. She could hardly speak. "And Lord, I pray for Annie. Heal that deep, black ball of guilt and unworthiness buried inside her—the lie Satan would have her believe. Lift it up and out of her, God. Set her free."

When Chelsea finished, Dave prayed. I followed, begging God to save my daughter. Jenna's breathing shuddered. When the prayers ended, she said amen with the rest of us.

"Thank you," I whispered to Chelsea. She nodded, tears running down her cheeks.

I took a deep breath, trying to pull my thoughts together. "We have to call people. Milt and Stephen. Chetterling. And Dave, somebody needs to call the church so they can start a prayer chain."

If only Gerri Carson were in town. She'd be here now. I needed her.

We made the calls. Again and again we tried Kelly's number—to no avail. Her phone wasn't even turned on anymore. Her message kicked in after the first ring.

She'd been missing for three hours.

How could my heart beat for the next minute? The one after that?

We waited.

The phone rang. I jerked, my hand flying automatically toward the receiver. The ID read, *Ryan Burns.* I exhaled slowly, nauseous with disappointment. "Hello, Ryan."

"Annie." His voice sounded squeezed. "I've just heard about your daughter—they said her name's Kelly?"

"Yes."

"I am *so* sorry. I can't even imagine ... Look, I'm going to do whatever I can. I just got off the phone with the Police Department. I've put up a fifty-thousand-dollar reward for Kelly's safe return. The police will give the news to the media right away. Somebody's got to know something, Annie. Neese's friends will start to talk. We *will* get your daughter home."

Tears bit my eyes. "Thank you, Ryan, so very much."

"You're welcome. I'm on my way down to the police station now. I'll ride along with one of the officers, help look for her."

"All right. I really do appreciate it. I can't tell you ..."

"It's okay. I have to do *something.*"

I hung up, a tiny ray of hope shining. Fifty thousand dollars was a lot of money. If Neese had said one word to some friend ...

The seconds ticked. I fell into stillness, staring at nothing. *Kelly, where are you? Can you feel me praying for you?*

The phone rang again. I snatched up the receiver. Chetterling. "Ralph, please tell me you know something!"

"Annie, listen." His words were hurried. "It looks like we've tracked Neese down to a house out in the country."

I gasped. "Is Kelly—"

"We don't know; we're not inside yet. I just want you to hang on. If Kelly's in there, I'll do everything I can to get her out. In the meantime I need to ask you to not try calling her cell phone. I know that will be hard for you. But we don't have the number to any phone in the house yet. We only know that Neese has been using your daughter's cell. We'll be calling that number to try to establish contact with him and negotiate him out of there."

"Okay." I could barely think. "Where's the house?"

He hesitated. "Is Jenna there? I should talk to her."

"Ralph, *please*."

"Okay, just—we got a tip that led some deputies to an address out on Boyle Road. Annie, you have to hang with me now. They found a shallow grave in the woods behind the house—it's not Kelly. They think it's Amy Flyte. But Neese starting shooting. He's holed up now. I'm on my way there, and so are plenty other officers and deputies."

The news washed over me. Kelly, a hostage in a shoot-out . . . Amy already dead . . .

"What's the house number, Ralph?"

"Annie, I do *not* want you going out there. Just sit by the phone—"

"Don't *tell* me what to do!" I didn't care that I was yelling. "It's my daughter's *life*. If you don't give me the address, I'll call Milt Waking. He's probably on his way there already."

Chetterling argued, but he knew I'd hear the information one way or another. In the end he told me.

Within sixty seconds the four of us were racing to my SUV.

Chapter 53

Jenna drove, with Dave in the front passenger seat, Chelsea and me in back. My sister and I had grabbed our purses, guns inside. A desperate prayer now repeated like a mantra in my head. *God, keep Kelly safe . . .*

Following the auto's navigation system, Jenna turned south on Old Oregon Trail, headed for Boyle Road. The house lay a number of miles to the east. Our bodies swayed as Jenna attacked the curves. Dave talked to Milt on his cell phone, relaying information to the rest of us. My own phone lay gripped in my hand in the wild hope that Kelly would call again. Milt, along with his cameraman, was already driving like a crazy man toward the site. As were dozens of police and sheriff's deputy cars and a helicopter. Not to mention all the other reporters now on the story. The tip had come from someone who'd recognized my drawing of Neese on FOX News.

God, keep Kelly safe.

"Okay," I heard Dave say. Then—"Hi, Stephen."

Stephen?

Realization pushed through my prayers. My son was with Milt. Now he was headed toward a possible shoot-out with some soulless *animal* who was holding Kelly hostage. Dear God, wasn't one child at risk enough? What if Stephen was hit by a stray bullet?

"No!" I gripped the back of Dave's seat. "I don't want Stephen with Milt; I don't *want* him there."

Dave half turned, nodded. He spoke into the phone, then handed it to me. Even as I accepted it, I knew it was too late. Stephen was already in Milt's vehicle. "Mom, don't panic." Stephen's voice rapid-fired. "I'm riding with Milt in his rental car. I'll be okay. Milt's cameraman and their rented news van are already there."

"Why didn't you stay away?" My words sounded thick. "You could get hurt—"

"I'm not going to get hurt."

My head swam. "Why are you with Milt anyway; what have you been doing?"

"He sweet-talked a woman at the Building Department into helping him. She remembered seeing some plans four or five years ago for a house with an oval basement window. She was looking for the file when we heard Neese had been found."

"Oh." I could formulate no further reply. Those plans wouldn't matter now anyway.

"I'll see you soon," Stephen said and hung up.

God, please keep Kelly safe.

On the back roads off Boyle, we knew we were close. The *thwap-thwap* of a helicopter beat through the car windows. Four times Jenna yanked the SUV over to let police vehicles with blaring sirens and flashing lights whip past. My head spun at the noise, fear zinging my nerves.

Up ahead I spotted a gravel driveway splotched with official cars, more spread across a vast lawn. Officers and deputies with guns drawn hunkered behind the vehicles, all of them focused on a large two-story house with columned porch. Red and blue lights whirled. A deputy waved us over to the side of the road, about thirty feet from the driveway. "Stay back where you'll be safe!" He pointed a finger at Dave, as if commandeering him to take charge of us women.

Stay back? That was my *daughter* in there.

I stumbled from the car, looking up. Two helicopters hovered, a close one from police, and one farther away, probably from the media. From the ground someone was speaking over a megaphone. *Tim Blanche.* A megaphone meant Neese wasn't answering their calls to Kelly's cell number. Behind me, news cameras whirred. I counted four, one of them from FOX. Blanche was getting what he'd wanted—national coverage. Good for him. He could be the next star of the universe, for all I cared. *Just bring my daughter out safely, Tim, or I will never forgive you.*

Dave pulled me down behind the SUV, Chelsea and Jenna beside him.

"Orwin Neese, this is Detective Tim Blanche. We have a lot of cars out here. Come on out before somebody gets hurt."

No response. The police helicopter beat bricks of air, the acrid smell of dirt biting my nostrils. Dave gripped my arm and Chelsea prayed. Jenna cursed at Neese.

"Mr. Neese! Come on, I'm here to help you."

I held my breath, squinted at the house. The window shades were drawn. Where was Kelly?

Blanche kept talking, talking. Panic sprouted through my limbs. What if Neese had slipped away? What if he wasn't here in the first place? Who had checked this out; did these people have any clue what they were *doing*?

Chetterling. I had to talk to Chetterling.

I pushed to my feet, scrambled toward the bumper. Dave caught the end of my shirt, pulled me back. "Annie, no, you can't go over there."

Frantically I fought him. "I have to get to Ralph! Let me go!" Three times Dave grabbed for my hands; three times they flew from his grasp. When he caught them for good, he held on so tightly, my skin burned. *"Annie!"* He pushed me down, stuck his sweating face in mine. "You. Are. Not. Going. Over. There."

Air rattled in my throat. "Dave, *please*."

"No."

My face crumpled. I fell against him and wept.

Chapter 54

He crouched on the floor in front of the TV, watching the live coverage. A wide pan of the house, its expansive yard, the police cars and officers and hovering helicopter. A man's voice called through a megaphone. "Mr. Neese! Let's talk."

Fine way of talking, with all those guns pointed at the house.

Better stay away from the windows, man, even with the shades closed. You know they got a SWAT team just waiting for your shadow.

His mind whirled. What should he do? This had happened way too fast, before he'd had time to carry out his plans.

The old voices started whispering in his head.

No, no, no, chill, man. You can handle this. Think it through.

On the TV a camera shot panned over cars parked down the road. He saw sudden movement behind an SUV. The camera froze, zoomed in. It was a woman. Annie Kingston. Scrabbling. Trying to do ... something.

He watched, openmouthed. A man yanked her backward and she folded to the ground.

Annie Kingston—out there. Squinting, he leaned toward the screen. She was with at least three other people. Was one of them Chelsea Adams?

The camera panned back to the house.

Annie Kingston.

His brain scrambled for a Plan B. So many cops and deputies focused on the house, so much confusion. Talk about a diversion. He slitted his eyes at the TV, thinking ...

"Mr. Neese!" The megaphoned voice called. "We want to talk to you."

Yeah, yeah, keep on begging.

The longer they were held off, the better. He could do something. He *had* to think of another plan.

His eyes roved as he considered the beginnings of an idea ...

Yeah. Okay. If it went sour, he might have to take down some people to get to the one he wanted.

But hey, nothing in life was easy.

Chapter 55

I slumped against the car, exhausted. Stephen had made his way over to us and now stood between me and Dave. Tim Blanche called Neese to no avail. I knew the officers and deputies wanted to move in. Would they have, if not for Kelly? One false move and my daughter could lose her life.

Please, God, just keep her safe.

If only they could spot Neese through a window, but all the shades remained closed. SWAT team members had positioned themselves around the property. If one of them could take Neese out, he would. Or if they could sneak inside the house through some back way and overpower the man …

Fifty yards down the road Milt yakked at the FOX News camera. "Mom—" Stephen gestured toward him—"he's going to be done filming soon. But he wanted me to tell you something important. This house was obviously built a long time ago."

"So?" Jenna squatted on the ground, facing me.

"The building plans with the oval window that woman was looking for?" Stephen spoke rapidly. "That house wouldn't be more than five years old."

My breath hitched. I shifted to my knees, peeked at the house through the car windows. The others did the same. Was there a third level in the back like our home? The lot looked flat as far as I could tell. I sat down hard, my neck tingling. "Doesn't look like there's a lower level."

"Maybe there is." Dave kept his voice annoyingly calm. "The basement could be all underground, with a window in back and the dirt cut away from it, like Chelsea saw. We only assumed the part about the sloping lot."

I focused on Milt. He was lowering his microphone. "This place is surrounded. If we could get to Chetterling, have him radio someone who's positioned in back and ask if there's a window—"

"I'll go ask."

"Stephen, no!"

But he darted around the car, bent low, before I could stop him. The four of us pushed halfway erect, peering through the car windows as he crabwalked to the row of official vehicles lining the driveway. An officer ordered him back. Stephen ignored him. He neared Chetterling, called something. Ralph whipped around, took in my son's wild gesticulations. With a glance at the house, he hurried, bent over, to Stephen. I watched them talk in a crouch, straining to hear their words when I knew it was impossible. *God, where is Kelly? Is she in there?* I couldn't even decide which would be worse—knowing Neese held her hostage in a surrounded house, or having no idea where the spider room was located. Either way she could *die.*

God, please!

"Chelsea, do you think she's here?"

She sank her fingers into my arm. "I don't know, Annie. I wish I did."

Ralph heard Stephen out, then spoke into his radio. A moment later he said something to Stephen.

Stephen scurried back to us. "No oval window," he puffed. "They're sure of it."

"Oh, God, help; then she's not there?" I sagged to my knees, Dave beside me. Jenna murmured something and ran down the road toward Milt. My brain turned vaporous, all oxygen sucked from my lungs. The next thing I knew, a stern-faced Tim Blanche had hunkered down to look me in the eye. "Annie, I *cannot* have your son running around here. He's likely to get himself killed."

"Hey!" Stephen shot back. "I was—"

"I don't care *what* you were doing. I don't want you in the way."

"We wouldn't *be* here if you'd protected my sister in the first place!" Stephen crouched like a wildcat ready to spring at the detective's throat. "You can't even get Neese to talk, so what good are you?"

"Stephen," I breathed, "don't—"

Blanche flapped a hand at me. His cheeks flushed scarlet as he glared at my son. "I don't need you to tell me how to do my job. Now all of you, go home. We'll call you with any news."

Anger tore through my veins. One more word from this man and I'd hit him. "*News*, Tim? You *told* me my daughter would be safe at school. Now she's been kidnapped, and you want me to just leave and wait for you to call? Why should I listen to you? You never listened to *us*, and now one girl's already dead!" Dave clamped a hand on my arm, but I took no heed. I only listed farther toward Tim, my anger smacking like waves against the brick wall of his pride. "We *told* you about that room and the spiders. Now my daughter's trapped there, and you *want me to just go home?*"

Dave put his arm around me, drew me back. "Annie, stop."

Blanche clenched his teeth. "I know this is hard for you. Maybe it'll help if you hear what I think. I don't believe there *is* a spider room. I think you two—" he waved a finger between Chelsea and me—"started this thing, and Neese picked up on it after reading about it in the paper. So he leaves a jar of spiders at your house as a taunt. We still don't have one iota of proof that the room exists."

What? This was supposed to *help?* My anger drained away, replaced by a ball of ice deep in my gut. I stared at Blanche, jaw unhinged, implications ricocheting through my brain. Was he actually refusing to admit the truth, just to save his own hide? What would that mean for my daughter? "Kelly called me, Tim. She *told* me she was in that room."

His jaw flexed. "Maybe so. Or maybe it was just a teenage prank; we don't know yet. We've tried and tried to call that number, and no one's picked up, so we can't even be sure Neese has the phone." He shook his head. "Look, if he is trapped in there and Kelly's really with him, he'll use her as a hostage. We'll hear about it."

"Haven't you already been treating this as a hostage situation?" Dave threw at him. "You haven't gone storming in there."

Blanche looked at him like he was an idiot. "We haven't gone storming in there because he's got a gun, and I don't want any of my men killed. But he'd better start talking to us soon." Blanche's face flattened. "Annie, all I'm saying is, don't be so sure you know everything. You were already wrong about that drawing you brought to me. Give us some credit. We're doing the best we can. But you're in the way.

Go *home*." He pushed to his feet with a final, hard look at Stephen and hurried off.

Chelsea watched him go, stunned. Stephen threw a curse at his back. I couldn't move, couldn't *think*. I pressed a hand against my forehead, staring at a pebble at my feet.

"Mom—" Stephen grasped my arm—"forget him. There's no oval window back there. Neese may be in that house, but I don't think Kelly is."

I raised my head, feeling the weight of it, the weakness of my neck. Logic had abandoned me. Vaguely I focused down the road at Milt Waking. He was talking with animation on his cell phone, Jenna leaning in close to him. He said something to Jenna, then fished wildly in his pocket for pen and paper. She took them and wrote something down. Milt flipped shut the phone, grabbed Jenna's elbow and propelled her in a run toward us.

"Guess what," Stephen sneered as they pulled up beside us. "That cop doesn't even think the spider room exists."

Jenna's eyes widened. Milt waved a hand, his expression tight with anticipation. "It doesn't matter. I just got the address of the building plans for that house with the oval window." He read off the piece of paper: "2378 Scander Lane. Jane—that's the woman at the department—said the rendering of the rear view clearly shows the window. I convinced her to take a close-up picture of it with her camera phone and send it right over. We should get it in a minute."

"Scander Lane." Dave's eyes roved. "That's outside of town on the west side." He looked straight at Chelsea. "You still absolutely convinced we need to look for that window?"

"Yes." She didn't hesitate. "I'm certain."

A tone sounded from Milt's phone. "There it is!" He flipped open the phone. "Okay, wait a minute." He punched a few buttons, ogled the display, then thrust it in Chelsea's face. "Is that the window?"

Chelsea took the phone and focused intently on the picture. I leaned in for a look, saw the upper half of the window above ground, the top of a semicircular retaining wall made of stone. *Oh, God, please tell us something.* Chelsea pulled in a breath. She looked into my eyes, her face pale.

"Annie, this is it. This is where we'll find Kelly."

Chapter 56

Kelly stood in the middle of the room, shaking violently. The awful man had come back. He was staring at her—and smirking. Any minute now her legs would give out and she'd fall to the floor. How many spiders would she land on? She couldn't bear to look.

The man sniffed. "You get bit yet?" He spoke in that raspy whisper.

Yet. How long before that happened? Nausea ate at Kelly's stomach. *I'm still standing, I'm still standing.* She shook her head.

He swatted at a fly. "Well, only a matter of time."

Kelly whimpered. "Please, let me out."

"So you can do what? Run home and tell Mommy all about me?"

"I–I won't tell anyone. I promise. Just let me *go.*"

"Don't you *get* it, girl?" He shook his head. "You're here till you die."

No, God, please. She swallowed hard. "Why are you doing this?"

He scowled at her. "I'll ask the questions, got it? Is Chelsea Adams still hanging around with your mom?"

Chelsea? How would he even know her? "I don't know. I think so."

"You're going to have to do a little better than that."

Kelly's breath shuddered. Her brain felt so twisted, she could barely think. "She was at the house when I left for school. Her car was supposed to be ready sometime today. That's all I know."

He blinked slowly at her feet. "Was she supposed to leave after she got her car?"

"Yeah. She was going home."

His shoulders tensed. "Really." He pulled the door open.

Fresh terror seized her throat. "Please don't leave me in here!"

He gave her a long look, his face like stone. "Sorry I had to use you for bait. You're a pretty girl and you don't deserve it." He took a step, stopped, then turned back. "By the way. That spider near your toe?" He pointed. "It'll kill ya."

She jerked her head down and screamed.

Chapter 57

Chelsea's words stabbed through me. I clutched Dave's arm, a dozen questions zinging through my mind. Was Neese not here, then, trapped in the house behind us? Or had he left some accomplice to guard Kelly in the oval window house? Was she locked in there—by herself? Could we *save* her?

Sights and sounds blurred around me: Blanche calling through the megaphone; the *thwap, thwap* of the helicopter; the sea of official cars and officers; Jenna and Stephen and Chelsea all talking at once. "We have to call the Sheriff's Department," I blurted. "They have to help us get Kelly."

"Let's go." Dave barked the words, his expression hardened with determination. "We'll call for help on the way."

We scrambled for our cars. Stephen ran back to Milt's car, the reporter yelling for his cameraman to "Leave the truck and come with us!" I hurried into the SUV with Dave, Chelsea, and Jenna, my sister driving again. She smacked the car into gear, surged into a U-turn. As we passed the other media, I caught a glimpse of their suspicious faces, as if they worried we were on to a major part of the story they would miss.

Jenna bent over the wheel, shoulder blades jutting beneath her shirt. Dave twisted around toward me. Sweat shone on his forehead, his fingers gripping the back of the seat. "Annie, *you* call the Sheriff's Department. We have to explain how we know Kelly's not in the Boyle Road house with Neese. If they'll listen to anybody, it's you."

I fumble-punched the number, prayers filtering through my head. Dispatch put me through to Ed Grange, one of the few deputies who hadn't been called out to capture Neese. I tore through the information, voice frantic, until he told me to slow down and start over.

"It's Kelly, my daughter." My words shook. "She's locked up in this horrible little room and we know where it is now. She's *not* in the house with Neese. She's in another house to the west of town. We're on our way there now and we need help."

"You mean that room with the spiders?" Ed, an older deputy, spoke so infuriatingly *slowly.*

"Yes. We know that room has an unusual small oval window, and now we've found the house where it is."

A pause. "How do you know it has an oval window?"

Oh, God, please. "Chelsea Adams saw it in her vision."

"Oh." Another pause. "Wait. I thought Ms. Adams said Orwin Neese had taken Kelly."

I gritted my teeth, explanations tumbling crazily. "Chelsea didn't say that, but Kelly called and said, 'He put me in the spider room,' and we know Neese had the spiders, but now Neese is surrounded in a house on Boyle Road, and that house doesn't have an oval window, and we know Kelly's in a room with the window, and now we know where that room is!" I gulped a breath. Surely I sounded like a blabbering idiot. "Look, we *know* she's there. Maybe the house belongs to some accomplice of Neese's who's guarding her. We need help getting her out! We *can't* go into this situation alone."

"Okay, okay; what's the address?"

My mind went blank. I asked Jenna, who spouted it immediately.

We flew around a curve. I hit the door, bumping my elbow. "It's 2378 Scander Lane."

Silence. "Say again?"

I repeated it. *Come on, come on.* Dave was still half turned toward me, listening. Chelsea perched forward, pasty knuckles wrapped around the back of Jenna's seat.

"Annie," Ed said, "careful now. Tell me that address—one more time."

What was *wrong* with him? I spat it out.

"There's no way." His tone dropped. "You have to be wrong."

"We're not wrong! Ed, *please.*" Tears scratched at my eyes.

"Look, I want to help you. But *that* address? I can't send a bunch of armed deputies out there just because it has some window your friend claims she saw in a vision. I'd lose my job for sure. How do you know the window's in that house anyway?"

"Milt Waking found—"

"Doesn't matter. I can't do it. Not unless a supervisor okays it, and right now everybody's busy capturing Neese. Who's *supposed* to have your daughter, by the way."

I gripped the phone, disbelief closing my throat again. After all the work I'd done with the Sheriff's Department, they didn't *trust* me?

"Annie, you listening? Please don't go out there and do anything foolish. I tell you I know that house. It's protected to the hilt. You so much as rattle a window, it'll set off the alarm, plus buzz a pager in the owner's pocket. Then you'll have some *real* explaining to do."

I couldn't be hearing this. There had to be a mistake—somewhere. "Ed, I'm begging you to believe me. *Whose* house is it?"

He cleared his throat. "Not house, Annie. More like an estate. And it belongs to Ryan Burns."

Chapter 58

So Chelsea Adams thought she'd skip town, huh? Go back to her Bay Area house, where she could dream up more visions about him. A little more time and she'd get it all right.

Think again, Mrs. Adams.

He perched on the top basement step, Kelly's cell phone in his hand. He'd turned the thing off long ago; its incessant ringing was driving him nuts. The megaphoned voice of Detective Blanche filtered into his ears. Guy had been on television half the morning—first interviews and now live coverage. His ego must be sky-high, with all those cameras on him.

"Mr. Neese! Please answer the cell phone you were using. We've been trying to call you."

Fat chance.

He opened his palm, stared at the phone. With one finger he scratched his chin, thinking. This plan would be last-ditch, all right. But with all the chaos it was now or never. If he let that woman get away ...

Abruptly he pushed to his feet and hurried to watch the TV. He saw more close-ups of officers and their cars, aerial shots of the whole mess. The entire world seemed to have stopped, the station showing nothing but the stakeout.

"Mr. Neese!" the megaphoned voice called.

How much longer would they wait before busting down doors?

Man, you better do this now.

Chapter 59

I lowered the phone and stared at it. Emotions unwound and writhed in my stomach—shock ... disbelief ... denial ... fresh terror.

"What did he say?" Dave twisted in his seat to search my face, gripping the headrest for support as Jenna sped around a curve. *Slow down, stop*, I wanted to tell her. *We have the wrong house!* But my tongue lay like stone.

"Annie!" Dave's voice tightened. "What did he tell you?"

My finger found the exit button on the cell phone. I clicked off the line, let the thing slide to the floor. My brain searched frantically for logic and found none. "Jenna. Pull over."

She threw me a look in the rearview mirror. "Why?"

"Pull *over*." I turned to motion to Milt's car behind us.

Jenna veered to what little shoulder the road possessed and we slid to a halt. Milt followed. Dave, Chelsea, and Jenna all leaned toward me, faces tense.

I drew a breath. "We have the wrong address." My voice sounded dry, dead. "That house on Scander Lane belongs to Ryan Burns."

Silence. Jenna gawked at me.

"Ryan Burns?" Chelsea's jaw went slack. "That man I met at the police station?"

"Yes. And the one who just put up fifty thousand dollars for Kelly's safe return. He's out somewhere right now with an officer, trying to find her. He told me that on the phone."

Dave blinked hard, as if searching for any detail that made sense. "The deputy just told you it's Ryan's house?"

"Yes."

"He's *sure*?"

"Yes."

We all breathed, in and out, in and out. Chelsea stared hollowly at her lap. Behind us car doors slammed.

"Chelsea?" Dave said. "You *knew* that oval window was the one. Right?"

She nodded.

Stephen skidded up to my door, tugged it open. "What's the matter; why did we stop?"

My brain threatened to burst open. Time was ticking. My daughter still prayed for rescue in some horror-filled room, and once again we didn't know how to find her. "Everybody out!" I pushed Chelsea toward the door, wrapped my fingers around Dave's arm. "Right now! We have to talk about this; we have to figure out what to *do*."

We scrambled out, huddling off the road like pursued convicts. Ed Grange's words tumbled from my mouth. "Now what do we do? Kelly can't be with Ryan. I *know* him; he wouldn't do this to me."

"You've been wrong before, Mom." Stephen stood beside me, his expression dark, sweat trickling down his temple.

"But not this time."

"I agree." Jenna dug fingers into her hair. "It can't be Ryan. We've gone off somewhere."

I leaned toward Milt, grasped his wrist. "Maybe there's a local builder who uses that oval window as a sort of signature. Maybe there's five, ten, a dozen homes in the area with windows exactly like it."

"Could be." He surveyed the ground, looking miserably disappointed.

"The builder's name should be on those plans," Dave told him. "Call your friend at the department, ask her who it is. Maybe we can track him down."

Maybe, but how *long* would it take? I rubbed my forehead, pleading with God for something, something ... Chelsea hadn't said a word. One hand lay at the back of her neck, her brows knit. I touched her arm. "Please *tell* us something! You've got to know. Is Kelly back at that house with Orwin Neese after all?"

She looked at me, pain in her eyes. Slowly she shook her head. "Not unless there's—"

A cell phone rang. Muffled, from inside the SUV. *Whose?* I jerked around, head cocked, listening. Another ring. "It's mine."

I sprang for the car door, threw it open. Half fell upon the seat, fingers scrabbling toward the floor for the phone. *God, let it be Kelly. Or Chetterling, with good news* ... I felt the cell's rectangular hardness, snatched it up to check the ID—and read my daughter's number.

Chapter 60

Kelly's bare feet throbbed. She shivered in the middle of the little room, shoulders drawn in, hands fisted at her stomach. Her desperate gaze roved the floor around her, looking for spiders. If only she had something, any little thing, to flick them away—

A tickling on her head. Kelly shrieked, flicked a palm across the top of her hair. A large black spider whisked down, landed on her leg. She screamed again, batting at it with both hands. "Get off, get *off*!" It fell to the floor, then scuttled toward her feet.

"*No!*" Kelly shuffled backward, then whipped her head around. What if she stepped on one? What if another one dropped down from the ceiling? Where was the one by her feet? What was that on her arm?

The black one reached her toe. She squealed and kicked it away. Frantically she ran her hands over her arms, her legs. *They're everywhere, they're all over me, they're going to bite me, I'm going to die!*

With a wail she threw herself at the door once more. "Let me out! *Please! Let. Me. Out!*" She banged it and kicked it and tore at the knob. "Please, let me *out!*"

Kelly sobbed and pleaded until her throat rawed and the words ran dry. She sagged against the door, exhaustion flooding her. She needed to lie down. She needed sleep. Even for just ten minutes ...

Her eyelids drooped.

What was that?

Her eyes flew open. A spider—by her cheek. "Aah!" She jerked her face away from the wood, jumped back. *Oh no, the floor.* Now she had to check it again ... And the ceiling ... Then the floor again ...

Her vision blurred. She looked up, down, behind her, trying to see through fresh tears. Then turned in a cautious circle. Searching. Praying. *God, please, let somebody find me. Let someone find me soon ...*

Chapter 61

It's Kelly!" I jabbed on the line. Jenna gasped. Everyone crowded in, hope and fear quivering the air. I leaned forward, smashed the cell phone against my ear. "Kelly? Kelly, where are you?"

A chuckle. "Annie Kingston." The same low voice grated every nerve in my body.

Oh, God, no. This could not be Ryan Burns. "Where's Kelly, Orwin? I want to *talk* to her!"

"She's alive and well. I'm gonna make this quick, so you better listen if you want her back. Is Chelsea Adams with you?"

Chelsea? My heart slammed against my ribs. "Yes, but *please*, I want to know Kelly's okay; let me—"

"If you don't listen," he hissed, "you'll never see your daughter again. *Do you hear?*"

"I ... yes."

"All right." He drew a breath, spoke rapidly. "As you know, I'm rather indisposed at the moment. Policemen are everywhere. But your daughter's not here. Now that I'm trapped, I'm thinking if I let her free, maybe the cops will go easier on me. Besides, I got a friend who could use that fifty-thousand-dollar reward. So bighearted me just told him where Kelly is. But he's dicey about all this and doesn't want any trouble. So here's the deal. Tell Chelsea to drive your car—alone—heading north on Tory Road, west of Redding. Go two miles. When she sees a falling-down old red barn on her right, she stops. Gets out of the car and opens every door, plus the back. My friend will have binoculars. When he sees nobody hiding in the car, he'll come out and give Chelsea a key and directions. The key will open an old warehouse and the room inside it where Kelly is. No use trying to find this place on your own. You don't follow these instructions, the guy will split and you'll never see Kelly again. This is your *one* chance. Got it?"

"Yes, *yes*."

"Good. The guy will be wearing a sweatshirt with a hood. Chelsea's not to look at his face. When this is all over, and he's sure he won't get in trouble, he'll come forward for the reward. You want your daughter back, tell Chelsea to be there in twenty minutes."

Click.

I lowered the phone in shock.

"Mom—" Stephen leaned down and shook me—"what happened?"

Adrenaline catapulted through my veins. Kelly was alive. We could bring her *home*. My back straightened. "We have to go. Now."

Amazingly, no one would get in the car without an explanation. I could have strangled them all. I stumbled out, shook Jenna by the shoulders. Words spurted from me—where Chelsea was supposed to go, what she was supposed to do. Tears raked my eyes and my voice shook. But as I repeated Neese's commands, reality hit. Wait a minute. Why did Neese want *Chelsea* to do this—alone?

And how could I possibly ask her to go?

Jenna screwed up her face. "Why did he ask for Chelsea; why not you?"

"Annie—" Dave looked appalled—"that's far too dangerous. We don't know who this guy is. No way can we let her do that."

Chelsea only stared, pale-faced. Her gaze fell to the ground and she drew away from us. Her lips moved in silent prayer.

Everyone else started talking at once. "Wait, wait!" Milt held up both hands. "None of this makes sense; we have to think it through."

"I know it sounds crazy," I cried, "but we don't have *time* to think it through. Chelsea's supposed to be there in less than twenty minutes!"

Jenna pushed past me toward the car. "Annie, give me a second. I think I know where Tory Road is."

She scrambled into the front passenger seat and punched something into the navigation system. Stephen ran around and climbed into the driver's seat to watch. Up popped a map, an address marked in a red bull's-eye. Jenna sucked in a breath. "Look! I put in the Scander Lane address and it's only a couple miles from Tory Road. In fact, that lane turns off Tory. Maybe that *is* the house."

"Yeah." Stephen jabbed a finger at the screen. "Can't be coincidence. She's gotta be there."

My throat threatened to close. "But that's Ryan's house. She *can't* be there. Neese said she's in an old warehouse."

"Why should we believe him?" Milt swiped his arm through the air. "We can't believe *anything* he says, including this latest scheme about Chelsea and some key. Whole thing sounds like a setup to me."

The minutes were ticking away. I wanted to scream. "We don't have a choice but to believe him. I just want to get Kelly!"

Dave held my shoulders. "We all want to get Kelly. But we can't send Chelsea into danger."

I knew that. I *did*. But my daughter needed us ...

Something in the very core of me turned over, went cold. I bent low, dropped my head in both hands. *God, help me! I don't know what to do!* A sob rattled up my throat.

Someone touched my hands gently. Pulled them away. I straightened, blinking.

Chelsea.

I looked into her eyes. She was shaking. Literally shaking. She opened her mouth, tried to speak, but the words caught. She firmed her lips, tried again. "Annie." Her whisper sounded barren, as if she stared death itself in the face. "God just ... I understand now. And—heaven help me—you're right. I have to go."

Chapter 62

Chelsea dug her fingers into the leather of the backseat. Every muscle felt stiff enough to crack. *God, I don't know how I'm going to do this.*

No one spoke. Jenna was pushing the speed limit, even as the arch of her shoulders belied her dismay of their plans. They'd driven through town and now were in a rural area again, on Redding's west side. Dave cupped his chin, vacantly watching the road. Annie had moved to the center of the backseat, one hand firmly on Chelsea's arm. Dread and despairing hope fell from her like molten drops. Chelsea knew Annie had everything to say—and could say nothing.

"It's okay," Chelsea managed to whisper and patted her hand.

Tears trickled down Annie's cheeks.

Dave puffed out air. "Look, I can't ... There's got to be another way to do this."

"Yeah." Jenna's voice was hard. "There's seven of us and one of him. I could take this guy all by myself. I'll just hike in, me and my gun."

"He'll have binoculars." Annie wearily wiped her eyes. "He'll see you way before you see him."

No doubt Annie was right. The man had probably chosen an open area where he could see for some distance. Plus the SUV's navigation system showed Scander Lane—a dead end—as the only turn off Tory Road. No one was going to sneak up on this man. Not them, and certainly not any sheriff's deputy in a car.

"We need to call 911." Dave turned to look at Chelsea, his mouth set. "I'm not going to let you do this, no matter what you say. 911 *has* to respond. We should have called them in the first place—forget talking to some deputy behind a desk." He reached for his cell phone.

"No!" Annie grabbed his arm. "Dave, we've already been over this three times. If deputies show up, they'll scare the guy away for sure. We'll *never* find out where Kelly is."

Sudden panic bubbled within Chelsea. Dave was right; she shouldn't go out there alone. Imagine if Paul knew. He'd *never* let her do this.

God, maybe I heard You wrong. There has to be some other way . . .

She closed her eyes. Waited.

Please . . .

The knowledge deep within her didn't budge.

Psalm 56 rose in her mind: *"When I am afraid, I will trust in you. In God, whose word I praise, in God I trust; I will not be afraid . . ."*

She swallowed down the fear. "Jenna, how much farther?"

"About three miles."

"Okay." Chelsea's mouth spoke as if from someone else's body. Memories of her visions, the closing walls of the dim spider room, snatched at her breath.

"For You have delivered me from death and my feet from stumbling, that I may walk before God in the light of life ..."

"There it is. The turn for Tory Road." Jenna pulled the car over. Milt parked behind them.

Chelsea pressed her palms together, brought them to her lips. *"When I am afraid, I will trust in You ..."*

Dave surveyed her. "This isn't right. I can't let you do it."

Yes, Dave, Chelsea wanted to scream, *please don't let me!* Annie's words from last Saturday—was that only two days ago?—echoed in her head. *"If we knew everything up front, we'd be too scared to walk off that cliff ..."*

Now she knew it all. Far more than she would tell them.

But she *would* walk off that cliff.

Chelsea forced herself to look Dave in the eye. "God wants me to do this. He'll be with me. I know it's frightening, but I'm going to trust Him. I *will* be safe. We have our plans. I'll be back with that key in no time. And if for some reason I'm not ... you know what to do."

They argued ... and argued some more. But Chelsea knew one thing—if God truly wanted her to place herself at the mercy of this man, He'd smooth the way so it could happen. Hadn't He brought them through everything else so far?

She won the argument.

Chelsea pushed her cell phone beneath the driver's seat. She was supposed to call Annie as soon as she was driving away with the key.

If only she could make the call.

They took a precious minute to pray. Another to gather sturdy pieces of wood from the surrounding area. These they threw into the trunk of Milt's car, beside Bill's camera.

Then with a final hug to Annie, Chelsea climbed into the driver's seat of the SUV.

Alone.

Chapter 63

There she comes.

His body tensed as the SUV came in sight around a curve. About time; she was almost ten minutes late. He lay on his belly, uphill from the narrow road, scanning the countryside through binoculars. Sweating bullets in the sweatshirt. As if his walk in the heat hadn't been bad enough. After all this trouble, he'd better pull this thing off.

Chill, man, you want the dirt ants to start? Think about ... something else.

Yeah, like wasn't this kind of whacked out? The woman had visions, said they were from God. So where was her God now? How come He was letting her walk into a trap?

The car pulled even with the old red barn. Stopped. Chelsea Adams got out. He fixed the binoculars upon her.

Wow. Pictures didn't do her justice. This woman was *fine.*

She left her door ajar. One by one opened all the others, plus the hatchback. She backed away from the car, head bent, focused on the road.

He peered at the front seat. *Check.* At the rear. *Empty.* In the back. He moved his head right, left, making sure he saw no still form. Then scanned the countryside once more. All clear.

Pum, pum, chaka-laka-laka. Here goes.

Chapter 64

I perched in the backseat of Milt's car, half on top of Dave. Jenna and Stephen were squeezed in with us. Milt sat in the front passenger seat, his cameraman, Bill, driving. I could barely breathe. My brain lay buried in rubble, dazed and bewildered. Stephen, Jenna, and Milt all insisted the close proximity of Tory Road and Scander Lane was no coincidence. I *knew* Kelly could not be in Ryan Burns's house, but I had no energy to argue.

Wherever she was, I just wanted her back.

Milt bristled with energy. Every word he spoke was clipped. "It's been five minutes."

Five minutes—the planned time for Chelsea to be starting her drive up the south end of Tory Road. And soon we should see the turn onto its north end.

"There it is!" Milt jabbed his finger toward the window.

Please, God, let everything work.

Now the next step. In about three minutes Chelsea should reach the barn. An estimated three more to receive the key, climb back in the car ...

Stephen checked his watch. "Okay, I'm counting down the six minutes."

Bill turned on Tory Road and we headed south. Milt leaned toward Bill, neck straining. Aloud he noted each tenth of a mile. "Eight . . . nine . . . one mile. Slow down; we should see Scander Lane soon." He peered ahead as we rounded a curve. "Whoa, there's the lane. Back up, back up!"

Bill stopped the vehicle, shoved into reverse. The car shot backward, then slowed. Milt had his door open before we stopped rolling. "Okay, I'm out of here."

I leaned forward, scanning through the windshield. "You sure we backed up enough?"

"You can't see the lane; nobody on the lane can see you." Milt clambered outside.

"Keep low!" Jenna called, but he was gone.

Bill rolled down his window. Milt's door remained open. Dave squeezed my hand. "You okay?"

I'll never be okay until Kelly's safe. I nodded.

Stephen held his watch close to his face. "Three and a half minutes left."

Maybe less, if things went faster than we thought. I shifted my legs. Heart rattling, I opened the hand that held my cell phone. Stared at it, waiting, *pleading* for it to ring. Jenna, Stephen, and Dave watched too, as if our singular focus would laser an urging force to Chelsea, enable her to make the call early.

Come on, come on . . .

Chapter 65

Cautiously he pushed to his feet. His eyes flicked from Chelsea Adams to the road, left and right. Nobody around. He eased his way down the hill. Chelsea never moved. Brave woman. He hit the road about twenty feet behind her, cat-footing it up close enough to touch her shoulder. "Don't turn around."

She jumped, her body going taut. Her head remained down. "Where's the key?"

He snarled at the steadiness in her tone. What, she wasn't scared enough at his stealthy approach? The bad boy whisper? "Shut up."

Suddenly he felt a thousand eyes at his back. He whipped his head left, right, behind him. Saw nothing.

Chill out.

He pulled a small jar from his sweatshirt's left pocket. Reached out to stick it in front of her face. She caught sight of the huge spider and her breath hitched. "See this? It's one of the world's deadliest. You don't do what I say, this thing goes down your back."

Her head nodded.

"Get in the car."

She hesitated.

"Get in the car!" He shoved her spine. "You're driving."

She moved, looking straight ahead. He veered off toward the passenger side. As he slid inside the SUV, he pulled the sweatshirt hood further over his face. Just to remind her, he raised the spider jar in his left hand.

She put the car in gear. "What makes you think you can get away with this?"

"Cut the comments!" He glared sideways at her. This woman was just a little too sure of herself. *We'll see how long that lasts.* "Go down and turn on the only road you'll see."

He turned to check behind them for cars. All clear. "How come Annie Kingston let you come out here all alone?"

She firmed her mouth. "She wants her daughter back. Not something *you* would understand."

He snorted. *Just wait till I get you in that room, Chelsea Adams.* She could have all the visions she wanted there. Yeah, she could see herself *die.* That gave him a laugh.

She turned right on Scander Lane. After a mile, his long, graceful driveway beckoned up ahead. "Turn left there." She made the turn, drove over and down a hill. The mansion swept into view. He pulled a remote from his right pocket and punched the button. The garage door slid up. "Drive in."

He pictured Kelly, shivering in the basement. Girl had better do like he'd told her.

Chelsea parked, turned off the engine. It occurred to him he'd have to take the car for a middle-of-the-night drive, send it into Shasta Lake. Too bad. It was a fine automobile.

He punched the garage door closed. Turned toward Chelsea Adams and slid off his hood. "Welcome to my humble abode."

Chapter 66

Two minutes, fifteen seconds."

I could not stand this. My mouth had run dry, air scraping my throat.

Jenna thumped her knee with a fist. "Bill, can you see Milt?"

"Yeah. He's lying down. Stretching his neck just enough to see around the corner, I think."

Chelsea had insisted that Milt watch Scander Lane, "just in case." Not that we needed to. In a few minutes she would come barreling down the road ...

"One minute, thirty seconds."

Oh, Kelly, my beautiful daughter. I pressed fists to my mouth, felt the cut of teeth against my lips. Was she still safe? Could she feel how close we were to rescuing her?

The car felt suffocating. I sucked in a breath, fingers gripping the phone.

"Thirty seconds ... twenty." Stephen's right leg jiggled. I closed my eyes. *Please.*

"Time's up," Stephen snapped. "She should be calling."

I stared at the phone. Tension vibrated from Jenna's body to mine. "Come *on.*" I shook my cell. *"Ring."*

Dave squeezed my knee. Apprehension rolled off him in waves. I knew he was thinking that he never should have let Chelsea go, that he'd never forgive himself if something happened.

Stephen exhaled in frustration. "Now she's over a minute late."

I prayed.

The phone remained silent.

God, why is this taking so long? What have we done?

Bill slapped the dashboard. "Hey, Milt's running back!"

We jerked up our heads, pushed to our knees. Milt slid to his open door and threw himself in the car. Swiveled toward me, breathing hard. "I just saw your SUV turn up Scander Lane."

Chapter 67

Chelsea's legs jellied as he pushed her down the stairs. She could *feel* the black spider at her back, scrambling in its jar, waiting to be unleashed. What was she doing; why had she let him bring her here?

God, where are You?

She hit the bottom of the steps and stumbled. He grabbed her arm, jerked her up. She gasped at his touch.

"Not so brave anymore, are you." His guttural whisper grated her ears. Strong fingers dug into her skin. "See that door?"

No. Not the door, not the room behind it. Terror clattered down Chelsea's spine. Her ankles shook.

"So much for talking to God, huh." He laughed. "Looks like the Big Guy hung you out to dry this time."

She licked her lips, tried to swallow.

He pushed her forward. Tipped back his head and yelled at the door. "Kelly!"

Silence. Chelsea raked in a breath.

A tear-filled voice muffled through the wood. *"Please let me out."*

Kelly! Chelsea's shoulders convulsed. She pushed down a sob.

The man rapped on the door. "Remember what I told you to do in there, girl?"

"Y – Yes."

"Good. Do it."

"I don't want to sit down, *please.*"

"Shut up and do what I told you!"

Chelsea cringed. *Oh, Kelly. Having to sit on that floor. God, help her, protect her . . .*

He pointed to Chelsea's feet. "Take your shoes and socks off."

Bare feet against a cold floor . . . Slowly she bent over and did as she was told.

"There you go." He smiled at her, a smile that cut to her soul. With a flourish he unlocked the door. Sank his fingers into Chelsea's arm and yanked her into the dim room. There, on the floor. Kelly, shivering, knees drawn up, head down. Joy and terror shattered like glass in Chelsea's brain. She fought to say something to Kelly, but her throat closed up.

When we are afraid, we will put our trust in You. In God, whose word we praise. In God we trust . . .

"All right, Chelsea Adams," the man sneered. "Don't try any two-against-one stupidity. She's been warned. She sits like that without a word, or this spider goes down your shirt." He held up the jar.

Like some sleepwalker, Chelsea nodded. Her heart tremored. She dropped her jaw open, sucked in oxygen.

A slow, vindictive smirk twisted his features. He closed the door and faced her with smug anticipation.

Chapter 68

In the backseat of Milt's rented car, I hung on to Dave. My mind scattered in a thousand fragmented thoughts. Could Kelly's captor really be Ryan Burns? How? *Why?* Had he posed as Orwin Neese over the phone all those times? Was the spider room in his house?

God, I don't understand!

Beside me, Jenna held on to the back of the front passenger seat as Bill hit the accelerator. We surged forward. My sister looked dazed. "I never thought we'd need to do this," she breathed. "It was just supposed to be a backup plan ..."

Milt flipped open his phone. "No reason now not to call 911." He hit the numbers, then unleashed a string of explanations. "Yeah, I'll stay on the line as long as I can, but we're not waiting for you." Pause. "I don't care; there's no *time* to wait. Maybe if somebody'd listened to us in the first place. Just get here!"

Stephen pressed against the car door, his expression drawn. He caught my gaze, shook his head. "We're getting Kelly out of there, Mom. We *are.*"

Chelsea too. I tried to swallow, but my throat froze up. *Chelsea too.*

"Yeah, yeah, I'm still here." Milt's voice edged. "He doesn't know we're following. We've stayed back far enough.

We know where he's going anyway." He gripped the dashboard. "No, we didn't see his face! But it's *his* house we're headed to, and we *know Orwin Neese doesn't have Kelly.*" He jerked the phone from his ear and cursed.

"Did they hang up?" Steven's eyes widened.

"No, they just ask the *dumbest* questions to keep you on the line." Milt smacked the phone against his head again. "Listen, if you—" His words cut short. He leaned forward. "What?"

The way his back tensed. *Oh, God, what's happening?*

"Have they been through the house?" Milt half turned in his seat, held up his index finger. "And?" He listened, frowning. "No kidding, tell us something new." He yanked down the phone again. Looked at me. "She just got word they stormed the house on Boyle Road. Neese was shot. Kelly's not there."

I sucked in a breath.

"Look." Bill pointed ahead. "I see a chimney over the hill."

"It's got to be Burns's house." Milt spat words into the cell phone. "We're almost there. We're going in. You guys better get here fast. And keep your sirens off!"

We parked and jumped out. My brain went on hold, hovering on some other plane. I could not believe what we were doing, even as Jenna and I pulled our guns from our purses, Stephen and the men snatched the pieces of wood from the trunk. "Take your camera," I heard Milt tell Bill, but the reality of his words didn't register.

The next thing I knew, we were sneak-sprinting toward the massive estate owned by Ryan Burns.

Chapter 69

Chelsea's eyes fought to adjust to the dim light. The room smelled of dust and thickness and terror. She pulled her gaze away from the man's face—and locked on to a dirty oval pane of glass.

The window in her vision.

Air sputtered in Chelsea's throat. She knew what was coming. Every word, every movement. Had known it since Annie received that last phone call. The vision now become reality.

Her reality.

God, save us.

"Little-known fact about spiders." The man spoke in his raspy whisper. "Some can't even bite humans. Their jaws are too weak. And then there are the deadly ones ..." He chuckled. "The trick is telling them apart."

Kelly shuddered.

"Hey, don't be moving down there." He poured sincerity into the words. "They're all around you."

He snapped on the bulb, filtering red light into the darkened room. Chelsea's gaze fixed on Kelly, the girl's head on her knees, her feet bare. Chelsea raised her eyes, took in the crawling bodies—on the walls, the shelves, in the corner. Dizziness washed through her. *Breathe.*

"They won't hurt you if you leave them alone." He stepped forward slowly, careful not to crush any of the spiders. "Most of 'em aren't out to get you. In fact, some are pretty shy. But if you scare one, like put your hand down on him, well, what do you expect?"

Chelsea focused on his shoe, air wheezing in her throat.

"The harmless ones bite, and you may not even feel it." He took another step. "Others sting like crazy, but their venom isn't toxic. I have quite a few in here, though—" he laughed—"whose bites are something else. After a while your skin swells and feels real tender. The wound fills with pus, and you end up with a gaping hole. You'll need a doctor. Unfortunately, I won't be bringing you one."

He reached down, stroked the back of a large brown spider. Chelsea shivered. "This is a hobo spider. Lots of people mistake them for the brown recluse."

Chelsea's skin began to crinkle and crawl.

"Only problem, the poor hobos get trapped in other spiders' webs and are gobbled up, 'cause their own webs aren't sticky. They can't walk on that stuff. So I have to keep replacing them."

He pulled the bottle from his pocket. "Now *this* one—see that pile of sand in the corner? It belongs to him. Cool-looking dude, huh? Like I said, one of the world's deadliest. The funnel web, from Australia. *Atrax Robustus*, if you want to get technical. When he bites, he rears way up on his hind legs 'cause his fangs only strike down. Things are seven millimeters long. Look at the venom oozing off of 'em."

He held the bottle before her face, then unscrewed the lid. Bent down and shook the creature out. It scuttled across the floor. Kelly peeked up to see where it went.

Chelsea shuddered violently. Dozens of little legs pinpricked across her skin. On her arm. *Aaah!* She swiped it away. On her neck. On her leg ... elbow ... knee ...

No, no, they're not real, they're not real.

He laughed low in his throat. "Imagining 'em already, huh? Just wait. I haven't even locked you in here yet. But since you're enjoying this so much, let me introduce a few more of your roomies. I got some special ones from Africa, called six-eyed crab spiders. They're as bad as the Australian dudes." He sighed with satisfaction. "It'll be more interesting if I don't tell you what they look like."

He stepped toward Chelsea. "Did you know when a spider bites a bug, it injects a liquid that dissolves its internal organs? Then it just sucks everything up, predigested. The African crab spider is so poisonous, that's kind of what it does to humans. The venom eats up body tissue. Causes massive internal bleeding."

Chelsea's lungs congealed. Every nerve came alive, skittering.

"Poor thing, you look pale." The man's voice dripped with false empathy. "Too bad I have to do this."

Chelsea's throat cinched. Her mouth sagged open, gulping for air. Kelly hugged herself, trembling.

Sudden anger blazed across his face. He waved a hand at Kelly. "This is your fault, you know. She'd have lived. You both would, if *you* hadn't started it." He glared at Chelsea, then thrust his hand to the floor, scooped up a long-legged black spider. He grabbed her arm, jerked it out straight.

Chelsea's knees started to give way. "What do you think?" he taunted. "Is this one poisonous ... or not?"

Slowly he turned his hand over, opened his fingers. The spider dropped onto her wrist and began to crawl.

Chapter 70

We flailed over the uneven ground of an open field. My lungs puffed air in and out like creaking billows, fear and desperate hope fueling my adrenaline. As we crested the hill, the house bounced into view—and any remaining denial whisked away. There lay the sloping lot we'd imagined, the house two stories in front, three in back. And near the ground, toward the rear—the top of an oval window.

My heart burst into splinters. *Kelly, are you there? Chelsea?*

"The window!" Jenna wheezed. I veered toward it.

Dave ran after me, grasped my arm. "Annie, we can't look in there; he might see us."

I kept moving, trying to shake free. "I have to see her, just for a—"

"*No.*" He yanked me back toward the others.

We stumbled down the hill, my legs moving through some force of their own. *God, please don't let him see us coming.*

At the manicured lawn we spread out, ducking as we ran. Dave pulled me toward the other side of the house. Milt and Jenna hurried up the porch. Stephen and Bill stayed on the first side.

Dave and I slid to a halt at a large window, chests heaving. He dripped with sweat, his face crimson. "Here goes.

Stand back." He raised his piece of wood like a baseball bat, swung it toward the pane. Glass shattered. A siren whooped in violation.

Crack. From the front came more sounds of breakage. And more distantly a third window smashed.

"Keep away!" Dave thrust the wood back and forth, knocking out glass, his expression set with fury. A flying shard gouged his arm and blood welled up. He threw down the branch. "I'm going in." Grabbing the window frame, he hoisted himself up and over. I heard his body thud onto the floor. His head came up, arm thrust down toward me. It ran with blood. "Give me the gun."

I pushed it into his palm.

Dave disappeared.

Chapter 71

His fingers sank into Chelsea's wrist. Her eyes opened wide, a rattle in her throat as she watched the spider crawl up her arm.

Maybe he should mess with it, make it bite her right off. Would serve her right, after all the trouble—

Whow-whow-whow-whow. The electronic cry split the air. He jerked up his head, froze.

The alarm.

He snatched his fingers from her wrist. Chelsea knocked the spider off her arm and shrank from him.

"You!" he yelled at her. "Get over there in that corner." He raked a look at Kelly. She was still on the floor, but her head was up, eyes wide. "And *you*, girl, don't move."

He scurried out of the room, locked it with shaking fingers. Dropped the key in his pocket. Of all the times for a false alarm.

His feet took the steps two at once. He burst through the door into the hallway—and heard the shatter of glass. The siren swelled in his ears.

No. *No.*

With a curse he launched himself into the kitchen. He banged open the end drawer and snatched up a gun.

Chapter 72

The world jumbled into a cacophony of sight and sound. Panic lifted me on my tiptoes. Glass littered the lawn at my feet, the siren shrill in my ears. I backed up, searching for a glimpse of Dave. Was he safe? Was Jenna in the house yet? Stephen?

I saw nothing.

Just get to Kelly.

I stumbled toward the back of the house. Around the corner, across the rear lawn. Streaked around a second corner. My foot caught on something and I tumbled to the ground, breath knocked away. Gasping, I shoved to my feet and ran. My body seemed to only hover, a cartoon character with pedaling legs and no motion.

Please, God . . .

Ahead I saw it. A little circular stone wall. The top half of a grimy oval window. My heart leapt in my throat. I threw myself on my belly before the wall, stretched my neck toward the glass. *It's so dark, I can't see anything!* I pushed myself forward, a ragged stone edge ripping my shirt, scraping skin on my stomach. I thrust my nose up to the window, cupped my eyes with both hands.

A dim little room, shelves on the walls. Two figures, standing up, clinging to each other. *Kelly!*

I pounded on the glass. Kelly's head snapped around, and Chelsea's. They shuffled toward me. Their mouths moved, but I heard only the wail of the alarm. My daughter's arms stretched toward me in desperate pleading.

"Kelly!" I pressed my hand against the glass, willing it to dissolve. Forget our plans, forget where Dave and the others were; I had to get to my daughter—*now.* Why hadn't I brought that piece of wood? I pulled away from the window, frantically searched for something to break the pane, even as I knew I'd never fit through the opening.

Nothing.

I slid back toward the glass, pushed my palm against it. "I can't get in this way! They're coming to get you; just hang on."

Oh, God, I don't want to leave them.

I slithered backward, pushed to my feet. Ran up the sloping lot, past the gaping window Bill and Stephen had broken, and around the corner to the front. The siren wailed in my ears. I leapt toward the porch steps. The door stood wide open. From inside—sudden noise. Feet running, Dave shouting. A thud. Stephen yelled something. A man's voice barked a command.

Ice rolled across my lungs. I slid to a halt, unsure what to do. Then carefully eased inside, head whipping back and forth. Straight ahead in the kitchen, I saw a flash of Dave's shirt. Then nothing.

My heart stabbed daggers into my chest. Sudden terror of the unknown shoved at my spine. I flung myself toward the kitchen and over the threshold.

"Stop right there, Annie!" A man's voice, one I recognized. I froze.

My brain took in all the sights at once. Bill pressed against a cabinet, his camera askew on the counter. Its filming indicator light still glowed. Milt and Stephen posed, unmoving, by the sink. My gun dangled from Dave's lowered hand, his limbs locked tight.

Across the room stood Ryan Burns, one beefy arm crooked around my sister's neck, a weapon pressed against her head. Jenna's arms hovered in the air, her face white. Her gun lay kicked away on the floor, behind them.

Ryan turned hard eyes to Dave. "I told you to put it down. Now." His face looked as I'd never seen it — contorted, hate-filled. Desperate. His shoulders heaved with each rapid breath.

Slowly Dave reached out, placed my gun on the counter. "Push it away from you."

Dave shoved it down the tile.

Nobody moved.

Whow-whow-whow. The alarm took an ax to my head.

"Ryan." His name burst from my mouth. *"Why?"*

He glared at me. "Why did you come here? Why didn't you keep yourself safe? The town needs you, Annie; you keep killers off the street."

I gawked at him, trying to make sense of his insanity. "Please. I just want my daughter back. And Chelsea."

"They're already dead."

No! I'd just seen them, alive and calling to me. But that gun in his hand ... My legs turned to water.

Suddenly Jenna shrieked. Jerked her head down. Ryan's gun slid from her temple. She shoved sideways into him. His finger pulled the trigger. *Crack!* A bullet rent the air, barreled into the wall.

Everything happened at once. Dave leapt for my gun, snatched it off the counter as Bill grabbed for his camera. Jenna rammed into Ryan again. His weapon flew out of his hand, clattered to the floor. Stephen scrabbled for it. Somebody yelled and my own mouth screamed. Ryan Burns launched toward the gun—and my son. Milt rushed the man and knocked him to his knees. Then kicked him in the side. Ryan collapsed like a sack of flour and rolled, groaning, onto his back. Jenna scraped her gun off the floor just as Stephen scrambled to his feet with the other one.

Three barrels pointed at Ryan Burns.

Whow-whow-whow. The siren screeched in my brain—then suddenly stopped. The abrupt silence blistered my ears.

From the front hall I heard stealthy footsteps, men's lowered voices. "In here!" I called. Two deputies materialized at the threshold, guns drawn. They took in the sight with sweeping gazes, jaws dropping in disbelief.

"Help me," Ryan moaned. "They broke into my house."

Voices talked at once, the deputies commanding all guns put down, Dave explaining, and Jenna protesting. I paid no heed, had only one thought. *Kelly and Chelsea.*

My head swiveled. Where was the basement? Milt was already jogging down a side hallway. He reached a door, flung it wide. "The steps are here!" He turned toward the deputies. "They're locked in down there."

Oh, God, please let them be alive.

Ryan pushed to his feet, demanding our arrest, his face the old innocence that I knew. "Don't *listen* to him!" I pushed myself into a deputy's face. "You have to make him give you the key! We have to *get them out!*"

"I don't have a key," Ryan insisted. "I don't know what they're talking about."

I stumbled past him and down the steps, Milt behind me. On my left, three closed doors. I fell upon one, yanked it open. A laundry room. "Kelly!" I screamed. "Kelly!" Milt skidded to the second, flung out his hand—

"Mom! In here!"

The voice floated through the third door. We both whipped toward it. Milt reached it first, but I shoved him away. I tried turning the knob. It didn't move. I pulled and rattled, but it wouldn't give. A deputy appeared at my side. "Do you *hear* them? We need the *key*!"

The deputy shouted to his partner, then headed up the steps.

"Kelly, hang on! Chelsea, we're coming." At the door I jittered and trembled, hands at my mouth, waiting an eternity. The deputy appeared again, hurrying down the stairs, a key in his hand. Ryan's loud protests fizzled down to my ears. The deputy thrust the key in the lock, flung open the door.

"Mom!" Kelly rushed out and into my arms. We held each other and erupted into tears.

"Are you hurt?"

"We're okay."

Chelsea stumbled out of the room and tripped. Milt caught her. I reached out with one arm and pulled her close. "Thank You, God," I hiccupped into her trembling shoulder. "Thank You, thank You, thank You ..."

"Bill, get down here!" Milt shouted.

Vaguely I registered more voices. A bright light. The whir of a camera. For once I didn't care. I could not let go of my daughter. Or Chelsea. The three of us did the only thing we could possibly do.

We clung to each other and cried.

Saturday, October 22

Epilogue

The house gleamed. The floor and wood wainscoting were polished, furniture buffed. Two dozen helium balloons were tied to various log posts, the balconies, and numerous lamps. All four of us had dressed up, decked out for Jenna's thirty-sixth birthday party. I donned the black dress I wore to my own birthday dinner four months and eons ago. And of course, the necklace Dave and Erin gave me that night.

Our party promised to be quite the gathering. Amazing, the friends you find when your family brings down a silent killer. And makes national headlines.

Again.

My sister was in the kitchen, bossing me as usual. "Those hors d'oeuvres should be in the refrigerator" and "Send Kelly over to Dave's for more ice."

"Jenna—" I shook my head—"knock it off. I really do have this under control."

She mumbled under her breath and I feigned a glare.

I knew the reason for her nervousness. Milt Waking was coming. He'd flown all the way out from filming some story on the East Coast and planned to stay three days in Redding. Fortunately, he was bunking in a hotel and not in one of our guest rooms. I owed him the world for helping us find Kelly, and I'd told him so. But having him around for three days was another matter.

Seven o'clock, and the guests started arriving, Dave the first. Erin had already been there for hours, helping with the house and food, and spending the last hour with Kelly, doing makeup and hair. Chetterling arrived with his date, a voraciously chatty social worker named Rowena. "An old friend," he told me somewhat sheepishly last week, "come back around again."

Good for you, Ralph.

It was Chetterling who told me every detail about the storming of the Boyle Road house. Neese had finally answered Tim Blanche's megaphoned calls, yelling through a top-floor window. But negotiations didn't get very far. Neese panicked and fired some shots, wounding a deputy in the shoulder. At that moment a SWAT team member got a bead on him and pulled the trigger. The bullet hit Neese in the forehead. He was pronounced dead at the scene.

Three weeks ago I attended Amy Flyte's funeral. According to autopsy and forensics reports, she'd been strangled soon after she disappeared. Such a horrible truth to realize—that she lay dead before anyone even knew she was missing, and all during those days we searched for the spider room, hoping to rescue her. A second body of the "possible missing young man" was never found. To this day we could only hope he was merely a lie in Orwin Neese's raging threats. But sometimes I woke in the night, wondering . . .

The doorbell rang again and I answered it. "Chelsea!" She stood on our porch, brightly wrapped present in hand, flanked by her handsome husband and sons. "Come in, come in."

They flocked into the great room, Chelsea first. She shoved the present into her husband's arms and hugged me tightly. "How are you and Kelly?" she whispered in my ear.

I pulled back, studying her face. As much as I'd thanked her, it would never be enough. I owed this woman more than I could ever repay. What she did for us, allowing herself to be taken into that nightmarish room ... Not until days later, when I began to sort the puzzle pieces out, did it hit me—when Ryan Burns insisted she come get Kelly instead of me, she'd *known*.

"I'm doing fine," I told her. "Kelly still has her moments. A couple times a week she crawls into my bed in the middle of the night. I just hold her and we pray. What more can I do?"

Chelsea's eyes glistened. She nodded.

"And how are *you?*"

She tilted her head. "Okay. As long as I don't see a spider in the house."

We exchanged wan smiles.

She introduced me to her husband, Paul, and her sons, Michael and Scott. The girls took one look at her boys, and their expressions outshone our hardwood floor. Soon the four of them were headed for the TV room.

"Where's the birthday girl?" Chelsea asked.

"I think she's down in the basement with some folks, finishing up a tour of the house. Want to go say hi? Dave's down there too."

"Oh no." Chelsea waved a hand with a little shiver. "I'll just wait for them up here."

More friends arrived, some from church, others who'd become Jenna's local clients. Gerri Carson and her husband,

Ted, showed up. Gerri hugged me even more tightly than Chelsea did. "How great to see your face, Annie Kingston."

"Yeah, well, next time you decide to go to Hawaii, check with me first, okay? You sure picked a week to be gone."

She leaned close to me, looking conspiratorial. "Is he here yet?"

"Who, Milt? No."

She raised her eyebrows. "I can't wait to meet him in person. He's absolutely gorgeous on TV."

"More so in real life," Jenna said, sidling up to hug Gerri.

"Oh yeah, he's terrific." I wagged my head. "Just ask Chelsea how much she adores him."

Jenna rolled her eyes.

Five minutes later Milt made his grand entrance, planting a kiss on Jenna's cheek and glad-handing everyone like a smooth politician. I watched him and sighed. The man was so annoyingly, arrogantly ... heaven-sent.

He greeted Stephen and Dave like it was old home week, pumping handshakes. Stephen pulled him aside with a dramatic whisper. "Did you bring it?"

"Yeah, it's in the car. Didn't want to give it to you in front of everybody."

I suppressed a shudder. I knew what *it* was—Bill's footage of our break-in at Ryan Burns's house. The smashed windows, drawn guns, Chelsea and Kelly released. As if Stephen needed a copy, after all the times the story had run on national TV. Still, I supposed my son couldn't see it enough. He'd show it to his friends and they'd crow. He'd earned that much.

As long as he played the thing at someone else's house, not mine.

By eight the great room was filled with people and laughter. Jenna opened her presents. Chelsea and I, helped by the girls, served hors d'oeuvres and drinks. Every now and then I saw Milt and Jenna exchange lingering glances across the room.

Oh boy.

I was in the kitchen putting stray dishes in the sink when I sensed Chetterling beside me. I turned to him with a smile. "Rowena's great. I like her."

He gave me a long look, then nodded. "Thanks. I do too."

I searched his face. He had something to tell me. "What?"

"Just some talk. I've been hearing interesting things about Ryan Burns. Warden at the jail says he whispers to himself about those bodies he buried. How they're coming to take their revenge. And he rubs his legs and feet real hard all the time. Yelling at dirt ants."

I creased my forehead. "Dirt ants?"

Chetterling shrugged. "You got me."

We were silent for a moment. I thought of Ryan and his chameleon-like personas. Pretending innocence in public, yet feigning the kidnapping of Amy Flyte in the privacy of his own home. *If* all the scenes from Chelsea's visions were to be believed. And I thought they were.

I picked up a plate, rinsed it. "I talked to Irene Kreger again this week. Every time, she's so sweet and grateful. I mean, she's heartbroken over what happened to her niece and nephew, but at least she doesn't have that black hole of not knowing after all these years."

"Yeah." Chetterling drew up his chin, gave me a meaningful look. "That's because of your work, Annie. You should be proud of that."

"I am proud—of *all* my forensic artwork. I just ... need a break. You can understand why."

He drew a long breath, let it out. "Yeah. I can understand."

I watched him amble back into the great room, the projector in my head replaying Irene Kreger's first phone call.

"For six years I prayed that I'd find out what happened to those kids. Now God has answered my prayer. He was such a good boy, my nephew Eddie. Took care of Emily, his sister. Most of the beatings from their no-good father went on his back. When his sister got pregnant, he knew their father would kill her. Who'd have guessed they'd run all the way from Kansas to California ..."

Eddie, eighteen, and Emily, fifteen, were apparently broke by the time they reached Redding. Eddie splurged and bought a lotto ticket at a convenience store. His wildest dreams came true—it turned out to be worth $56 million. Irene got a call from Eddie. He was ecstatic, saying he'd come into a lot of money, and he would phone her back when it was all settled. Tell her where he and Emily were. He'd pay Irene's way to come to them, and they'd all live together in a big fine house ...

She never heard from him again.

Ryan Burns's broken-spirited confession gave the rest of the story. Thinking he was protecting himself, Eddie made a fatal mistake. He walked into a copy store and ran a duplicate of the ticket—just in case the lottery folks tried to cheat him out of his winnings. He need not have worried about the State of California employees as much as the helpful clerk named Ryan Burns who saw what he'd copied and struck up a detail-seeking conversation. Pretending to watch out for them, Ryan lured Eddie and Emily to his apartment and killed them both. He buried their bodies in the middle of the night—one at our airstrip and one clear across town—and went on to be one of the biggest winners of the California State lottery. Redding knew him as generous with his money, always ready to help fight crime.

Good deeds from a guilty conscience.

Since the day of Ryan's arrest, Tim Blanche and I hadn't spoken. I wasn't ready for that yet. I knew I should apologize for my mistakes. Yes, he was right that Chelsea's vision had nothing to do with Orwin Neese. But he wasn't exactly perfect. I had to admit I felt a certain vengeance in seeing his takedown of Neese overshadowed by the national fascination with Kelly's and Chelsea's rescue. Served him right.

Sorry, God. Guess I need to work on that.

I'd turned it over and over in my mind—all that God allowed to happen. I didn't understand everything. But I did see that He sent Chelsea her visions so justice could be won for young Eddie and Emily. Without those visions, Milt wouldn't have aired my drawing of John Doe on FOX News. And without national coverage, Irene Kreger in Kansas wouldn't have seen the face of her missing nephew. Ryan Burns later led Chetterling to Emily's grave on the other side of town. He'd certainly gone to great lengths to cover his deeds. Both Emily's and Eddie's remains were shipped back to Kansas for burial.

Closure for another grieving family.

As for myself, I saw how the terrifying events led Chelsea to pray for me—a prayer that changed my life. That deep, constant sense of unworthiness had faded, almost disappeared. When it threatened to raise its ugly head, I'd learned how to claim victory against it. Amazing to me, how a focused healing prayer, even in the midst of chaos, released me from its grip.

Chelsea and I talked about it on the phone a couple weeks ago. "Annie," she said, "Satan fights Christians daily. Don't forget he's a liar, the father of lies. He wants more than anything to keep us from being all we can be in Christ." She gave a little huff. "Don't *let* him."

I won't, God. Thank You for answering her prayer. Thank You for everything, especially my family's safety.

And for Dave.

As if I'd spoken his name, Dave wandered in to stand behind me, circling my waist with his arms. I squirmed around, looked up into the eyes I'd grown to love.

"Know what?" He gave me an almost weary smile. "You and I have waited *far* too long for a party."

"We sure have."

I tilted up my face and kissed him.

Read an excerpt from

Violet Dawn

Book 1
of the new Kanner Lake Series

by
Brandilyn Collins

Prologue

They called him Black Mamba.

One of the world's deadliest snakes. Even its head is coffin-shaped. Its neurotoxic bite is one hundred percent fatal without antivenin. It's also the world's swiftest, reaching up to seven miles an hour in short bursts. Fast enough to catch a fleeing human.

A black mamba plays with its prey.

It bites with the longest of fangs, then waits. Confident. Silent. Watching the paralyzing squirrel or rat stagger away, hide in a burrow. Then, uncurling its sleek body—up to fourteen feet long—it smugly slithers after the animal. Drags it out. And swallows it whole.

He approved of this name.

Even more scintillating to him were the rumors of the reptile, wide-eyed whispered around the world. That black mambas stalk humans, killing whole families. That they are mean and aggressive, eely machines created to kill. Here, he thought himself closer to myth than reality. Indeed, his strikes had risen to mythic proportions of their own.

He had no known address. No permanent phone number. A certain someone needing the most elusive killer in the country need not search a directory. Like the stories of his namesake, Mamba's latest contact information was

murmured from sibilant lips to anxious ears. Those fortu-
nate enough to find and hire him were rewarded two-fold.
Their targets were ruthlessly killed. And headlines of the
deed dripped with poisonous entertainment.

Tonight, tomorrow, he would deliver no less.

Chapter 1

Paige Williams harbored a restless kinship with the living dead.

Sleep, that nurturing, blessed state of subconsciousness, eluded her again this night. Almost 2:00 a.m., and rather than slumbering bliss, old memories nibbled at her like ragged toothed wraiths.

With a defeated sigh, she rose from bed.

Wrapped in a large towel, she glided through the darkened house, bare feet faintly scuffing across worn wood floors. Out of her room and down a short hall, passing the second bedroom—barren and needing to be filled—and the one bathroom, into the small kitchen.

She unlocked the sliding glass door. Stepped outside onto the back deck. Cicadas' grating rhythm rose to greet her. Scents from the woods—an almost sweet earthiness—wafted on a slight breeze.

The dry Idaho air was still warm.

A large hot tub sunk into the corner of the deck was her destination—a soothing womb of heat to coddle and comfort. There, looking out over the forested hills and Kanner Lake, Paige could feel sheltered from the world. No probing stares upon her, no cradle of lies. Even the closest neighbor on either side was a good half-mile away.

But first, captivated by the night, she padded to the deck's edge and gazed up at the heavens.

A slivered moon hung askew, feeble and worn. Ice chip stars flung themselves in all directions. The Big Dipper poured into Kanner Lake, whose waters seemed almost brooding under the spangled sky. Across the sullen waters, a few downtown lights resolutely twinkled.

Intense yearning welled within Paige, at once ancient and new. It rose so suddenly that she nearly staggered in its presence. She clutched the towel tighter around her body, swaddling herself against it. The universe was so vast, she thought, the world so small. A mere speck of dust, Earth churned and groaned in the spheres of infinity. Upon that speck, mothers and fathers, children and friends, laughed and cried and celebrated one another. No bigger than dust mites they were, compared to the vastness of space. Their lives, their loves — insignificant.

So why did she long to be one of them?

Paige stared at the downtown lights across the water. In eight hours she would return there, among the families and lovers. Surrounded with people who *belonged*. Separated from them by a mere two feet of counter space ... and a chasm. Behind the Simple Pleasures counter on Main Street, she would sell gift items and pretty home accessories to tourists and local residents. Parents with tagging children, couples hand in hand. Sometimes from the corner of her eye she would watch them shopping. Pointing out an oil lamp candle to a husband. Exclaiming with a friend over a glitz-studded handbag. And something inside her would swell and ache like bruised skin —

Stop it, Paige.

With resolution, she turned away from the lake and town.

As she edged across the deck to the beckoning hot tub, she consoled herself that all would be well. She had settled in Kanner Lake only two months ago. She *would* make friends. She *would* make a life here. Most of all, for the first time in her existence, she would build a family to love. Her yearnings may feel weakening, but in their pursuit, she would be strong as steel, forged from the fires of life's hardships. Gone were her years of powerless longing.

Paige reached the hot tub. Sunk into the deck, it protruded up from the wood about one foot. A heavy vinyl top, divided down the middle, covered the tub, protecting its heat. When she'd rented the house, her landlord had warned her to leave it on when not using the tub. Her energy bill would be less if she did. Paige heeded his words. Letting her towel fall, Paige leaned down and used both hands to fold back the cover, revealing half the water. Because of the cover's weight, she would not take it all the way off. Besides, the tub was large enough that even half of it provided her with plenty room to relax. Inviting steam rose into her face. She would not turn on the jets—she never did. She wanted quiet solace, not roiling waters.

She held on to the smooth side and stepped into the tub. At that end, a body-formed "couch" seat ran its length. There, she lay back, sinking up to her neck in the hot water and pillowing her head against a black vinyl head rest. *Ah.* She closed her eyes. Stretched out her legs and floated her arms in the warmth. Tried to concentrate only on the sensations.

But the memories came once more. In vivid flashes, haunting smears. Days of despair. Nights on the run.

No.

She would not be sucked into that cavernous maw. Her best defense, when the memories could not be repressed, was to distance herself. Imagine watching a film of someone else's life, hearing a narrative voice-over. But how hard it was to divorce one's past! To be reduced to a few carefully chosen details to satisfy the curious. She was Paige Williams, born and raised in Kansas, date of birth November 12, 1980. Orphaned at three. Now twenty-five years old...

This is who you are, and no one can take it from you. Hold on to it, build a new life. Hold tight.

She pulled a deep breath and held it, filling her lungs with cleansing air. Her body lifted in the water. Slowly she exhaled, and her torso sank.

Her thigh tickled. Paige flicked her fingers over the spot.

She wrenched her mind away from memories of her past. Gazed at the silver studded sky and rocked herself gently in the hot, soothing water. If only her soul could feel so warm, so coddled. If only—

Something sinuous brushed against Paige's knee. Her leg jerked.

What was *that*?

She shot up to a sitting position, groped around with her left hand.

Movement again. Fine wisps wound themselves around her fingers.

Hair?

She gasped, yanked backward, but the tendrils weighted her hand. Something solid bumped her wrist.

With one frantic motion, Paige shook her arm free, grabbed the side of the hot tub and heaved herself out.

Her body hit the deck with a wet thud. She rolled, sucked a shaky breath. Whipped a stare toward the tub, eyes stabbing the black water. What was in there? Something underneath the cover?

Paige pushed to her knees and cautiously leaned toward the tub.

A head surfaced.

Brink of Death

Brandilyn Collins

The noises, faint, fleeting, whispered into her consciousness like wraiths passing in the night.

Twelve-year-old Erin Willit opened her eyes to darkness lit only by the dim green nightlight near her closet door and the faint glow of a street lamp through her front window. She felt her forehead wrinkle, the fingers of one hand curl as she tried to discern what had awakened her.

Something was not right . . .

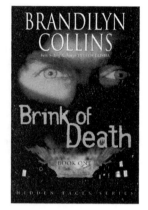

Annie Kingston moves to Grove Landing for safety and quiet—and comes face to face with evil.

When neighbor Lisa Willet is killed by an intruder in her home, Sheriff's detectives are left with little evidence. Lisa's daughter, Erin, saw the killer, but she's too traumatized to give a description. The detectives grow desperate.

Because of her background in art, Annie is asked to question Erin and draw a composite. But Annie knows little about forensic art or the sensitive interview process. A nonbeliever, she finds herself begging God for help. What if her lack of experience leads Erin astray? The detectives could end up searching for a face that doesn't exist.

Leaving the real killer free to stalk the neighborhood ...

Softcover: 0-310-25103-6

Stain of Guilt

Brandilyn Collins

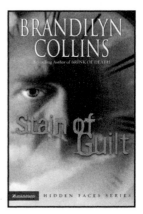

As I drew, the house felt eerie in its silence. . . . A strange sense stole over me, as though Bland and I were two actors on stage, our movements spotlighted, black emptiness between us. But that darkness grew smaller as the space between us shrank. I did not know if this sense was due to my immersion in Bland's face and mind and world, or to my fear of his threatening presence.
Or both . . .
The nerves between my shoulder blades began to tingle.
Help me, God. Please.

For twenty years, a killer has eluded capture for a brutal double murder. Now, forensic artist Annie Kingston has agreed to draw the updated face of Bill Bland for the popular television show *American Fugitive.*

To do so, Annie must immerse herself in Bland's traits and personality. A single habitual expression could alter the way his face has aged. But as she descends into his criminal mind and world, someone is determined to stop her. At any cost. Annie's one hope is to complete the drawing and pray it leads authorities to Bland—before Bland can get to her.

Softcover: 0-310-25104-4

ZONDERVAN™

GRAND RAPIDS, MICHIGAN 49530 USA

WWW.ZONDERVAN.COM

Dead of Night

Brandilyn Collins

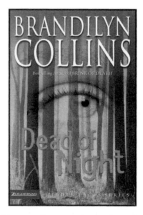

All words fell away. I pushed myself off the path, noticing for the first time the signs of earlier passage—the matted earth, broken twigs. And I knew. My mouth turned cottony.

I licked my lips, took three halting steps. My maddening, visual brain churned out pictures of colorless faces on a cold slab—Debbie Lille, victim number one; Wanda Deminger, number three . . . He'd been here. Dragged this one right where I now stumbled. I'd entered a crime scene, and I could not bear to see what lay at the end. . . .

This is a story about evil.

This is a story about God's power.

A string of murders terrorizes citizens in the Redding, California, area. The serial killer is cunning, stealthy. Masked by day, unmasked by night. Forensic artist Annie Kingston discovers the sixth body practically in her own backyard. Is the location a taunt aimed at her?

One by one, Annie must draw the unknown victims for identification. Dread mounts. Who will be taken next? Under a crushing oppression, Annie and other Christians are driven to pray for God's intervention as they've never prayed before.

With page-turning intensity, Dead of Night dares to pry open the mind of evil. Twisted actions can wreak havoc on earth, but the source of wickedness lies beyond this world. Annie learns where the real battle takes place—and that a Christian's authority through prayer is the ultimate, unyielding weapon.

Softcover: 0-310-25105-2

Cast a Road before Me

Brandilyn Collins

A course-changing event in one's life can happen in minutes. Or it can form slowly, a primitive webbing splaying into fingers of discontent, a minuscule trail hardening into the sinewed spine of resentment. So it was with the mill workers as the heat-soaked days of summer marched on.

City girl Jessie, orphaned at sixteen, struggles to adjust to life with her barely known aunt and uncle in the tiny town of Bradleyville, Kentucky. Eight years later (1968), she plans on leaving—to follow in her revered mother's footsteps of serving the homeless. But the peaceful town she's come to love is about to be tragically shattered. Threats of a labor strike rumble through the streets, and Jessie's new love and her uncle are swept into the maelstrom. Caught between the pacifist teachings of her mother and these two men, Jessie desperately tries to deny that Bradleyville is rolling toward violence and destruction.

Softcover: 0-310-25327-6

Pick up a copy today at your favorite bookstore!

ZONDERVAN™

GRAND RAPIDS, MICHIGAN 49530 USA

WWW.ZONDERVAN.COM

Color the Sidewalk for Me

Brandilyn Collins

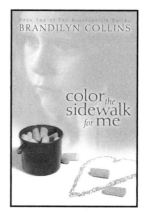

As a chalk-fingered child, I had worn my craving for Mama's love on my sleeve. But as I grew, that craving became cloaked in excuses and denial until slowly it sank beneath my skin to lie unheeded but vital, like the sinews of my framework. By the time I was a teenager, I thought the gap between Mama and me could not be wider.

And then Danny came along. . . .

A splendidly colored sidewalk. Six-year-old Celia presented the gift to her mother with pride—and received only anger in return. Why couldn't Mama love her? Years later, when once-in-a-lifetime love found Celia, her mother opposed it. The crushing losses that followed drove Celia, guilt-ridden and grieving, from her Bradleyville home.

Now thirty-five, she must return to nurse her father after a stroke. But the deepest need for healing lies in the rift between mother and daughter. God can perform such a miracle. But first Celia and Mama must let go of the past—before it destroys them both.

Softcover: 0-310-24242-8

ZONDERVAN™

GRAND RAPIDS, MICHIGAN 49530 USA

WWW.ZONDERVAN.COM

Capture the Wind for Me

Brandilyn Collins

One thing I have learned. The bonfires of change start with the merest spark. Sometimes we see that flicker. Sometimes we blink in surprise at the flame only after it has marched hot legs upward to fully ignite. Either way, flicker or flame, we'd better do some serious praying. When God's on the move in our lives, he tends to burn up things we'd just as soon keep.

After her mama's death, sixteen-year-old Jackie Delham is left to run the household for her daddy and two younger siblings. When Katherine King breezes into town and tries to steal her daddy's heart, Jackie knows she must put a stop to it. Katherine can't be trusted. Besides, one romance in the family is enough, and Jackie is about to fall headlong into her own.

As love whirls through both generations, the Delhams are buffeted by hope, elation and loss. Jackie is devastated to learn of old secrets in her parents' relationship. Will those past mistakes cost Jackie her own love? And how will her family ever survive if Katherine jilts her daddy and leaves them in mourning once more?

Softcover: 0-310-24243-6

ZONDERVAN™

GRAND RAPIDS, MICHIGAN 49530 USA

WWW.ZONDERVAN.COM

Eyes of Elisha

Brandilyn Collins

The murder was ugly.
The killer was sure no one saw
him.
Someone did.

In a horrifying vision, Chelsea Adams has relived the victim's last moments. But who will believe her? Certainly not the police, who must rely on hard evidence. Nor her husband, who barely tolerates Chelsea's newfound Christian faith. Besides, he's about to hire the man who Chelsea is certain is the killer to be a vice president in his company.

Torn between what she knows and the burden of proof, Chelsea must follow God's leading and trust him for protection. Meanwhile, the murderer is at liberty. And he's not about to take Chelsea's involvement lying down.

Softcover: 0-310-23968-0

Dread Champion

Brandilyn Collins

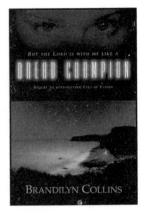

Chelsea Adams has visions. But they have no place in a courtroom.

As a juror for a murder trial, Chelsea must rely only on the evidence. And this circumstantial evidence is strong—Darren Welk killed his wife.

Or did he?

The trial is a nightmare for Chelsea. The other jurors belittle her Christian faith. As testimony unfolds, truth and secrets blur. Chelsea's visiting niece stumbles into peril surrounding the case, and Chelsea cannot protect her. God sends visions—frightening, vivid. But what do they mean? Even as Chelsea finds out, what can she do? She is helpless, and danger is closing in . . .

Masterfully crafted, *Dread Champion* is a novel in which appearances can deceive and the unknown can transform the meaning of known facts. One man's guilt or innocence is just a single link in a chain of hidden evil . . . and God uses the unlikeliest of people to accomplish his purposes.

Softcover: 0-310-23827-7

Pick up a copy today at your favorite bookstore!

ZONDERVAN™

GRAND RAPIDS, MICHIGAN 49530 USA

WWW.ZONDERVAN.COM